PRAISE FOR PAPER, SCISSORS, DEATH

"*Paper, Scissors, Death* is not only an engaging mystery—it also gave this die-hard non-scrapbooker some idea why scrapbooking fans find their hobby so addictive."

—Donna Andrews, Agatha and Anthony award-winning author of the *Meg Langslow* and *Turing Hopper* series

"Charming, funny and very enjoyable! Slan combines mystery, romance, suspense, and humor in this wonderful debut, and her scrapbooking heroine Kiki Lowenstein is a real cut-up."

—J. A. Konrath, author of *Whiskey Sour*

"*Paper, Scissors, Death* is charming, clever, witty, and exciting—with a cliff hanger at the end!"

—Monica Ferris, author of *Knitting Bones*

"You'll love Kiki Lowenstein! A spunky, down-on-her luck widow with a young daughter to raise, she's not going to let a murderer get away with, well…murder!"

—Shirley Damsgaard, author of *Witch Way to Murder*

"*Paper, Scissors, Death* is a page turner, who-done-it, filled with colorful characters and scrapbooking tips. The plot line races along as Kiki, a personable if unlikely heroine, struggles to take care of both herself and her daughter while dealing with death, betrayal, and injustices. Along the way the story is filled with insightful glimpses into the heart of a true scrapbooker and a touch of romance."

—Rebecca Ludens, Scrapbooking Guide for About.com

FORTHCOMING BY JOANNA CAMPBELL SLAN

Cut, Crop & Die, June 2009

paper Scissors eath

A Kiki Lowenstein
Scrap-N-Craft
Mystery

Joanna Campbell Slan

MIDNIGHT INK
WOODBURY, MINNESOTA

First Edition
Second Printing, 2008

Book design and format by Donna Burch
Cover design by Kevin R. Brown
Cover images © PhotoDisc
Editing by Connie Hill
Midnight Ink, an imprint of Llewellyn Publications

Library of Congress Cataloging-in-Publication Data:

Campbell-Slan, Joanna.
  Paper, scissors, death : a kiki lowenstein scrap-n-craft mystery / Joanna Campbell Slan. —1st ed.
      p.   cm. — (A kiki lowenstein scrap-n-craft mystery ; no. 2)
  ISBN 978-0-7387-1250-5
  1. Husbands—Crimes against—Fiction. 2. Murder—Fiction. 3. Life change events—Fiction. 4. Scrapbooks—Fiction. I. Title.
  PS3603.A4845P37   2008
  813'.6--dc22   2008014416

Midnight Ink
Llewellyn Publications
2143 Wooddale Drive, Dept. 978-0-7387-1250-5
Woodbury, MN 55125-2989 USA
www.midnightinkbooks.com

Printed in the United States of America

DEDICATION

Mom, I told you on the way to chemo and radiation that this book was for you. You hung in there and survived. Now I'm proud to put it in your hands. I hope you like it.

Love, Jonie

PROLOGUE

Two days before Thanksgiving, a man doesn't think about dying. And if he did, he certainly wouldn't pick the Ritz-Carlton in downtown Clayton, an exclusive suburb of St. Louis, as a venue. The shimmering fountain out front, an elegant cigar room, and two four-diamond restaurants all reminded guests that life was very much worth living.

But on this clear November day, with small puffs of clouds like fuzzy cotton balls on a cerulean sky, George Lowenstein's life was ending. The agony that gripped him wasn't indigestion from his meal at Antonio's. It wasn't a sore muscle from his most recent round of golf at the St. Louis Country Club.

His vision blurred, his hands shook, and his gut twisted in pain.

Leaning back on a Frette pillow case, George moaned, "I don't feel so good. I feel dizzy. Sick to my stomach. Call 911."

His companion only smiled at him. But it was a grin tinged with malice, and it hurt George more than the spasm in his chest.

That's when George Lowenstein knew he was dying.

A wave of fury accompanied the next twisting grip of pain. In response, George clawed at the expensive Egyptian cotton sheets. He tried to lift his arm, to move to the phone, but a pressing wall of agony kept him pinned against the headboard. A rage swept through him. Why hadn't he seen this coming? He thought of all the people who counted on him—and hated himself for not being more prepared.

From outside the room came the lonely rattle of a maid's cart. For one shining second, George thought help was on the way. He opened his mouth to scream, to yell for help. A piece of silken fabric was stuffed down his throat, smothering his cry.

In the hallway, a Hispanic woman wearing a black dress with a white collar and white apron checked a clipboard. The small laminated sign with its perky "Do Not Disturb" message on George's door encouraged her to move along. The last thing she wanted was for a guest to complain. Not when she was so close to having enough money to go back to Toluca. Her pen hesitated before touching sheets of paper covered in scribbles. She tucked a stray lock of hair into the bun resting on her neck. She'd have to come back later. The maid leaned on her cart to rub her ankle and then straightened.

She pushed her supply cart down the hall corridor, its wonky wheel squeaking all the way.

ONE

"THANK YOU, MRS. LOWENSTEIN!" seven pre-adolescent girl voices piped in unison. "Thanks, Mom," added my eleven-year-old daughter, Anya. The girls were delighted with the pages they'd created with my help.

"You are welcome," I said. All in all, it had been a pretty terrific play date at Time in a Bottle, my favorite scrapbook store.

I felt positively glowy. Approval was a scarce commodity in my life, and the fact that I was getting my strokes from children didn't diminish my joy one bit. I was sharing the second great love of my life, scrapbooking, with the first love of my life, Anya.

Jennifer Moore, mother of Nicci, echoed the girls' praise. "That's right. Mrs. Lowenstein deserves a super-big thanks. She put together this whole project." Turning to me, she added, "Really, Kiki, you outdid yourself. Boy, are you creative. Their pages look really cool. No wonder people call you the Scrapbook Queen of St. Louis."

Wow. This was a nice turn of events.

Jennifer had never paid one bit of attention to me, no matter how hard I'd tried to strike up a friendship with her. From the tips of her French-manicured nails to the zebra-striped flats on her toes, Jennifer exemplified what I think of as essence of Ladue lady of leisure. The mothers in this tony suburb are *tres chic* and tres sleek. Try as I might, I don't quite measure up. Oh, I try to make up for my shortcomings by being a willing volunteer and going out of my way to be nice, but not everyone is interested in what I have to offer. Jennifer sure wasn't. But the day she heard another mom asking me questions about scrapbooking, her ears perked up. She was looking for a pre-Thanksgiving activity for her daughter, Nicci, and did I think I could help?

In a flash—photo flash, that is—I said, "Sure!" Now my daughter was spending time with the coolest girls from her class at the Charles and Anne Lindbergh Academy, locally known as CALA, our city's most exclusive private school. This was definitely a day to remember. And I had lots of practice saving memories.

"Girls, would you please stand over by the wall? I want to take your picture."

"For your own scrapbook?" asked Nicci.

"That's right." I moved the girls into a formation that allowed each child to display her prized piece of artwork. As I looked over the variety of results, it was a real struggle to contain the grin that threatened to stretch my face to unladylike proportions. No matter how extensively I plan a session like this, the individual vagaries of each participant's taste and skill level determine the outcome. And what a wide-ranging outcome it was.

Kaitlyn Godfrey chose to make her turkey a vivid lavender and added a hot-pink wattle and orange-striped tail feathers. Ashlee

Hueka spelled the upcoming holiday "Tanksgiving" and steadfastly rejected any attempts to bring her English in line with more conventional standards. Claire Kovaleski couldn't make up her mind about placement and moved each piece until nubs of torn paper dotted the whole layout. Linsey Murphy pouted until I replaced her turkey die-cut with a panda bear. Minnie Danvers confused the journaling paper (ivory, so handwriting would show up) with the photo matte paper (deep green). Nicci Moore decided to decorate her turkey with sparkly ballpoint pens she carried in her purse. Britney Ballard explained she hated Thanksgiving because her father, Bill (my husband's business partner), always made her eat dark meat, and she used lettering stickers to give her turkey a protest sign, "Eat more BEEF!!!"

All in all, the special outing for the group of pre-teens had turned out well, even though it had been a lot of work.

"Don't you ever get bored with this?" Jennifer asked.

"Nope." I clicked the shutter on my digital camera. "Wait, girls. I want to take another. One of you closed your eyes. It's always a good idea to take extra pictures."

Nicci left her pals to give her mother a hug. "Mom, this was awesome. Everybody had a great time. Can you and I scrapbook when we get home? We've got all those photos in the basement."

Jennifer smiled down at her daughter. Nicci seemed like a sweet kid. I hoped this might foster a friendship between her and Anya.

"I guess we could, honey, but I don't know where to start." Jennifer turned to me. "You've really gotten these girls excited."

I smiled. I had no illusions that my young friends were going to run right out and fill albums with photos and their written reflections on life, but I did hope that one or two might be tempted to try scrapbooking. We all have lives of value, no matter how different our journeys. From the variation in their pages, each of the girls seemed well on her way to a highly individualistic and exciting life. Every girl, that is, except my Anya.

Only Anya constructed her "make and take" page in an exact replica of my design. That worried me. Other mothers complained about sassy mouths and rebellious behaviors—witness Ashlee Hueka's disastrous haircut, an experiment gone wrong at a recent sleepover. And Linsey Murphy's two detentions for skipping classes to watch boys play hacky sack.

But dear, dear Anya exhibited only the most biddable behavior.

I worried about her. Was this a prelude to becoming a woman? Were her hormones starting to rear their ugly heads? Or was it a reaction to her father's recent moodiness? My husband George had seemed distant and preoccupied lately, although a good round of golf the other day had perked him up considerably.

Watching my lovely daughter push a strand of platinum-blonde hair away from her face, I felt a surge of protective love. What happened to that little rabble-rouser who organized a strike in kindergarten to get chocolate milk? Who melted all her crayons into one big lump in first grade by using the microwave in the teachers' lounge? Who let the crawdads out of the aquarium in fourth grade because "all God's creatures want to be free"? What happened to my rowdy, playful Anya? What was wrong? Why didn't she jabber and horse around like the other girls?

Maybe over the Thanksgiving holiday we'd have a chance to talk. Without the dodge of "loads of homework," or the evasion of "my favorite TV show is on," maybe Anya could be coaxed into sharing what bothered her, what had made her so quiet lately.

"Can I get a copy of that photo? Where are you taking it to be developed?" Jennifer asked. The whole time the girls had been working on their projects, Jennifer had been on her cell phone. Jennifer was one of those mothers who was part fashion stylist, part career counselor, and part social director in her daughter's life. She seemed very organized.

"Of course you can have copies. I'll get them to you."

"Kiki, you sure are an expert scrapbooker."

"I'm pretty crazy about it."

I've only been good at two things in my life: scrapbooking and getting pregnant. This was the one skill I could share without nasty social repercussions.

"No kidding," said Dodie Goldfader, Time in a Bottle's owner. Dodie was a big woman with a voice rivaling a boom box. "Last year Kiki chased the Oscar Meyer Weinermobile down Highway 40 at seventy miles an hour because she wanted a photo. That speeding ticket made for an expensive page embellishment."

I said, "I've always wanted a weenie whistle."

Jennifer laughed. "I like photos and all, but gosh, it looks like you put a lot of time into this. Do you and Anya work on your scrapbooks together?"

"Once in a while. Anya's been scrapbooking for years. And she loves the scrapbooks I've made. Every kid likes to be the star of a scrapbook page." As we talked, I picked up supplies and returned them to their original places.

What surprised me was that Jennifer didn't lift a finger to help. That was just one of the ways we were different. Another was how we talked about people. As the girls were being dropped off, I overheard Jennifer and a couple of the other mothers snicker about

Dodie. One woman bet she was related to the Woolly Mammoth they unearthed at nearby Principia College. Okay, Dodie is large and unusually hairy for a woman. Even so, that was not a nice thing to say.

And I'm a big believer in nice. That's me, Kiki Lowenstein, the original Mrs. Nice Guy. Heck, I've apologized to empty carts I've bumped at the grocery store.

Dodie passed out class calendars, discount coupons, and small goody bags to the girls. Competition for scrapbook dollars is keen. As the hobby grows, everyone wants to get in on the act. Keeping her clients happy with small freebies, great classes, and a never-ending flow of new products is the key to Dodie's success. In every way but one, Time in a Bottle is the preeminent scrapbook store in the St. Louis area. All Dodie lacks is an in-house scrapbook celebrity and expert.

Dodie offered Jennifer a goody bag. "Nobody knows more about scrapbooking than Kiki. I keep asking her to come work for me. I get all sorts of scrapbookers who want to teach in exchange for supplies, but no one is as talented as she is. Kiki's work has been published in every major scrapbooking magazine. She's famous."

I couldn't help but blush. If Dodie only knew how important scrapbooking was to me, she'd charge me by the hour for therapy instead of paper supplies. Time in a Bottle was my home away from home.

"That so?" said Jennifer. "You are published?"

"Darn tootin," said Dodie. "Look at this." Dodie directed her attention to one of my albums. "Aren't these pages adorable? See how each layout tells a story? That's what makes her work special.

Believe me, I could keep her busy twenty-four-seven making custom albums and teaching private lessons."

Jennifer slowly flipped through the pages. She was viewing my most recent and elaborate work. Her eyes took in the mix of patterned papers, the designs, and the embellishments. "Do you teach adult classes? I mean, I have supplies but I don't know where to start. A lot of my pictures are in those magnetic albums."

"Oh, boy. You want to get those out right away." I explained how the sticky background and plastic covering for magnetic pages is a deadly combination that can cause photos to fade.

"Hmm. Could I pay someone to do that for me? To take the photos out?"

"I can help you do that. It's really easy." I gave a surreptitious yank at my blouse because it was riding up. I'm self-conscious about my weight. George tells me I'm beautiful, and I'm fine the way I am, but all the other mothers at CALA are built like pencils. In their world, anything above a size zero is borderline obese.

Through the front door came three more CALA moms, chattering like a flock of busy starlings. They were all beautifully dressed, well-groomed, and thinner than a single sheet of vellum. I gave another yank at my blouse. Seeing how thin they were made me feel awkward. The shame of being overweight made me hungry.

Who am I kidding? Everything makes me hungry. There's an emptiness in me I can't seem to shake.

The front door to Time in a Bottle opened yet again to admit Linda Kovaleski, Claire's mother. Linda always seemed a bit confused. "Is this the party place?"

Like the other mothers, Linda was tan, underweight, and stylish in her designer clothes. My hair is an outrageous cap of curls; theirs smooth, perfectly cut, and shaped to enhance their best features. And their makeup was always perfect. From the tips of their fingernails to their creamy lips, the women of CALA were impeccably groomed. Maybe that's why I feel like I don't belong. My mother-in-law, Sheila, would be the first to tell you I lack polish.

Jennifer promptly forgot about her magnetic albums. She hurried over to join her friends.

"Anya, honey, ready to go home?" My daughter was standing alone, pretending to be engrossed in the latest paper crafting magazines. I hoped she hadn't picked up on my insecurity. Time to put some spin on the afternoon. "This was fun, wasn't it? I can't wait to make a page of this day. I wouldn't want to forget it."

But as it turned out, I wouldn't need a page to remember the day. In fact, I would give anything to blot that day from my mind. As Anya and I climbed into my Lexus SUV, a uniformed policeman approached the car and gestured for us to talk.

"Yes?" I rolled down the window. "I'm not speeding. I haven't even turned on the engine."

"Mrs. George Lowenstein? Ma'am? I'm afraid I have some bad news. It's about your husband. You need to come with me."

———

KIKI'S INSTRUCTIONS FOR REMOVING PHOTOS
FROM MAGNETIC ALBUMS

1. Start by photocopying the pages. This is particularly important if you have identifying information accompanying your pictures. Once you remove your photos, it may be difficult to match information with images.

2. Set a hairdryer on low and train it on your pages. Move the air stream at all times to keep from overheating any one spot. As the background softens, test to see if you can pull up the plastic page cover and photos.

3. Slide a piece of dental floss or an old credit card under the photos to separate them from the background.

4. Try Un-Du, an archivally safe solvent for loosening adhesives, if your photos still stick to the background.

5. Restore your faded or damaged photos by scanning them and manipulating them with photo-imaging software. Some scanners also include photo restoration software.

TWO

"MY HUSBAND IS DEAD? Are you sure? Sure it's George? I mean, you could have made a mistake. Right?" I couldn't believe what I'd just heard.

Detective Chad Detweiler of the St. Louis County Police Department shook his head solemnly. "No, Mrs. Lowenstein. I'm sorry. There's no mistake. A housekeeper found his body in a room at the Ritz-Carlton. We're sure it is—was—your husband. His clothes were hanging over a chair, and his wallet was in his pants pocket."

I swallowed hard. I'd managed to keep calm on the ride to the police station. I kept reassuring my daughter there must have been a misunderstanding. Now I felt like I was coming apart at the seams. I couldn't focus. I kept repeating, "Dead? My husband is dead? There must be some mistake."

"No, ma'am."

The room swam and turned flips. I tried to process what the detective told me. In my struggle, I focused on the trivial. It seemed more manageable than the big picture. "I, uh, don't understand. Why were his clothes over a chair? You mean he ... he didn't have them on? Did he ... uh ... have on *any* of his clothes?"

The detective shook his head, his eyes never leaving my face. He seemed to be taking my measure, sizing me up.

The large mirror on the adjacent wall of the interview room bounced my image back to me. My hair was always curly, but today it had turned into ringlets. My skin looked blotchy from the cold. And I'd chewed my lips until I could taste the blood in my mouth.

I took tiny sips from the glass of water the detective had offered and swallowed repeatedly to dislodge the lump in my throat. I tried to focus on a far-off object, as I blinked back tears. There were so many questions. Part of me didn't want to ask, didn't want to know. But a voice inside reasoned it was better to hear the worst of it here, from an impartial officer of the law, than in a public place from a "friend." I thought about the mothers I'd left at the scrapbook store and shuddered.

Detweiler sat across from me patiently, silently.

Obviously, someone had made a mistake. That was all there was to it. This man couldn't be talking about George. Not *my* George.

"How can you be so sure? I mean ... don't you need someone to identify the body? You probably just think it's George. As soon as he answers my call, we'll get this straightened out." I reached for my cell phone and punched in his number one more time.

The phone rang and rang.

Suddenly, my whole body grew heavy, and I was incredibly tired. All I wanted was to go home and sleep for a million years. Maybe this had all been a bad dream.

Detweiler sighed. "We got hold of your husband's business partner, Mr. Ballard. I was there when he made the ID. If you'd like to see the body..."

I shook my head vehemently.

"I'm sorry, Mrs. Lowenstein." He didn't press the issue. He could tell I was queasy. Or maybe he worried I'd make a scene.

Poor Bill. A part of me felt guilty that I hadn't been the one to take on this intimate and final task of marital life. It seemed, in some way, the least I could have done for George. And Bill had done it for him. For me. For us. It seemed wrong. It felt like one more failure. I put a hand to my stomach and pressed hard to control the revolt within.

A strand of chestnut hair fell over Detweiler's eyebrow, a dark accent mark to his unwavering gaze. "There'll have to be an autopsy. The law requires one in these circumstances." Detweiler took a sip of his coffee and set the mug down gently on the battered Formica tabletop. A circle of brown indicated the depleted level of the liquid. It reminded me of George's wedding ring.

I fingered my own gold band. I was trying desperately to take in what the detective was saying. George. Was. Dead. What was I going to tell Sheila, my mother-in-law?

"Does George's mother know?"

I did not want to be the one to tell Sheila her son was dead.

"Mr. Lowenstein's mother has been notified." The detective cleared his throat. "Evidently our police chief is an old friend."

Thank God, I thought. She didn't have to hear the news from a stranger.

"A woman at your house," he turned to a page in his steno pad, "a Mert Chambers, told us where to find you."

A thought flittered across the tickertape of my mind and fell on the floor in a pile of other ideas. How could we have Thanksgiving? George always carved the turkey. And what about Hanukkah? He loved shopping for his daughter. How would Anya learn about her Jewish heritage? Who would teach her golf? Take her to Cardinal baseball games? Help her cheer on the Rams on Monday Night Football?

An endless stream of problems presented themselves.

"And you brought us here? Rather than talking to me at home? Why?"

"We have a few questions."

I was afraid to guess what that might mean. Time stood still. I was at the top the roller coaster looking down, suspended, waiting.

In my peripheral vision, I saw Detweiler rub his mouth. He was struggling, trying to decide what to say. I did not look up. I was bracing myself for what was to come.

But I got it wrong.

"Mrs. Lowenstein, did your husband's partner tell you money was missing from the business?"

My head snapped up. "What?" Stars danced in my field of vision.

Saliva flooded my mouth. I struggled not to bolt from my seat. I looked around desperately for the nearest trash can. Any second now, I'd heave my guts all over the floor. Where was the ladies' restroom? I swallowed hard.

"Money? Missing? How much?"

"A half a million dollars."

I jumped up and ran, praying I'd make it to the john.

THREE

Mert drove Anya and me home from the station. She sent her son Roger and one of his friends to pick up my car from the scrapbook store.

After Anya cried herself to sleep, Mert and I sat in my kitchen and talked.

"It don't make sense. George was in good health, wasn't he?" Mert asked.

"He had a complete checkup not six months ago."

"Why you suppose he was there? And naked? You said it was the Adams Mark?" Under stress, Mert's diction emphasized her hardscrabble background.

"Ritz-Carlton," I corrected. I stared at the big silver Viking refrigerator, noting our wavy reflections. It's like my life is happening in a carnival fun house, I thought, and nothing seems real. My husband is dead. And money is missing. None of this made sense.

I needed to talk to George.

But he was gone.

And only this morning everything was fine.

I was dumbstruck by the magnitude of the situation.

Mert's calloused hand reached over to squeeze mine. "When you want to talk, and if you do, I'm here."

We sat quietly, listening to the ticking of the wall clock. She still wore her work clothes, tight black jeans and a rhinestone studded T-shirt, plus five pairs of silver hoop earrings.

Sheila tells me you aren't supposed to pal around with the hired help. My Ladue neighbors would have been shocked to see me and my cleaning lady giggling over margaritas at El Maguey's Mexican restaurant. Frankly, my dear, I don't give a hoot. I liked Mert from the moment I met her in the cleaning product aisle at Lowe's. "Black marks on your porcelain sink? You need Zud. Comet'll make your sink white, 'cause it's got bleach and such, but those black marks from your pots and pans won't ever come out unless you rub a quarter-sized glob of Zud on them."

I do so admire professional excellence.

Mert handed me her card, "Got Dirt? Get Mert! Housecleaner Extraordinaire at a Price That's Fair." It understated her abilities. Mert was also an expert organizer, and a woman of many talents, most too bizarre and unusual to come to light until you desperately needed them.

Best of all, for the past six years she had been my uncritical friend, my go-to gal who is always there for me. If she hadn't been such a terrific cleaning lady, she could have been a very successful therapist. Mert had a way of helping you see things, getting you to cut through messy emotions and move on. Now she asked gently, "Could someone have been there with him? In that hotel room?"

"Maybe."

"You know her name?"

I shook my head. "Over the years there was this sort of on-again, off-again feeling that he was … you know. But I never wanted to ask. And I couldn't be sure. See, I've always felt guilty about how I got pregnant in college. Deep down, I guess I've always felt like I tricked him into marrying me."

Mert changed the subject. "And who found him?"

"A housekeeper."

"I wonder if it was anybody I know. Us folks in the cleaning industry stay right tight."

FOUR

THE AUTOPSY WAS POSTPONED until after the Thanksgiving holiday. Anya and I lived in a suspended state, a twilight of grief, waiting for the funeral service. Five days passed before we could bury George. Sheila raged at the delay, but Missouri law took precedence over the Jewish custom of burial within twenty-four hours.

A few days after the burial, I opened the front door to Detweiler in a suit instead of the khakis and blazer he'd worn at the station. He shifted his weight from foot to foot. His eyes darted from his oversized gold police-issue Impala to my oversized marble foyer. He took in the spiraling staircase of oak with its coiled banisters, the large mahogany table with a graceful vase of fresh flowers, the wide crown molding around the ceiling.

Yeah, our house was a real show place. It just wasn't much of a home. Especially now that George was gone.

He cleared his throat. "May I come in?"

I settled him on an overstuffed sofa and brought him a cup of instant coffee, before pouring a glass of ice water for myself.

"The autopsy says your husband died of natural causes. Looks like he had a heart attack."

I squinted at him. "That makes no sense at all."

"Things like this happen. Maybe he had a heart abnormality. I know it's hard to accept—"

"No. Not hard to accept. Impossible to accept. George had a heart scan and a stress test six months ago. He insisted his doctor do a complete workup after one of his friends had a scan, and they found an aneurism."

"Yes, well, the autopsy was quite thorough. He had a heart attack."

I jumped up and scribbled on a piece of paper. "Here. This is George's doctor. Call him."

Detweiler nodded and tucked the paper in his pocket. "Right. But he had a heart attack."

"How? He was in perfect health."

The detective shook his head. His hands sat loosely on his knees. "We found no signs of foul play."

I gritted my teeth. I'd practiced this next question. I knew I could spit it out. "Were there any signs of sexual activity?"

"No."

"Then explain to me what he was doing alone and naked in a hotel room."

"I have no idea."

"Doesn't that seem awfully suspicious to you? It sure does to me!"

"It doesn't make much sense, but sometimes there just aren't any answers. We're still doing interviews. So far everyone we've talked to says Mr. Lowenstein was alone."

It was my turn to shake my head. "That can't be right. Why was he there? What was he doing? Why would he have taken off his clothes?"

Detweiler cleared his throat. "Could he have been despondent?"

"He'd just broken par on St. Louis Country Club's golf course. The man was ecstatic. Not despondent. All his dreams had come true. In fact, he was talking about flying down to Florida to play during the holidays."

"Really? And this doc will say his health was good?" The detective rubbed his chin thoughtfully. I could see him thinking, puzzling over these pieces that didn't quite match up.

"Absolutely. Are you sure you aren't missing something? You personally talked to everyone at the hotel?"

"Here's how this works. The housekeeper found the body and called her manager. He called us. An officer secured the scene and phoned in a report. Another detective and I interviewed hotel personnel. So, no, I didn't talk to everyone myself."

"Well, somebody has to know something. I mean, isn't this odd? Have you ever had a case like this before?"

Now his hands were tense, and they gripped his knees. I felt mesmerized by his gorgeous green eyes with their dancing gold flecks. I gave myself a hard mental shake. What was I, nuts? This was hardly the time to be distracted by a good-looking man.

"Tell you what I'll do. I'll check with the other officers. I'll tell them about Mr. Lowenstein's recent clean bill of health and state of mind. I'll go back over everything we've got."

"And could I see the police report? I know it probably won't make much sense to me, but I want to. I feel like I should." I knew my own copy of the autopsy was probably sitting in that official envelope at the bottom of a pile of mail I was too cowardly to open.

"Look," Detweiler spoke in a controlled voice, his eyes locked onto mine, "is there something you aren't telling me? Any reason to think someone might want your husband dead?"

"No," I said softly. I noticed he hadn't answered my question about seeing the police report. "I can't imagine anyone wanting to hurt George. And with that missing money, I'd think there was a good reason to keep George alive. But I might be overlooking something. George and I…" I searched for the words. "We sort of led separate lives. I mean, we had our own friends and interests."

I couldn't go on.

"I see." Detweiler's eyes were piercing. I could tell he was thinking hard, processing all I'd said. And he knew I wasn't going to say more.

We walked to my front door.

Pausing on the threshold, Detweiler ran a finger around his collar, clearly feeling choked by his tie. He turned to me with a pitying expression on his face. I swallowed hard and focused on an imaginary spot on my lawn which was splotchy brown and pale yellow from the cold weather. A thick rim of dark clouds hung low in a sky as heavy and wet as fresh concrete. Soon it would snow, a soggy blanketing of flakes, a final tucking in for the earth and all its life forms.

"I'll talk to the officer who secured the scene." His voice was low and firm, his hands jammed deep into his pockets. "But you call me if anything comes to mind. And I mean anything. If I don't have something to go on, a line of questioning to pursue, there's not a lot I can do."

I nodded. We stood, caught up in our individual thoughts, unable to communicate further.

——

I sat in the empty living room and watched droplets run like tears down the side of my half-empty water glass. Not for one moment did I think my husband had died of natural causes.

Someone had planned this. Someone had murdered George. And I wasn't about to let his killer get away with it.

FIVE

After opening the mail, the most worrisome task on my "to-do" list was talking to George's partner, Bill Ballard, about the money my husband "borrowed." A week after Detweiler's visit, I drove to Clayton. I purposely planned my route so that I didn't have to go past the Ritz. Clods of half-melted snow studded with salt crystals dotted the sidewalks. I pulled into George's reserved parking space at the offices of Dimont Development Inc. The business took up all of a storefront that sat in the chilly shadow of taller buildings. This was a prime location because of the nearby municipal offices and headquarters of many Fortune 500 companies.

"If you repay the half million, no one ever needs to know," Bill said. I couldn't look the man in the face. Instead I focused on the beautiful screensaver floating across his computer monitor. In that far-away place, the sky was a cornflower blue, the sand was white, and a strange white structure made of poles beckoned further exploration. If only I could jump into that scene and run away!

"I need a little time. I'm going through all our bank statements and paperwork right now." What I didn't share was how bleak my financial situation seemed. From what I could tell, we owed for George's Jaguar, my Lexus, the new pool he'd insisted we put in last spring, the furniture, and all our country club memberships, as well as our ongoing house payments, utilities, food bills, and the cost of Anya's school.

Our savings were severely depleted by the cost of George's funeral. Not wishing to upset Sheila further, I'd allowed her to make most of the arrangements. She'd given her son a grand send-off.

"Maybe I can help you," Bill interrupted my thoughts. "The attorney who drew up George's will does a lot of work for Dimont. How about I contact him for you? He probably won't charge me to go through whatever needs to be done."

"Such as?"

"Oh, like making sure the death certificate is in order so you can claim any property jointly held and filing for his life insurance. How about it?"

"Under the circumstances, that's very, very kind of you, Bill. I can't thank you enough." Maybe, I thought, maybe the attorney will find money for us to live on. I sure hoped so, because my preliminary analysis told me all we had was the money in my household expenses account. I hadn't gotten up the nerve to open my husband's checkbook. It felt strangely invasive, like a breach of privacy. I assumed there was money in his account, but each time I picked up the leather folio, I felt too nauseated to look. Perusing the check ledger might tell me more about my husband's personal life than I wanted to know.

My carefully constructed ignorance might crumble even further. I wasn't ready for that. I felt like a kid on a bike with training wheels. I knew the time was fast approaching when I'd have to go solo, but I hadn't yet found the courage to wean myself.

Bill smoothed his slicked-back hair with both hands and worked his jaw. "I don't want this to get out, Kiki. If people think they can't trust Dimont Development with their money, well, I hate to think how it could impact the business. And if the banks we work with find out? Good lord, the auditors would swarm this place like flies on a corpse—" he blanched. "Sorry."

I forgave him. I heard a lot of stupid things in the aftermath of George's passing.

"Can Sheila help? Half a million is a lot of money."

I'd gone over and over this in my mind. On one hand, Sheila had the money. Her late husband (and George's father) Harry had left her well off. A half a million wouldn't even put a dent in her savings. Why not ask her for help? Wasn't that what family was for?

On the other hand—and this hand seemed preternaturally big to me, like the right hand of Michelangelo's David—George was Sheila's son. She was already despondent. Wasn't it better to handle this myself? And if she did get involved, what repercussions might follow? The woman didn't like me, never had. I needed a good relationship with her so we could both be there for Anya. My own mother paid little attention to either Anya or me. Sheila was all Anya had. Going to her for money could only make a bad situation worse.

No, I didn't want Sheila involved. I told Bill I'd handle it. All I needed was a little time.

Surely, George's life insurance policy would yield enough money to pay Bill back.

And it would have.

But the money didn't go to me.

SIX

GEORGE'S INSURANCE ALL WENT to Sheila. I dropped the phone when the insurance policy representative delivered the blow.

By my calculations, I could make one more house payment. Basically we had nothing to live on. Scratch that, less than nothing. I was in the hole a half a million dollars.

I called Pamela Bertolli, a real estate agent for whom I'd once helped make a business scrapbook. That afternoon, she brought over a suggested selling price and a marketing plan. I listened carefully as her head bent over the figures.

Pamela wore her hair in solid swerves, a style faintly reminiscent of the modern art museum in Balboa. On anyone else it would look ridiculous, but she was a paragon of good taste.

I did the math. The classic BMW convertible George had purchased on a lark had no Blue Book value so I decided to sell my Lexus and drive the Beemer. If our humongous home in Ladue sold for within ten percent of the asking price, I could pay all our obligations plus the money George owed Bill. Sheila had offered to take over paying Anya's tuition, and I'd taken her up on it. I'd have just enough for a few months' rent on a handyman's special in a less-affluent neighborhood. (That's real estate speak for "a dump in a bad area of town.")

The phone rang just as Pamela tucked the signed copy of the sales contract into her leather briefcase.

Detweiler didn't waste time on small talk. "I've been looking over our department's report. I want to make a few phone calls. Something doesn't feel right. I'm going to the hotel this afternoon. I'll let you know what I find out."

———

A few days later I ran into Elise Maddis picking up her preschooler at CALA. Okay, reporters can be scum-sucking, ambulance-chasing vultures, but some are kind and decent people. Elise was the latter. We'd worked together on a project to bring scrapbooking supplies to the Ronald McDonald House. For a person who covered the society beat, she was amazingly uncomplicated and unpretentious. She dressed nicely, but her eyeliner and lipstick were always on crooked, making her eyes and mouth seem off kilter. On the other hand, maybe her makeup reflected her world view. Who could tell?

I waved her over to a quiet corner. There, huddled beside the enormous white columns that marched the length of CALA's administration building, I found the courage to ask, "Elise, do you know anything about my husband's death? Anything the police don't know?"

She glanced around. "Nothing we could print. A source did tell me that George had lunch with friends earlier that day over at Antonio's on The Hill."

The Hill is an ethnic neighborhood and home to many of St. Louis's best restaurants. Three-quarters of the residents are Italian, and such baseball greats as Yogi Berra and Joe Garagiola grew up there.

"Friends?" I hugged my arms tightly around my body. It was cold out on the portico, but I didn't want to blow my chances by asking her to meet later. That might give her time to reconsider talking. I shivered. "Uh, and who would that be?"

Elise winced. "Two women. Young. Well-dressed. I tried to get their names but I couldn't. A waiter saw the three of them all drive away in one car."

"Really?"

"Yes. But this is strange. When I called back, my source dried up. Couldn't convince anyone else at the place to talk either. Their mouths were tighter than a Mississippi mud flat in an August dry spell."

————

Not long afterward, Mert and I cleaned George's closet.

"You think George didn't go to the hotel alone." Mert folded a dozen silk ties I'd given her for her son.

"Yep. I mean it could have been a business meeting, but if so, why wouldn't his friends talk to Elise? Why did the waiter and everyone else clam up?" I put rolled-up socks in a pile for Roger. The kid had a habit of ramming his big toe through them, and Mert was always buying new pairs. This would hold him for a while. "And I bet Bill knows something. He and George went to high school together. At CALA, of course. But I can't ask him now. I need to wait until I sell the house and pay him back."

"Maybe Sheila paid people at Antonio's to keep quiet."

I nodded. "That wouldn't surprise me. She's always been over-protective. It was probably just an innocent business meeting."

Mert snickered. "Right. The only kind of business a man does with two young women is monkey business. Girl, you gotta wake up and smell the coffee."

I cleared my throat.

"Sorry," she said. Mert could be blunt sometimes, but she means well.

I'd have taken her words better if handling George's clothes didn't make me so emotional. They smelled like him. I pressed one of his slightly worn oxford shirts to my face. I wanted to cry, but I'd wait until Mert left and I was alone. Anya was spending the night at her grandmother's. Having her visit seemed to be the only thing that brightened Sheila's days.

I missed my daughter's father and worried about how I'd come up with the money to pay Bill, but I was lucky compared to Sheila. I hadn't lost my child. I couldn't even imagine that. A pain in my throat choked me, and I gasped for air each time I imagined what Sheila must be feeling. Poor Sheila! If I lost Anya, I'd lie down and die. I wouldn't be able to go on. Yes, Sheila had it much worse than I did.

In fact, compared to most widows, I was lucky. I hadn't lost my soul mate. But I had lost my parenting partner and my friend. I lost the person I talked to daily about life's ups and downs, the local news, the weather, and most of all, our child. Just knowing someone was coming through the front door at the end of the day was one of marriage's greatest blessings, and I definitely mourned that loss.

Despite our problems—and they were many—I had loved George.

"What's next?" asked Mert. "The house is on the market, and you're waiting for that police report. What else can you tell that detective to help him see this weren't no natural death?"

I finished shoving suits into the bag for Goodwill. "I don't know. I finally got the courage last night to open George's checkbook."

"And?"

I turned my back to pull down sweater boxes from the top shelf of my husband's walk-in closet. I didn't want to face Mert. I didn't want to see her expression. "He's been writing big checks to someone on a regular basis."

"Got a name?"

"The ledger said 'orb.'"

"Like shorthand for orbit? And you didn't call that cop and tell him?"

"I left a message on his voice mail and asked him to call me."

Seeing her skeptical expression, I added, "I couldn't get to it until this morning. I've been busy."

SEVEN

PAMELA EXPLAINED THE CONCEPT of staging a house. "Make it look like a movie set. Inviting. Cozy, homey, romantic. Glance through a home décor magazine and you'll get my drift. We want potential buyers to see themselves living here. And clear out the personal effects. Prospects don't want to be reminded you live here. That ruins the fantasy."

Yeah, well, my fantasy was definitely gone with the wind, but if helping other people along with their personal delusions would sell my house, so be it.

Pamela was stopping by later with a couple who'd expressed interest. If they didn't buy, I couldn't make my next payment. I could no longer afford Mert, and my whole life had been taken over readying my home for lookie-loo's.

I fluffed and folded fresh towels, lit candles, and took a Pyrex dish of noodle kugel out of the oven. Cooking one of George's favorite dishes was oddly comforting. The scent of cinnamon and vanilla filled the house.

I worked my way from the top floor down and dragged the vacuum after me, leaving a barely discernible nap in the deep carpet. Everything on the top floors was perfect, but as I finished mopping the kitchen floor, I slipped and spilled an entire bucket of water on myself.

I wasn't about to run upstairs to my closet and leave footprints in the carpet.

I was soaked to the skin. Since I cranked down the heat to save on my gas bill each day when Anya left for school, I was freezing. Goose bumps rose as I stripped and threw my soggy clothes into the dryer.

The doorbell rang.

I stood buck naked in my laundry room. From the hanging rod, I grabbed a damask tablecloth I'd just washed and wrapped it about me like a sari.

The bell rang again, more insistently. Whoever was out there had seen my car and knew I was home.

I shuffled toward the front door, the tight wrap curtailing my stride. My bust wasn't big enough to hold up the makeshift dress. The whole shooting match started to slither away from me. I grabbed the fabric and re-tucked the white length of cloth into the selvage around my bust.

"Coming! Coming!" I swung the door wide.

Detweiler stared at me. For a moment, he said nothing, the gold flecks dancing in the bottle-green of his eyes. Then, "Your husband was found naked. Hmmm. Are you a family of nudists?"

"Not hardly. Look," I said with a sigh. "I was just leaving."

"In that? That's a tablecloth, right?" His finger inched toward my bustline and the wad of cloth I clenched in my fist. "And you were going out? Aren't you a bit underdressed? This is Ladue after all."

"No. I mean, yes. I was just getting my coat."

"Oh. And mittens? To complete the ensemble? That's kind of a new look for you, isn't it?"

A release of tension told me the cloth around my chest was giving way. I needed to hurry this conversation along. "People are coming to see the house."

He nodded. He was biting his lip to keep from laughing. "And you are what? The greeter? Like at Wal-Mart? Let me guess, it's a toga, right?"

"Uh-oh," I could feel more fabric starting to slip. I grabbed a hunk in my free hand. Now I was using both hands to hold the tablecloth in front of me like a shield.

A breeze tickled my rear end.

This was bad. Really bad.

"How 'bout you come back later."

He watched me struggle, his eyes twinkling. "Why? Is there a floorshow?"

"My clothes are in the dryer. I'm having a bad day, okay? Give me thirty minutes and I'll meet you at St. Louis Bread Co."

He smiled. "No problem. You might also want to grab a pair of shoes. Or maybe sandals would go better with your ... uh ... out-fit." Then, he winked at me. "Remember, no shoes, no shirt, no service."

EIGHT

"THERE'S AN INTERVIEW MISSING." Over a smoked turkey sandwich on focaccia and a cup of broccoli cheddar soup, Detweiler was all business now. He insisted on paying so I ordered a tall glass of green tea and a sourdough bread bowl of low-fat vegetarian black bean soup.

He continued, "Another detective was supposed to talk to the housekeeper who found your husband's body. And we're missing information because of the shift change. The hotel records show the assistant manager was on duty when Mr. Lowenstein died. But—and here's where it gets interesting—the responding officer only talked with the manager."

"So what happens next?"

"I follow up. I talk to the housekeeper and the assistant manager. Now, what did you want to see me about? Anything I need to know?"

The nearness of his body, the smell of his cologne, the sound of his voice were all getting to me. I wanted to reach over and touch him.

Which was silly. Really silly of me. This was business. And he felt sorry for me. That was all.

I cradled a heavy coffee mug in my hands. I'd shivered after the iced green tea. Without a word, he'd gotten up, ordered two coffees, and placed one in front of me. I took a sip and decided to trust the man. "I heard George had lunch with two people, two young and well-dressed women, the day he died. They left the restaurant and got in a car together. My source tried to follow up and no one would talk."

There. I'd made a contribution to the investigation.

"You heard this? From who?"

"I need to protect my sources." After all, I'd been a journalism major in college. Time to use what little education I had.

"Your ... sources? That's rich." Detweiler tapped my hand softly with his index finger. "Did your sources have any idea who your husband might have been with?"

My stomach flipped. "No." I glanced up at him. "No," I repeated more firmly.

Detweiler moved on. "Something else that's bothering me, I don't remember seeing a report on the key cards."

"Key cards?"

"They're coded. I couldn't find where anyone checked whether Mr. Lowenstein was issued one card or two. Or if anyone entered the room just before the housekeeper did."

"You could learn that from those silly plastic cards?" I was impressed.

"Maybe there's a reason all this isn't in the report."

"Such as?"

"Could be sloppy police work. With ninety-one different municipalities in the greater St. Louis area, stuff falls through the cracks."

"Or?"

"Or maybe someone is covering up." He sighed. "I hate to think that. But I'm not naïve. This *is* St. Louis. People here have—"

"Connections," I supplied.

"What high school did you go to?" We chanted in chorus. That question was the standard opening gambit for anyone in the area. By learning what high school you attended, a native of St. Louis could tell what religion you were, your ethnic background, how much money you had, and what your social status was.

Detweiler nodded and continued, "People in St. Louis go to school together, worship together, marry each other, and spend the rest of their lives hanging out together."

"Exactly." Which went a long way toward explaining why I never fit in.

I took a deep breath. "There is one other thing..." I told Detweiler about the regular checks George had written to "orb." Then I swallowed hard and added, "And I have no idea who or what 'orb' might be."

My imagination must have kicked into high gear. I could have sworn he stared at me with sad eyes as he said, "I'll check into that."

———

A few days later Mert and I pulled up in front of a small apartment building not far from the Busch Brewery. A set of rickety wooden stairs once painted white climbed past the first floor to a bent aluminum storm door on the second. The glass was missing, if indeed it had ever been there. All that stood between the apartment and the cold winter wind was an insubstantial wooden door that didn't even meet the floor. Splinters of wood along the perimeter told me the door was hollow. Mert rapped sharply and the sound of her knuckles echoed.

A dark-haired woman with drooping, worried brown eyes answered. Under an oversized man's sweater, a faded housedress clung to her, draped like a thin painter's cloth. As I glanced down to step over the threshold, I could see angry purple veins running up her legs like a trellis.

"Irma, this here's my friend Kiki."

I took the woman's rough hand and shook it. "Thank you for agreeing to talk to us." A wonderful smell of bacon and onions filled the air as we followed Irma into her kitchen. Through an archway to our left, four children under the age of ten sat on a sagging sofa and watched a flickering television.

We pulled up chairs. I watched Irma cook and realized the dish she was making was very similar to one I'd seen in a magazine. I made mental notes because it smelled so good. Mert shocked me by speaking Spanish to her colleague.

Why on earth had I taken French in high school? "Jacques has the red crayon" hadn't gotten me anywhere in life. Somehow I doubted it ever would come in handy. At least not at the rate my life was going.

I caught "señora" and "señor" and my last name as they rattled along.

Mert translated. "Irma didn't find George, but she knows the woman who did. The other gal's afraid to talk with us. The police have already been to see her. She ain't talking with them neither. She's worried she'll be deported."

"I don't want to cause any trouble, Mert. Please, reassure her. I just need to know if Irma's friend saw anything suspicious."

Mert and Irma exchanged accented volleys. Both waved their hands in the air. I was beginning to think they'd forgotten me, when Mert said, "There's one thing. She doesn't want to get her friend in trouble—"

The Latina raised her eyes to mine. Her mouth was set tightly, and her fist clenched the wooden spoon.

How could I convince her to talk?

I crossed my heart in a childish gesture. I raised a hand as if taking the pledge. I broke down and begged, "Please. *Por favor.*" That used up every bit of my Spanish vocabulary.

Finally I offered my little finger. "I pinky swear."

Irma's face relaxed and we met halfway, linking small digits. She tapped the wooden spoon against the side of an iron skillet. "Ho-kay. It was woman's scarf. Silk. My friend, she say, she find scarf in el hombre's mouth. The color was, how do you say?"

Mert translated, "Aqua and black. Striped. Like a zebra."

Back in my BMW, Mert hesitated. "I'll be jiggered. And the manager took the scarf, and musta hid it afore the police got there. Sounds pretty suspicious-like to me. Whatcha reckon happened?"

"Sheila," I said tiredly. "The assistant manager was on duty. He called the manager when it happened, and I'd bet anything the manager called Sheila. Probably knew her from some charity board. She used her money and connections with the police chief to protect George's reputation."

"Unless he was into flying solo, your hubby wasn't in that hotel room alone," said Mert. "That sound like him? Was he a wild man?"

"Huh, George thought patterned boxers were obscene." I stared out my windshield at the line of cars clogging Highway 40. "I'll have to tell Detweiler what we learned. And I have to figure out how to tell him without getting an illegal alien in trouble. That'll be tough. I'm not sure I can pull the 'protect my sources' gambit twice. I've got information, but I can't share it. And without what we've just learned, he can't turn this into a murder investigation."

I thought for a minute.

Mert heaved a tired sigh. "Okay. I'll go to a pay phone and call in an anonymous tip. You s'pose that'll work?"

"Absolutely." I sent up a prayer of thanks for such a terrific friend. "Of course there's nothing stopping me from snooping around too. I always did like Nancy Drew."

"Not me," Mert cleared her throat. "She ain't my type. I always had a hankering for them Hardy Boys."

NINE

PAMELA BROUGHT ME AN offer for the house and counseled me to accept. She didn't have to ask twice. I was on it like needles on a pine tree. In what I'm sure was an act of charity, she also helped me find a small place to rent. I would be able to pay back Bill as soon as the paperwork cleared. But I still needed money for Anya and me to live on.

I was willing and eager to work. But where? And at what?

Dodie became the most unlikely of saviors. I'd been going on an endless and humiliating round of job interviews when she stopped by.

"I need help at the store." She watched me tape a packing box shut.

The couple buying my house fell in love with my furniture. With Pamela's help, we came to an accommodation and I sold most of it. That extra money would tide me over until I got a job. Roger was helping me transfer my things into Mert's garage until I could move into my new home, a smallish brick box set on a crumbling street in a diverse neighborhood. The new place needed a major cleaning and paint job. I was up at dawn and busy every moment of the day and getting more panicky by the minute because I hadn't found employment.

Dodie continued, "I don't know your situation, or if this appeals to you, but I talked this over with my hubby Horace, and I'd like to make you a business proposition."

I'd never seen Dodie outside of Time in a Bottle. She moved about like a wild animal in an unfamiliar environment. As she talked, she paced my living room floor, while turning her key chain over and over in her meaty hands. Having a six-foot-tall linebacker wearing a lopsided floral dress and following a path round and round in circles made me nervous. My kingdom for a tranquilizer dart. As she walked, she scratched various body parts intermittently. This seemed to be a nervous habit, but given her hirsute physique it could have been fleas. Later I would learn that Dodie had grown up dirt poor, like I had, and her method of overcoming her fear of poverty was to attack financial matters head on.

Mine was to run and hide. Head down in the sand, bottoms up. Not a very secure or smart position. And not one that seemed to be working.

But she wouldn't let me take cover.

She asked what I thought I needed to survive.

I told her I didn't know.

"Let me guess. You went straight from under Mom and Dad's roof to under George's, with a brief layover in a college dorm."

"Is it that obvious?"

"Unemployed and clueless. Pitiful combination, sunshine." She rattled off a Yiddish proverb and translated it for me: "Ask advice

43

from everyone, but make up your own mind." With a grunt, she added, "When you decide what to do, call me."

———

True to his word, Detweiler phoned a couple of weeks after our meeting at Bread Co. His frustration leaked from every word. "The housekeeper working that day at the Ritz-Carlton has moved back to Mexico, a place called Toluca. I've heard rumors she found an article of clothing in the room, but I'm not at liberty to say what. But no one saw another guest with your husband, and no one saw anyone leaving the room."

"Which leaves us … where?" I prayed the housekeeper moved to Mexico of her own free will and hadn't been deported.

"That leaves us bupkis. Nowhere."

What little I knew about Yiddish was right down there with Jacques and his red crayon, so I refrained from explaining that *bupkis* literally means "goat droppings."

"How about fingerprints?" I tried to be helpful.

"We've got fingerprints."

"So can't you track someone down with those? They do it all the time on television."

"Yeah," he said, extending the word to two syllables. "We call that the CSI effect. An unreal expectation based on a television program. See, unless a suspect committed a crime before, or unless the individual has had prints taken for a job or what-have-you, the prints aren't in our system. So, okay, we've got prints from the room—lots of prints—but when we ran them they didn't match anyone."

"Any luck on finding out who or what 'orb' is?"

"No."

I stood in the middle of my empty living room. The house had been sold, my culled-down belongings were in Mert's garage, and for the past two weeks I'd been fixing up my new domicile. The landlord had "graciously" allowed me to both pay rent and make improvements. I didn't want my daughter to see the place before I spruced it up. She'd go into shock. Bad enough her whole life had turned upside down and her dad was dead. Adding a move to the slums was going to be a crushing blow—unless I could provide enough eyewash to distract her.

Temporarily, Anya was staying at Sheila's. Valentine's Day had come and gone, delivering a pang as I remembered how George always sent me a dozen red roses. The Easter holidays were nearly upon us. Sheila was taking my child to Florida for spring break. I'd called my mother and sister just to check in. and succeeded only in re-opening old wounds of family strife and sibling rivalry.

I had never felt so alone in my life.

And now, now I'd let George down all over again. I was failing at helping Detweiler catch his killer.

I could hear the detective breathing softly into the phone and waiting.

"Is there anything more that can be done?" I whispered. My throat tightened and ached.

"You could exhume the body and pay to have more tests run."

I ended the conversation with my thanks and sank down to my knees on the carpet of the empty room in the empty house. No way would Sheila sit still for an exhumation, especially one that was little more than a witch hunt. All that was left of our life as a family was this vacant building and my beloved scrapbooks. A tear rolled down my cheek and splashed onto my hand.

It was left to me to find out who or what 'orb' was.

And I needed to find out who was with George in that hotel room. I could no longer avoid the truth; my husband was involved with another woman.

What I needed was a name.

Suddenly it dawned on me. Time in a Bottle would be the perfect cover for investigating George's death. Everybody who was anybody patronized the store. The wealthy elite of St. Louis moved in a circle as tight as a pair of control-top panty hose. Surely one of them knew who my husband was seeing, who the aqua-and-black-striped scarf belonged to. And it would be easy enough to discover what they did know. People record their personal and social lives on their scrapbook pages. Someone, somewhere, had to have seen my husband with his girlfriend.

Okay, Detweiler was stymied. But I could snoop around on my own. Who would suspect me? I was just a mom.

Shoot, I was as good as invisible.

I called Dodie and named a figure.

She laughed, a deep rumble like thunder. "I couldn't pay Martha Stewart that much, sunshine. Welcome to the real world. Who do you think I am, your fairy godmother? I can't promise you that in salary, but..." She limned out a plan that had me working as a freelance scrapbook consultant, as well as full-time help in the store. Dodie figured I could also teach classes, especially to newbies who wanted to start scrapping. The benefits were slim, but mindful I had a child, Dodie compensated with flexible hours.

It wasn't perfect, but it was a plan.

KIKI'S LIST OF SUPPLIES
FOR BEGINNING SCRAPBOOKERS

You don't have to spend a lot of money to get started scrapbooking. Many people become overwhelmed and buy what they don't need, neglecting what they do need. Here are basic supplies which will be enough to create a nice scrapbook:

1. Scissors: Get a pair of scissors with large blades, and a pair with tiny blades for small cuts.

2. Adhesives: Buy several kinds. HERMA Dotto Removable Adhesive is super for beginners because you can reposition items until you get them exactly where you want. In addition, buy a package of photo splits and a liquid adhesive such as Elmer's Craft Bond, which dries clear and doesn't run.

3. An 8" × 8" album: Try the Perfect Scrapbook by Jill A. Rinner. Although 12" × 12" is standard, 8" × 8" is less intimidating for a beginner. Plus, you can trim your 12" × 12" paper and use the extra for mattes.

4. A paper trimmer: Choose one that cuts 12" paper.

5. A craft knife: X-Acto makes a good one with replaceable blades.

6. Archivally safe pens: Sakura has a great line called Pigma Micron.

7. A pencil and an eraser.

8. A ruler: Get a metal one so you can't cut through it.

9. A paper kit: Buy a package with several sheets of coordinating papers and embellishments. The best kits show you what you are buying so you know if you like all the patterns and colors. If you are making a specific album, take your photos along when you shop for a kit. Hold the pictures up to the paper—you'll quickly see if they look good together.

10. A half-dozen sheets of archivally safe paper: Buy white (or ivory) and solids that match your kit. The white can be used for journaling. The solids make great photo mattes.

TEN

THAT'S HOW I CAME to be standing in a cardboard box, six months to the day that George died.

"This has to be the most embarrassing moment of my life." I stared through two peep holes. Covered in white and silver paper with an enormous white bow on top, my prison was wrapped like a gigantic bridal shower gift. The container and I were situated on a narrow grassy strip in Elizabeth Witherow's back yard. In front of me was a flower bed thickly planted with fragrant petunias, salvia, geraniums, and marigolds. Behind me a collection of koi splashed around in a pool at the foot of a trickling fountain. The running water made me need to tinkle. A dangling length of ribbon held the front flap of the "gift" closed. When Dodie pulled the ribbon, the front wall would open flat, and I would burst from my hiding place.

At least, that was the plan.

Geez, was it ever hot inside. The heady sweetness of the flowers filled the air. The blossoms warmed in the sun while bees buzzed about busily gathering pollen.

"No way. I'm positive this isn't the most embarrassing moment of your life. Not by a long shot," said Dodie, talking to my eyeballs, her garish mouth larger than the jaws of a giant carp. "And remember, I'm paying you big money to do this. Big money."

Big money, I thought, huh. My salary was peanuts, but to me it was a king's ransom. This special event would bring in extra—enough to pay my rent with a little left over to take Anya to see that new Pixar movie.

I adjusted my body, as I struggled to see the garden and the pretty table set up directly across from me. The eye holes drilled into the cardboard were small. I faced the blinding sun. St. Louis is known for manic-depressive extremes of weather, and this spring was no exception. We had four inches of snow on St. Patrick's Day. Hail pelted us two weeks later. Here we were the last week in May with a scorcher. My prison had warmed to a temperature so hot that sweat dripped into my eyes. I flapped my arms to dry my pits, but I didn't have much room to move around. Angry bees tapped persistently on the outside walls. I was standing in their salad bar.

"I hear the guests coming. Remember to hop out and scream, 'Surprise!' Okay?"

Like I would forget what to do.

The moment of my liberation couldn't come quickly enough. I counted the seconds until my escape. Sweat moistened my waistband and trickled down the backs of my calves. My bra was soaked from perspiration. I strained to listen as distant voices grew louder. I heard women giggling, talking all at once.

In a stage voice, Dodie said, "Merrilee Witherow, what have we here? Another gift for you? The tag says this present is for our little bride-to-be. Don't just stand there! Open it!"

Yes, I begged Merrilee silently. Please, release me, let me go!

Ribbon rubbed against ribbon. A sliver of light sliced the top of my chamber and grew steadily larger. The panel fell slowly. I waited until the flap was parallel to the ground before leaping out. I lunged forward and yelled, "Surprise! It's scrapbook time!"

Staring in speechless astonishment was a seated row of neatly dressed women, cool and collected in their linens and silk.

I brandished a big photo album open to a page announcing, "Merrilee's Bridal Shower" in large gold letters.

What a sad sight I must have been. My clothes dripped with sweat. I could tell my mascara had smeared under my eyes, and my curly hair stuck out like a '60s Afro. I probably looked like Bozo the Clown after an all-night binge.

The guests' eyes traveled down and up my body. Their faces reflected shock and awe. While my personal grooming stunned them, the capper was the geeky gift bows Dodie had insisted on pinning all over my clothes.

No one moved. The women gawked at me, their faces blurred by the sweat in my eyes. I struggled to keep a huge smile plastered across my face.

Okay, maybe it looked like a grimace, but I tried, I really tried to smile. Sweetly.

An insect crawled along the back of my knee. I held my pose until that nasty sweat bee jabbed his stinger into my flesh. Then I yelped with pain. I dropped the album as I reached behind to swat him. I aimed to kill, but I missed by a mile. He was a poor sport.

51

He must have called in reinforcements. My whole body was attacked by sweat bees.

"Ow!" A dozen angry flying objects zapped me. A zillion volts of venom pulsed through me. "Ow!" I hopped from one foot to another. Molten lava raced through my flesh. The throbbing pain made me dizzy. A bee landed on my neck. "Ow," I stepped to one side, then the other, trying to dodge my torturers. Searing stingers plunged into my skin. A bee nailed me under my arm. Another punctured my lower lip. One landed under my ear. I slapped at them furiously.

"Get off my flowers!" An angry woman in a purple silk A-line dress shouted. "Move it! Now!"

I staggered like a drunk, battling bees, clutching my painful stings.

Dodie screamed, "Watch out! Pay attention!"

"Ow!" The insects swarmed me. Desperate to escape, I hopped back into the box. A bee sank his stinger into my eyelid. "Ow!" I swatted at him. My cardboard jail rocked side to side. Other bees took up the chase.

Dodie chanted, "Be careful! Be careful!"

But I heard, "Bee! Careful!" I spun and writhed, bumping each wall of the box in turn.

"Help!" The box and I tipped too far to recover. I fell into the fish pond with a loud splash.

———

"The swelling is going down. Nothin' better than meat tenderizer for a bee sting. How do you feel?" Mert dabbed a cotton ball full of liquid on the bump by my eye. She was kind enough to buy tenderizer on her way to my house.

You don't need tenderizer when all you eat is hamburger.

I considered myself lucky to have driven home without an accident. My half-closed eye and overblown lower lip hurt like the dickens. My depth perception was distorted, making the world one-dimensional. I couldn't judge distance accurately. I compensated by driving very, very slowly.

"I feel woozy. Benadryl makes me sleepy. How's Anya?" I tried to peer into the living room where my daughter was. I perched on the edge of a straight-back wooden chair, while wearing nothing but an old T-shirt and panties. Drinking ice tea was difficult with my overblown bottom lip. Using a paper napkin, I caught a trail of drool before it slid down my chin. My reflection in my spoon assured me I looked like I'd been in a bar fight. And lost.

Mert poked her head around the doorway and checked on Anya. "Hey, kid, you okay in there?"

Anya smiled at Mert and gave the older woman a thumbs-up. Her shoulder-length hair framed her oval face with two smooth wings of silken blonde strands. She was sitting cross-legged on the sofa, a book open in her lap. Her coltish legs were still pale from the winter, her knees knobby and childlike. "Better than Mom. Just trying to finish my English assignment. I hate tests on Mondays. They wreck your whole weekend."

"Tell me again," said Mert, hugging a glass of iced tea to her chest, savoring the cold. She was wearing a low-cut top with sparkling beads and sequins around the neckline. Platinum polish turned her fingernails into ice-cube talons. "Old Mrs. Witherow told you she didn't have any Benadryl or Caladryl—"

"Or baking soda. Nothing. Nothing to put on my stings. No aspirin or ibuprofen either."

"And she couldn't spare anything to help the pain. Or wouldn't. She's a real 'begins with B and rhymes with witch'."

The vehemence in Mert's voice awakened Gracie from her slumber. The big girl lifted her sloppy muzzle to rest it on my knee.

I shivered as I remembered my slow crawl out of the koi pond. "Dodie yelled at me for ruining everything. She was so nervous. She's not usually like that. The guests went inside to eat and watch Merrilee open gifts. Mrs. Witherow's maid directed me to the guest bathroom. I toweled off with toilet paper."

"I can see." Mert shook her head at the clumps of wet paper still stuck to my skin.

Gracie stretched as she rose from her dog bed. Milton and Bradley, the two Chihuahuas I'd been dog-sitting for Mert, stood up along with her. The little dogs raced to wrap themselves around Gracie's front ankles.

From their positions near her feet, the two canine lover boys stared up at my Great Dane with intense expressions of passion.

So close and yet so far away.

At this rate they'd never get to doggy Nirvana. They clung to her like twin Ugg boots. Gracie took a robotic step forward, dragging the two hairballs along for the ride. They remained attached, whining and yipping for all they were worth.

Which was not much in my opinion. Gracie concurred. She rolled her eyes and took another shuffling step, trying to knock off her freeloaders.

Poor Gracie. She was so ill-used, and so patient.

"Hey, you two, stop that." Mert bent over to peel the Chihuahuas off my dog. I took one from her so that we both held puny excuses for man's best friend on our laps.

Thinking about Mrs. Witherow's behavior toward me brought on a wave of remorse for not paying more attention to the plight of the hired help in my upscale former neighborhood. "Mert, is that the way people always act toward you? I mean, was it like this—is it like this when you clean for people?"

Mert's five hoop earrings marched in formation up her earlobe. They tilted to one side as she shrugged. Her penciled-in brows puckered to consider the question and then relaxed in surrender. "Some do. Some don't. You never did. Some folks make you come in through the back door. And a couple check your purse before you leave. One woman I worked for patted me down each time I left. Another gave me leftover food and tried to take it out of my wages. It don't pay to dwell on it." She closed the topic with a wave of her hand. "What happened after you dried off?"

I handed over Bradley—or was it Milton? Mert arm-wrestled the wriggling dog into her lap.

"I went into the family room where they'd set up work tables for scrapbooking. My page kits were in the boxes I delivered last week."

"You call them make 'n' takes, right?"

I nodded. "A make 'n' take includes all you need to create a pre-designed page except for adhesives, paper trimmers, and ink products. All the crafter does is assemble the page."

"Or project," she corrected. "A make 'n' take can be a project, right?"

"Right. Like a customized candle or bracelet or a notebook."

My make 'n' take was a particularly nifty page design, if I do say so myself. The theme was a garden party, so I used silk flowers, matching ribbon, and four patterned papers plus pre-cut letters spelling "Bridal Shower."

Mert refilled my mug with ice tea. After George died, she brought me a special coffee cup that says, "No More Mrs. Nice Guy." After I read the slogan, she leaned close and said, "For the next year, you are my project. I'm going to turn you into a woman who can stand on her own two feet. No more life as a human doormat, just waiting for people to wipe off their shoes on you. Makes me sick at heart, but you got to toughen up or you ain't gonna make it. And you got no choice but to make it because your little girl depends on you. Hear?"

That was hard, but she was right. That's what a real friend does— she tells you what you don't want to hear, even risking your friendship, because you are important to her.

I heard. And I obeyed. I'm the star pupil in Mert's School of Hard Knocks, better known as Tough Tamales University or TTU. I'm hoping to graduate Magna Cum Laude. Or as Mert says, "Magna cum LOUDLY. That rhymes with proudly."

I'm her only pupil, but I'm sure enrollment will increase when word gets around. I bet I'm not the only woman in the world who has a wishbone where her spine should be.

She handed me the mug, and I dutifully drank. When Mert's around, I'm only allowed to drink out of my special mug or I get demerits. "Best to flush out your system. You got all them bee sting juices in you." She poured herself another glass of ice tea as well. "Now tell me about this floozy. What's her name?"

"Roxanne. Roxanne Baker." I'd seen her photo a million times in the society section of the Ladue newspaper.

ELEVEN

"Here's what happened." I peeped around the corner to make sure Anya wasn't listening. "I was swollen, lumpy, and covered with globs of wet toilet paper when Mrs. Witherow introduced me to the women. One by one, they gave their names, then got real quiet when it was Roxanne's turn."

"What'd she say?"

———

I thought back over that day. Roxanne was tan and thin except for what looked like a pair of over-inflated beach balls popping out the top of her skimpy aquamarine sun dress. A chain of opals hung around her neck and nestled between her twin assets. Her eyes narrowed, and she gave me a wicked once-over before hissing, "So this is the famous Kiki. My, my, my."

How bizarre. I wondered what was up. I could see all the other women suppressing any signs of emotion. I tried to be polite. "Your name sounds familiar, as well."

She smirked.

Suddenly, I remembered. "Didn't you used to date my late husband, George?"

She stared down her nose at me and sneered, "That's one way of putting it."

The other women hopped up and began chattering over their make 'n' takes. Merrilee especially needed a lot of attention. I didn't have the chance to say more to Roxanne because I was busy helping the women get started.

———

Their lack of dexterity had flummoxed me. As I told Mert, "You'd think they'd never handled a pair of scissors in their lives. Except for Roxanne and Tisha."

"Comes from having other people do everything for you," snorted Mert. "They're all dang-near helpless. Can't even find their own backsides with two hands. Who all was there?"

"Mrs. Witherow, her daughter Merrilee, Roxanne, Bill Ballard's wife Tisha, Sally O'Brien, Markie Dorring, Jennifer Moore—the woman who organized the play date the same day George died—and Linda Kovaleski. Her daughter Claire is in the same grade as Anya. We used to sit beside each other in the carpool line."

My turn to pour us both more ice tea. "The good news is that Merrilee was so thrilled with the make 'n' takes that she wants me to make her wedding album. She's stopping by tomorrow to work out the details. As a surprise, Dodie slipped the memory cards out of all the guests' digital cameras while they were eating. She downloaded the images so I could make bridal shower albums. The women had no idea we could include pictures they'd been taking during the party."

"And the bad news?"

"I blew it. Roxanne was really nasty to me, and I told her off."

———

Dodie has convinced me my work is my best advertisement. As the women finished their make 'n' takes, she brought out my albums for them to look through. Roxanne pointed a jubilant finger at an old picture of me and said in a loud voice, "What a porker."

I cringed. My weight has been an issue much of my life.

"How could George stand being married to such a chubby?" Roxanne continued.

I turned away and bit my lip. My weight wasn't the cause of my marital problems. George always told me it was fine, even though I didn't believe him. Whenever something bothered me, I turned to food for comfort. Bad idea. A minute on the lips and a lifetime on the hips. Sure, food felt good going down, but after I swallowed, the guilt erased every smidgeon of satisfaction.

Ironically, after George's death, even the thought of food made me sick. In a dark recess of my mind, I worried I wouldn't be able to feed Anya, so I quit eating. I know that sounds silly, but I wasn't thinking straight.

Before long, my pants sagged around my waist. That's when Mert stepped in. "Either you start eating, or I'll drag your scrawny self to the hospital psych ward."

I forced myself to eat regular meals until my appetite returned.

So, yeah, I was skinny now. Whoop-de-do. Thin wasn't near as much fun as I thought it would be. I liked having room in my clothes, but being svelte didn't solve all life's problems like I thought it would.

When Roxanne's mean remark didn't faze me, she struck again. "How does a person get that big? What did you do? Sit around and stuff your face all day?"

Well, duh.

Once after a fight with my mother, I went to Wal-Mart and filled a shopping cart with half-price Halloween candy. The check-out clerk asked, "You planning a party?" She was half-right. It was a pity party, and I was the guest of honor.

I ignored Roxanne's comment and concentrated on gathering leftover paper. Thanks to my meager income, I was putting the "scrap" back into scrapbooking.

"Poor George," said Roxanne. "He looks miserable in all these photos."

He did not. The woman was either blind or a liar.

Tisha Ballard tried to change the subject. She said "I swear, Kiki, you are so creative. These layouts are gorgeous. Were they hard? Can you help me learn to scrapbook? Too bad my birthday was last month, or I'd ask Bill to give me lessons as a gift."

Jennifer Moore turned to Tisha and said, "Nicci had so much fun at the scrapbooking play date. We should get the girls together and take a lesson."

I responded to the cue for a sales pitch. "I'd be delighted to do a mother-daughter class. I don't know if you've stopped by the store recently, but we're getting new paper in all the time."

Dodie took advantage of the compliments to hand coupons and goody bags to Sally, Markie, Jennifer, Linda, and Tisha.

Roxanne moved in and stood too close to me, invading my personal space, as I stacked adhesives in the Cropper Hopper. I could smell alcohol on her breath.

"Look, everybody." She held up an album and pointed to a picture of me nine months pregnant with Anya. "She was as big as a whale—"

That was too much. Most of the guests were mothers themselves. They remembered being bigger than bread trucks. Roxanne's remark struck pay dirt. The women recoiled. Even Merrilee pouted with concern and said, "Roxie, darling, let's go upstairs. I want you to see the brochures I have from where Jeff and I are going for our honeymoon."

But Roxanne was spoiling for a fight. "No. I don't want to go upstairs," she said, flicking her red hair over her shoulder with one exquisitely manicured hand. "I want to stay right here."

Sally O'Brien took Roxanne's hand and said, "Come on, honey, we're done here. Let's go—"

"No!" Roxanne jerked her hand away. She struggled for balance. Her stiletto heel gouged my foot. I grimaced in pain. Slamming into me, she came to rest with an arm draped over my shoulder. I eased her off. Sally helped Roxanne right herself. Roxanne stared into my face and homed in on me the way a cat does a field mouse, head swiveling to follow my every move.

Linda tried to distract her. "Roxanne, sweetie, can I see those pictures on your camera again? Let's go over them together, okay?"

Roxanne bellowed at her, "Leave me alone!"

Merrilee and Sally each grabbed her by the arm. "Come on, Roxie."

But Roxanne wouldn't be deterred. She leaned close and shook a finger in my face. "George only took up with you back in college because I dumped him! What do you think of that? Huh? I dumped him! You got my leftovers!"

Now the women went silent, waiting for my response. I was too embarrassed to meet their eyes. I kept stacking supplies in the Cropper Hopper.

"Don't you have anything to say? Anything?" A spray of Roxanne's spittle landed on my face.

That did it. I turned to the evil woman beside me and said, "Leave me alone. Why don't you just eat bugs and die?"

KIKI'S SUGGESTIONS FOR PAPER CRAFTING WITH GROUPS

1. Keep your project simple.

2. Provide your guests with stable, smooth, and clean work surfaces.

3. Choose a project with visual dazzle and a limited number of pieces. The more pieces you have the more potential problems you have. Gluing small pieces together in advance will help.

4. Think through your supplies/tools carefully. How many of them can be shared? How many will you need for each individual?

5. Break your paper down into parts of pages. For example: If each guest needs a half a sheet of red paper, you can save money and time by dividing a sheet of red paper in half and giving each person a portion rather than wasting a full sheet.

6. Package small items in individual zippered plastic bags. Put the small bags into larger bags so it's easy to hand each person all the project pieces at once. (Be sure to have extra pieces on hand, but keep them separate so you don't get them confused with complete sets.)

7. Show samples of your project in various stages of completion. Some folks are visual learners and need to see how things go together to follow your oral instructions.

TWELVE

MERT PUT MILTON AND Bradley, the Mexican jumping beans, in their travel carriers and paid me for three days of dog sitting. "That money's hardly enough for Gracie's dog chow, but at least it's something. And the tenderizer is on me. I'll take the rest home. Roger and I are having steaks tonight."

At nineteen, Roger was a strapping young man, six feet tall and still growing. Anya had a big crush on him, and I could see why. He was as sweet as he was handsome.

"Hey, the cash is a big help. Gracie appreciates the ongoing contribution to her upkeep. She's my favorite mistake, aren't you, baby?" I reached down to stroke the big dog's floppy ears.

The last thing I needed after George died was another mouth to feed. Gracie weighs one hundred twenty pounds. A smarter woman would have found a smaller dog. But the Great Dane and I had a common bond: no one wanted either of us because we were just too big.

So my finding Gracie was *bashert*. That's Yiddish for "fated" or "meant to be," and the term usually refers to finding the love of your life or your truest, best-est friend.

A week after George's funeral, I was driving past a pet store with an adoption activity in progress. I paused to let a family with kids in tow navigate the crosswalk. One look at poor Gracie, her black-and-white body squashed inside a small pen, her uncropped ears falling softly around expressive eyes, and I was out of the car filling out forms.

The adoption volunteer quizzed me gently. "Ever own a Great Dane?"

"Nope."

"Um, a dog this size could cause a lot of damage."

"Yep."

Sure, Gracie weighs more than Anya, but the soft light in her eyes told me she was a gentle giant. Once out of the tiny crate, she quickly proved herself to be a loving and patient companion. As I completed the paperwork, she leaned her body against mine, her weight nearly knocking me over. She gazed up at me, her eyes filled with adoration. My heart melted.

Although Gracie's size is intimidating, her disposition is strictly low-key. If I'd wanted a watchdog, I was in big trouble. To date, we've never heard her bark. When Mert offered to subcontract the overflow from her dog-sitting business, Going to the Dogs, I worried how Gracie would take to furry rugrats sharing her home. Huh. Gracie ignores them the way a horse flicks away flies on a summer day. Even as Milton and Bradley clung to her legs and tugged on her ears for all they were worth, Gracie simply mustered a look of "whatcha gonna do?"

"I hope this heat breaks soon." Mert paused at the front door, steeling herself for the blast furnace that waited outside. Her fake tennis bracelets and faux Rolex clattered as she hoisted a dog carrier in each hand.

"I bless the man or woman who created A/C every day in the summer. As long as our window units keep humming, we can breathe. On the other hand, just thinking about my electric bill makes me shiver. See you at the crop Monday night?"

"'Spect so."

"I'm bringing my Lemon Poke Cake."

"Yum, yum. I better not tell Roger. He's liable to take up scrapbooking just to come eat."

The rest of Saturday evening passed quickly. My priority was to safeguard the images Dodie downloaded from the guests' memory cards. Much as I would have liked to stop and peruse the pictures, I've disciplined myself to first make backup CDs and label them. My fingers itched to examine closely the images from Roxanne's camera, but all I could give them was a cursory once-over.

I was torn between wanting to view them and spending quality time with Anya. Really, there was no contest. My priority was my child.

The copying didn't take long. There were only six memory cards with thirty-two images on each, because Merrilee and her mother hadn't taken any photos.

Dodie had explained our procedure to the group. "Each of you probably snapped a few photos your friends would like. We're making it easy to share. We've downloaded your memory cards to Kiki's computer. Kiki will post the photos to a website called Snapfish. Log into Snapfish tomorrow. Use the room code I've written on the back of my business cards. My home and store phone numbers are also there in case you have questions. You'll be able to view each other's photos in a gallery. Select twenty-eight photos you like and write down their ID numbers. We'll develop them and put them in a bridal shower album customized for each of you."

"Each album will be different?" asked Tisha.

"That's right," said Dodie. "The basic page layouts will be the same, but you can choose your favorites from among the photos each of you took."

Linda's eyes were wide. "Everyone can see all our photos?"

"That's right."

"It's my gift to each of you." Mrs. Witherow weighed in with a smile. "Thank you for being such good friends to my darling daughter."

My thoughts returned to the here and now as I turned off my computer and stashed my CD copies of the memory card images in my bedroom dresser. By separating the duplicates from my work area, I avoided the possibility of grabbing CDs by mistake and "writing" over them.

I checked on Anya. Her face scrunched in concentration as she worked on her father's old laptop. She didn't even look up when I came in. I eased myself down on the sofa and put my arm around her.

"Mom, will you quiz me tomorrow on geography? I have to know the names of countries in the Middle East. This will be the last geography test for the year, and I'm glad."

"I know you're looking forward to the end of school, honey."

"Mrs. Carter has a countdown on her blackboard. Only fourteen more days, not counting the half-days for tests."

I smiled to myself, thinking that poor Mrs. Carter was probably as excited about summer vacation as was her advisory group.

"A lot of country names and borders have changed since I was a kid, but I'll try to help." I wanted to grab my camera and take a picture of my daughter hard at work. Anya is the star of many of my pages, and rightfully so. My daughter is as lovely on the inside as she is on the outside. For this, I would forever be grateful to George. Not only had my husband been a very handsome man, but George insisted we raise a kind, thoughtful and decent child. "Going to CALA, she'll always run with a privileged crowd," he said, "but she needs to know money doesn't grow on trees."

Well, George, your daughter is learning how tough it is to make a dime the hard way, I said to his ghost. (I spent a lot of time talking to an ethereal version of my husband.) Oh, we'll make it, Anya and I, but I really wonder, where was your head?

On second thought, George, don't answer that.

THIRTEEN

How Gracie figured out which day was Sunday, I'll never know. I bet David Letterman would pay mucho dog biscuits to have a calendar-reading Great Dane on his show. Promptly at eight each Sunday morning, her cold nose would touch whatever body part I'd exposed during my nightly struggle with the sheets. If I ignored her gentle prompt, she'd wedge her gigantic head under my arm and jiggle me. If that didn't get my carcass moving, she'd hop on the bed and lick me in the face.

The Benadryl gave me a medicinal hangover that made me feel like I was wearing a paper bag over my head. My tongue stuck to the roof of my mouth. My eyes felt gritty as if rubbed with sandpaper. The bee stings were still tender, and now, as I was coming back to consciousness, little pinpricks of pain zipped their way through my nervous system.

But Gracie didn't care. She knew her rights. Sundays are German apple pancake and bacon mornings, followed by a family romp at Babler State Park.

The late spring morning felt blessedly chilly. It was difficult to regulate the temperature inside our home. As far as I could tell, this cracker box was built totally sans insulation. My landlord, Mr. Wilson, was a crusty old coot. The house had belonged to his parents. This inheritance formed the linchpin of his real estate holdings. I'd been attracted to the low rent and the fenced-in back yard. Mr. Wilson allowed how the place needed a "woman's touch." He got that right. A woman wielding a wrecking ball. The place should have been razed. I worried each time I turned on my computer that I'd blow fuses to kingdom come.

I slipped on fuzzy house shoes and my blue chenille bathrobe with the yellow "rubber duckies." Who wears all those skimpy nighties and sheer silk robes they sell at Victoria's Secret? Maybe that's the point: They're to be discarded, not worn.

I'm as cold as Nanook of the North. In the winter I sleep in a thread-bare sweatsuit and thick socks. George and I had two twin beds pushed together in our master bedroom. Often, I'd look over at his sleeping form and want to cuddle. But I'd never initiate it. Occasionally he would. Mostly, we lived like roommates with a shared purpose, parenting Anya. In some ways, our arrangement worked very well. What is it most experts say that couples fight about? Money and sex? Those weren't issues for us.

Marriages work or don't work for the strangest reasons. We all have different needs. To find another person who'll fulfill all those needs … well, I think that's nearly impossible. To find a person who closely matches your needs and who has a commitment to the same goals is somewhat more likely. George and I both needed stability, a home base, a listening ear, a cooperative household, and a child-centered life.

Gracie gave me her patented, "Where is my food?" expression immediately after her good-morning piddle. I fixed her a Sunday special, a bowl of kibble, a tablespoonful of canned food, with a dog biscuit on top.

She sighed as I put the rest of the canned food back in the fridge. A tablespoon was all my budget and her digestive system would allow. Two months ago, Gracie got into the garbage and helped herself to a midnight snack of leftovers. I awakened the next morning to a kitchen floor turned toxic waste dump. The whole surface was a sea of brown and pinned in one corner was poor Gracie. I cleaned a path to her.

"Poor baby," I soothed her. I understand food issues. Left to her own devices, she'd eat anything not nailed down and not worry about the consequences.

I felt her pain.

I'd been there myself.

Now we keep a bottle of Pepto-Bismol near the dog chow for those days when Gracie manages to steal human food. Even Anya knows how to fill a needleless syringe with the pink fluid, peel back a gooey dewlap, press the tube against teeth, and push the plunger hard and fast to give Gracie the squirt that cures. Inevitably, Gracie responds with a violent shake of the head which sends splats and splotches of pink flying.

The scent of bacon mixed with the cinnamon and apple fragrance from the oversized pancake. Gracie sniffed the air eagerly. "Poor lamb," I said as I patted her. "I'd love to share our bacon with you, drool face, but your innards wouldn't like it as much as your chompers would."

Anya wandered in, wearing cute pink jammies festooned with hearts and kisses. Sheila had impeccable taste. She made sure Anya not only fit in at CALA but was a pacesetter where fashion was concerned.

My child is a slow waker-upper. Rubbing her eyes, she pushed food around on her plate. She did pick out one piece of bacon and one slice of apple. With her fork, she foraged around in the pancake for another slice or two before taking her plate to the sink.

I, on the other hand, ate every scrap of my helping. I savored the mix of maple syrup flavor, cinnamon, vanilla, and butter.

I pointed to the untouched food on my child's plate. "What's the matter, sweetie?"

She gave me a weak smile. "I'm not hungry."

I didn't want to make her a member of the clean plate club like I'd been. The portions we serve in this country are outrageous. Encouraging children to overeat in order to save starving kids in Africa has contributed, in my humble opinion, to much of our problem with obesity. I slid the rest of the giant pancake into a plastic container for later.

"Get dressed, Anya-Banana. Gracie's ready for her run."

Forty-five minutes later, we were on Babler Access Road, passing a sign that announced "Dimont Development Inc.'s Babler Estates. Luxury homes in a beautiful setting." Oh, George, I thought, you worked so hard on this subdivision full of luxury homes—and now your kid is living in substandard housing.

We found a place to park and let Gracie roam the hills of Babler at the end of a retractable lead. Anya and I walked hand in hand. The earliest spring flowers—jonquils, crocus, and snowdrops—had faded on yellowing stalks. The next wave was gathering courage to burst into bloom. Bare tree branches were tipped in a watercolor wash of celery, celadon, mint, lime, and olive. In a week or two, the skyline would shout hosannah with verdant life. In spring and fall, there is no more beautiful place on earth than the hill country of Missouri.

"Don't you just hate those mean old bees for stinging you?" Anya's jeans stepped in unison to mine as we followed in Gracie's feverous wake.

"Nah. It wasn't personal."

One side of her mouth rose in a "huh?"

"Anya, baby, those bees were trying to protect their food, their homes, and their families. I was an intruder. They would have stung anybody in that box. How can I be mad at them for trying to protect what they love? I'd do the same."

"Makes sense. But they were still awful nasty to you." She walked beside me quietly. We both treasured spending time together now. I worried how this might change when she became a teen.

We followed Gracie quietly and watched her joyous explorations with smiles on our faces. The big dog stopped at one point and sniffed the cup of a late-blooming jonquil, a real straggler of a flower.

"Do you miss Daddy?" She asked me this frequently.

"Of course I do."

"I miss him … a lot."

I put my arm around her. "I know you do."

"But Daddy watches over us."

"I think so." And you're doing a really poor job, George, I muttered under my breath. Get on the stick, pal. Or turn the job back over to a real guardian angel and find another line of work.

"Gran misses Daddy. When I sleep over, I hear her cry at night."

Ah. Poor Sheila, I thought. Tough as nails in the light of day, but letting it all go in private. Too bad we didn't know each other or like each other enough to share our grief.

"I'm sorry to hear that, but I'm not surprised. I can't imagine losing a child. Losing you would be the worst thing that could ever happen to me. Nothing anyone can do to a mother is as bad as hurting her baby."

Anya gave me a long, searching look. She made a fist and bumped my shoulder. "Don't worry, Mom. You're stuck with me."

"No, baby. We're stuck with each other."

At that moment, Gracie bounded up to us and planted her muddy front paws in the middle of my chest.

"Aw, Gracie. What have you done?"

Anya giggled. "And Gracie's stuck with both of us, right?"

"Right."

FOURTEEN

"We grow accustomed to our troubles," said Dodie in Yiddish. She translated the proverb for me as she turned off the television. A real news junkie, she started each day with the *St. Louis Post-Dispatch* and the *New York Times*. While working in her office, she kept one eye on the television or her ear tuned to the radio.

"Good job at the bridal shower Saturday," Dodie continued. "You ruined the gift box, and Mrs. Witherow suggested that I take it out of your wages. Even so, I'm betting we do a lot of business with the Ladue ladies now they've had a taste of your work. When we were loading up, a couple of them said they're coming in to talk with you today."

Mrs. Witherow thought the box should come out of my wages? Crud. Welcome to the world of the poor and powerless. The less you have, the more you owe everybody around you. When we were rich, the freebies flowed fast and furiously. Now, when I needed the help, the stream of complimentary goodies had dried up.

Life was not fair. No wonder the poor couldn't get ahead, and the rich stayed furlongs out front.

I took a deep breath. "Dodie, what do you know about Roxanne Baker?"

Dodie gave me a long, thoughtful look. "Not a whole lot. Used to come in all the time and splash the cash. Haven't seen her in a while."

"Um, did you ever see any pictures of her ... and George?"

"I don't gossip about my customers." Dodie pointedly examined her watch.

I took the hint.

No sooner had I counted the change drawer and flipped the window sign to OPEN, than Sally O'Brien burst through the front door of Time in a Bottle, chattering a mile a minute. Right behind her was Markie Dorring. Both women had packs of photos in their hands.

"What a fantastic idea! Candid photos? Our shower albums will have photos from all of us? And you loaded them so fast! We were only out of the room for a minute." The two women took turns talking, their excitement bubbling over.

A minute? Their luncheon seemed to take ages, but then I was cold and hungry in the basement, setting up make 'n' takes, and watching my bee stings swell to ugly proportions. Were rich people always this oblivious?

Instead of dwelling on the remark, I said, "Yes. Candid photos are super. Now you'll have pictures of yourselves as well as each other. You don't want to be missing in action from your own life."

Sell the sizzle, I reminded myself. This was my livelihood. I need to keep them coming back for more.

Dodie came out of her office and greeted the women. She left me to the mundane chores of getting the store ready for another day while she answered their questions.

"You got my reminder message last night? Still got the card with the room code and site name?" Sitting at the powerful computer and professional-quality monitor, she walked the women through the selection process. While our customers oohed and aahed over the downloaded images, I worked on page layouts, being careful to leave spaces for their yet-to-come photos. Dodie had promised Mrs. Witherow a twelve-page album for each guest with fully designed pages capable of holding up to twenty-eight photos. For an additional fee, Dodie would also make available extra album pages that I would design.

The women wanted to see the strap-bound albums Mrs. Witherow had selected. "The Tiffany blue and cream covers match the color scheme Merrilee selected for her wedding. The covers can be personalized, if you wish, with a title embossed in gold," I explained.

The women were impressed. I assured them I'd get the albums done as soon as possible. "Of course, since we already have a theme, the garden party, the pages will go together pretty quickly. Here, I'll show you my work in progress."

I fanned out the patterns and solids I'd chosen to work with.

"How do you know what to choose?" asked Markie. "I mean, there are scads of papers and products. How do you know where to start?"

I explained my system for mixing and matching papers. I favor the squint method. It's highly scientific. You select a few papers, take a step back and squint. Usually you can tell right away if the patterns are harmonious.

I guess I dazzled them with my brilliance. Or I buffaloed them with my baloney. Either way, Sally and Markie signed up for one-on-one scrapbook lessons.

Seeing the women ready and raring to go tickled me. They were as enthusiastic as two little girls.

"What if we can't do this?" asked Sally. The negative thought brought her up short. "I mean, I'm not very creative."

"What if we mess up?" asked Markie.

"There are no scrapbooking police. No one is going to come to your door in the middle of the night and arrest you because you didn't make your pages a certain way," I said. "There is no right way to scrapbook! This is playtime for grownups. You decide what you want on your pages, and what you want your family to remember. Keep in mind, it's only paper. You goof it up—pish—you buy another sheet. Your mistake won't break the bank."

I studied the well-heeled ladies and corrected myself. Any mistakes they made wouldn't break *their* banks. Unfortunately, a lot of mistakes would leave me flat broke.

Oh, well. I continued, "In our one-on-one time, I can help you develop your own personal style." I didn't add I could also steer our conversation to their pal Roxanne when we were alone.

Markie was back to worrying about choices. "But how do you know what products to use? Which papers?"

"There's a universe of colors and patterns that could work with any photo. There's also a universe of design styles. Within those universes are your preferences, choices that reflect your unique self."

They still seemed concerned.

"I have homework for you." I handed each woman a sheet of questions I'd devised to get them thinking about their color and style preferences. I also handed over a sheet of sentence prompts to get going on their journaling, the written commentary vitally important to memory albums.

A few minutes later, Dodie rang up two large sales. Both women signed up for private classes and purchased pre-made page kits to get started.

I thanked the women for their business and told them I looked forward to our one-on-one sessions. My stomach was grumbling for lunch. The clock struck noon. But right after Sally and Markie walked out, Linda Kovaleski walked in. She asked the same questions Sally and Markie had about Snapfish. Linda, however, had trouble grasping how the website worked.

"I'm, um, a real computer idiot," she said. "My daughter Claire uses the Internet all the time, but I don't get it. I mean, I kinda get it, but not really."

I made a mental note that we needed a one-sheet with a detailed explanation of how Snapfish and similar websites worked. We could hand it out and save ourselves a lot of time and trouble instead of answering the same questions over and over.

"And you keep all the photos on your computer? What if they get lost? I mean, they could, couldn't they?"

Here was a scrapbooker as concerned about being careful with images as I was.

"They are on Snapfish *and* in my computer." I didn't mention the duplicate CDs.

"Snapping fish?"

I was about to explain my system for making duplicate CDs, but the doorminder buzzed. I whipped my head around to see who was coming in. Each time I heard the door, my muscles tensed. My encounter with Roxanne had made me skittish. For some reason, I half expected her to stop by the store to continue her harassment.

But instead of Roxanne, Bill Ballard strolled in. I nodded a quick hello and held up my index finger as the universal symbol for "just a minute." He came over and stood two inches from Linda and me, all the while shifting his weight and staring at us. I could feel his breath on my arm as I tried to assure her the photos were safe.

Bill tapped his toe loudly right behind us. I could smell his expensive cologne.

"The fish place is a website?" Linda still didn't understand exactly what Snapfish was or how it worked. I admitted the photo-processing service sported an odd name.

Bill stretched his arm to look at his watch and harrumphed loudly.

Linda got the message. She eyed him nervously and edged toward the door.

"I'll come back, okay?"

Bill seemed proud that he'd run Linda off. Something about the way he intruded on our conversation made me uneasy. Almost like he held power over her. As she walked quickly to the door, he didn't even try to hide the way he leered at her retreating backside. Once she was out of sight, he turned to me.

"All my wife Tisha could talk about was your fabulous albums. My, my, aren't you the little artist? Who would have guessed? Nobody knew you were so talented. Anyway, I want a private lesson for her. Make time for her this week. It'll be her birthday gift," and he gave me a big wink like we were best buddies. "Got to keep the old lady happy, right?"

I noticed he didn't ask me if I had time. He told me to *make* time. Bill's steady gaze was accompanied by a struggle to pull his wallet from the inside pocket of his pin-striped suit.

"Is there a discount for old friends?"

I couldn't believe he was trying to get me to reduce my fee. He had to know I was already living on next to nothing.

"Dodie sets the pricing. You'll have to talk with her."

"I'll do that. Got your check."

I had the vague sense he was pointing out that I owed him a favor.

"Glad to hear it." I tried to be gracious. I introduced him to Dodie, and she helped him with a gift certificate. I was happy to hand him off.

Maybe I was feeling leftover discomfort about the half-a-million dollars. Even so, the twist of my gut made me wish he'd conclude his transaction and go away. The farther the better, too.

I tried to disguise my relief when he waved goodbye. I had to be gracious. He was a paying customer. And he had done me a favor. He'd kept his mouth shut about my husband's mistake.

"Thank you, Bill. Tell Tisha I'm looking forward to working with her. Say hi to the kids, Britney and Paul." Being so overly cheery exhausted me. I was hungry and needed a lunch break.

But it was not to be. In walked Merrilee.

The bride-to-be indicated she wanted to talk privately. I led her to the cropping area in the back of the store.

"About Roxanne ... she's had a rough time."

I tried not to change my expression. A small voice inside screamed, "She's had a rough time? Hello? I just lost my husband!"

Something about my face betrayed me. Rats, there went my career in poker.

"Uh, sorry. I forgot." Merrilee had the good grace to turn red.

I took a deep breath. "So Roxanne and George were ..." I couldn't say the word.

"So romantic," Merrilee cooed. "Like in the movies. Childhood sweethearts. Roxanne thought they'd be together forever. Even when you came between them. They were Camilla and Charles, you know? And you were ..."

"Princess Di?"

She snickered. "Hardly."

Thanks a lot, I thought. I didn't bother to add that my character had conveniently died. Merrilee's expression told me the faux pas didn't register. She wasn't exactly the sharpest pencil in the cup.

"She was really down when George ... you know."

Yes, I did know. I would have hardly described my grief as being "really down" though.

"But she was so courageous."

Oh, goodie, a new synonym for insensitive.

Merrilee rattled on, "It took her a while, but she got involved with some new guy. They went on vacation together. Somewhere sunny with a beach. She came back with such a great tan. Really bronze and gorgeous. Lasted a long time, too. The tan, that is— not the relationship. But, I never met him. Roxanne was really secretive. I think he was married."

No kidding. What else was new? And here stood a bride-to-be acting like this was no big deal. I wondered what her vows would be like? Forsaking all but a few others?

She sighed, "But she found out he was cheating on her. He had another girlfriend. I mean besides his wife. Can you believe it? Who would cheat on Roxanne?"

I bit my lip. Did she see the irony here? Hello?

"Roxanne was terribly hurt. She's very sensitive. A real people person."

I could tell. She definitely got my vote for Miss Congeniality.

Merrilee sighed. "That's when her drinking got out of hand. She's always been a party girl. I think she had a little something before the bridal shower."

A little something? Her second-hand fumes nearly gave me a buzz.

"We've been friends ever since high school, even though she's older than I am. This is my second marriage. I moved home and took back my maiden name. I'm ready to settle down. But not Roxanne. Like, the rest of us grew up, but she didn't. She blew through what she inherited from her dad. He was this famous botanist. Developed all these drugs from plants. Now she's busted. I think all of us have loaned her money."

Could these women even spell J-O-B? Had it never occurred to Roxanne to go to work?

Merrilee smiled. "Poor Roxie. She doesn't really know what to do with herself. Kind of weird that both of you scrapbook."

Right. Weird. That covered it. Not so much.

"Anyway." A flip of her hand showed off the huge sparkler on her ring finger. "I want you to do my wedding album."

I had a hunch the words "I want" came out of her mouth a lot. Like on an regular basis.

She continued, "And I want a bachelor album for Jeff. And I want an album devoted to his boyhood. From me to his mom. Can you do all that?"

By the time Merrilee left, she'd committed to nearly three thousand dollars worth of custom scrapbooking. Dodie told her we needed a nonrefundable deposit. Merrilee pouted. I was panicked we'd lose the commission, but our customer gave in.

"You'll thank me," Dodie said after the bride left. "I know these people. They change their minds on a whim and expect you to eat the costs."

I guess she had conveniently forgotten that once upon a time, I'd been one of "these people." I decided not to remind her.

It was too late for lunch. I needed to pick up Anya from her grandmother's. I hoped to spend an hour and a half of quality time with my child before the babysitter—an older teen I made a prom album for—showed up, and I returned to the store to oversee the crop. Plus, I needed to pick up the Lemon Poke Cake I'd made when it was cool this morning.

On my way to Sheila's, I sent God a thank-you prayer. What had seemed like a horrible, embarrassing Saturday afternoon at the Witherow home was now going to pay our rent for the next three months. Almost equally important, Merrilee's rambling commentary about Roxanne convinced me I needed to know a whole lot more about the woman—and Time in the Bottle was the perfect base for my sleuthing.

FIFTEEN

I STOOD ON MY mother-in-law's front step, ringing the doorbell for the second time that afternoon. Sheila's smooth green lawn rolled on and on behind me like the vast turf of a golf course. White columns tall as sequoias framed her front door and extended to the third floor with enough space in the middle to accommodate a balcony overlooking the front yard. Glazed pots of varying sizes overflowed with trailing petunias, pungent geraniums, and spiky dracaenas. From the scale to the textures, everything about the Lowenstein family home lived up to the word "grand."

To my surprise, my mother-in-law opened the door herself rather than having her maid, Linnea, act as butler. The heat wave beginning that morning had picked up vigor during the day. I was wilting.

"Back so soon?" she asked. I'd just picked up my daughter less than an hour ago.

"Sheila, I need a favor. The electricity is out in my house. It's hotter than blue blazes inside. Can Anya spend the night with you?"

My mother-in-law's hard face softened as she spotted her granddaughter pulling a rolling overnight case from the trunk of my ancient BMW. I stood holding Anya's book bag and mopping sweat from my brow.

Despite the unseasonable heat, Sheila wore full-length white linen pants topped with a silk blouse in a soft shade of green. On her feet were embroidered mules, gold with green sequins and beads. As per usual, George's mother looked cool, confident, and wealthy. I could tell she was coming out of her depression because she'd taken to wearing clothes with color again.

By contrast I looked pretty LMC, lower middle class. After losing so much weight, nothing fit me. My new wardrobe could be summed up in a birdcall: Cheap, cheap, cheap. I had on a cute pair of cotton pants I found marked down at Target and a sleeveless blouse with a Talbots label I picked up for $3 at Goodwill. On my feet were navy-blue Keds.

Sheila glared at me.

Even though I wished I could turn and walk away, I stood my ground. Whatever else Sheila was, she was a doting grandmother. Anya was her only grandchild, and as far as I knew, her only living relative. The love in the older woman's eyes as she watched her granddaughter trudge up the paved sidewalk made my heart ache. How Sheila missed George! He'd been such a devoted son, taking his mother to dinner at least once a week and calling her daily. How I wished Sheila and I could turn to each other!

When we first met, I thought maybe she'd be my "adopted" mother. George spoke highly of her, and from what he'd told me, there was much to commend. The hope of having a loving relationship with a mother figure had my heart all aflutter, but the instant Sheila laid eyes on me with my unruly head of curls and my baby face, I knew I was going to have to take a pass on maternal concern. At least in this lifetime.

My own mother, Lucia Montgomery, never paid much attention to me. Only recently, as the vagaries of old age weakened her, had she discovered any reason to pay attention to my younger sister, Amanda. Mom phoned just last week from her home in Arizona to share the exciting news that "we are related to Anne Hutchinson, the Alford, England, native who came to these shores as a pilgrim and whose fervent belief in the rights of women made her an outcast."

I appreciated hearing about Anne, since she and I seemed to have that outcast thing going for us, but hello? I couldn't help thinking: Mom, my husband died seven months ago, and I'm kinda struggling here, so could you pause in your genealogical exploits long enough to ask how I am? No. She couldn't. If my daughter and I passed my mother in an airport, she wouldn't recognize us. She's simply not that interested in our lives. That's why she upped sticks and moved to Arizona right after Dad died, and she could sell the family home in Illinois. Being close to me wasn't a priority.

Correction: I wasn't a priority. Never had been. Never would be. In fact, I didn't even show up on her radar screen.

Sheila Lowenstein was my mother's polar opposite. She had built her life around her son, and now she transferred every smidgeon of that affection to the deep love she already felt for Anya.

Yet, somehow, she managed to overlook the fact Anya was the product of two people. And I was half of the genetic team. In her eyes, Anya was as close to perfect as a child could be. For that, I loved her. No matter what Sheila did to me, I'd never deny the older woman access to her grandchild.

"Of course, my darling granddaughter is welcome to spend the night. My home is her home. Come on in, sweetheart," and Sheila stooped to hug my sweaty child. No matter what condition Anya was in, Sheila never skimped on the physical affection. Heck, I'd even seen her holding Anya when my baby reeked of upchuck. As picky as Sheila was about her clothes, she never thought twice about whether Anya might ruin her outfit. She simply opened her arms to my child. I noticed and loved her for that. Yes, loved her. Even if she had no use for me. I found myself in this cosmic holding pattern where I established infinite attraction to folks who didn't return my affection. Go figure.

Sheila directed Anya toward the cool, vast entryway of her stately home. I could feel the chilled air within, and it had a revitalizing effect on my person.

"Tell Linnea to get you a big glass of her homemade lemonade, okay? I'll be right there. Are you hungry? I'll have her make us a salad with tuna. Is that all right, darling? Just leave your things in the foyer for now and get cooled down. The store dropped off a few new pairs of shorts, love. Why don't you try them on and see how you like them?"

Anya blew me a kiss and sauntered off.

In a wink, the loving grandmother changed to a harridan. "What did you expect? Of course your house is inadequate. That tacky shack you live in is one step up from public housing. I can't believe my grandchild has to put up with that. The neighborhood is dangerous, and you live in a dump."

"It's all I can afford," I hissed. I was tired of hearing her complain about my house. Actually I lived in a fine little area. Okay, the neighborhood was transitional, but I was near Anya's school and my work, and the brick bungalow was snug and secure behind its six-foot-high chain-link fence. Not that Sheila cared about my home's good points.

This quarreling over my housing had become a tired argument. A smarter woman would have bitten her tongue, but I was hot and tired. I rose to the bait. After working all day, finding my electricity out, and facing five more hours on my feet, I responded to the need to justify my meager existence. This really wasn't about the poor quality of Anya's housing. It was about Sheila's ongoing battle to gain total custody of her grandchild.

"If you weren't so selfish, she could live in comfort and security." Sheila's lip curled in an unattractive sneer. I hoped her face would freeze like that. The ugly moue didn't match her well-groomed eyebrows, perfectly lined eyes, and lightly dusted cheekbones. "You are keeping my granddaughter from a better life."

This really pushed my buttons. She knew how it felt to lose a child, but she didn't think I'd mind giving mine away? Huh! "If by a better life, you mean a life without her mother, you're exactly right. I am keeping my daughter by my side. So get used to it. Every kid deserves a mom. George had one!"

"He certainly did. Too bad he didn't have a good wife! If he had, my poor baby would be alive today!" This, too, had become well-trod ground. Sheila insisted that her son had been perfect, and his death was the result of my failure as a spouse.

I wasn't exactly sure how she'd made that causal link, but she had. And by gum, she stuck to it. In her mind, the responsibility for George's death rested squarely on my shoulders.

I wiped my brow. Sweat streamed down the backs of my legs. My bee stings had shrunk to small angry lumps that I could mainly ignore, but the salt made them complain anew. I'd had enough. Right now I was too hot to quarrel. "Okay, all right. I'm a loser. A waste of oxygen. An idiot. We agree. Feel better? I do appreciate you keeping Anya overnight. Do you want to take her to school tomorrow or should I stop by?"

Temporarily mollified, and believing she'd won because I refused to go round two with her, Sheila calmed down. "I'll take her."

With that, she slammed the door in my face.

———

The Monday night croppers had met regularly for months. As promised, Mert was there. Bonnie Gossage brought her baby, and we all took turns holding six-week-old Felix. (What possessed her and Jeremy to name their son that? He's going to hate his parents when he grows up, and we would all understand why.) Karen Michelletti brought photos from her Hawaiian vacation. Elora Jones was working on a retirement album for Dwayne, her husband. Miriam Finkelstein was finishing a bat mitzvah album for her daughter and asked me when Anya would be ready for hers. (I mumbled, "Soon," and prayed God would be understanding. I hadn't forgotten it. I'd just fallen a bit behind.) Vanessa Johnson had posed shots of her son, Jared, and the family car, along with close-ups of his driver's license and car keys which he'd subsequently lost the next week for rounding the corner to the driveway on two wheels. Reba Katz was working on an album dedicated to the family dog, Hates.

"Hates?" I asked, studying the photo of the sweet-faced Afghan hound with its long, flowing coat.

She nodded. "We adopted this Afghan when he was an adult. Jake, my teenage son, insisted on this particular name. I couldn't figure out why until we picked up our pet at the vet's office. The receptionist called back to the grooming area for our dog. She kept announcing, 'Hates Katz! Hates Katz! We're ready for Hates Katz!'"

We all groaned.

Reba laughed. "A wealthy-looking woman with a Siamese got up and stomped right out. The receptionist ran after her yelling, 'Wait, wait!' My son was rolling on the floor in hysterics."

"Boys will be boys," said Dodie, but the smile on her lips didn't match the sadness in her eyes.

What was that all about? I filed it away to contemplate later.

Each woman represented a different socioeconomic stratum. Among us was a rainbow of skin colors. We each had different subjects to scrap and different projects going. But we were there for one reason: to sing a hymn of gratitude to life. Scrapbookers compose paeans to the quotidian. Being around other scrappers is always fun because in the main, scrapbookers are positive people.

Even when the going gets rough. I've seen scrapbookers work through life's toughest blows by committing their feelings to paper. Last year when Bethany Gibbon's mother was dying of breast cancer, she worked diligently to create a legacy album while her mother was still conscious and could contribute. When Rose Mitchell miscarried, she made a special album dedicated to the baby she never had the chance to hold. And Marcia Primm created a loving life album to accompany her Alzheimer's-impaired mother to a special care facility. "This way the staff can see beyond who she is now and honor her as the person she once was," Marcia explained to us. I still wipe tears away as I remember her saying that.

I could go on and on. Scrapbooking allows you to step back and see the big picture.

Life is good, and the bad times don't last. At least, not for long.

Even though crops are a lot of work for me, I always look forward to them. The ladies and I took turns bringing goodies to eat. Since everyone was kind enough to share their favorite recipes, I'd developed quite a repertoire of wonderful baked goods and desserts.

Dodie decided all of our crops would include a technique lesson. This evening I taught the scrappers how to use stick-on lettering and ink to create a negative space page title. The demo went over well to the excitement of scrappers who wondered what on earth they were going to do with page after page of letter stickers in useless colors.

Cleanup went fast. At a little after eleven, I started collecting bits of paper the other croppers had discarded. I always found a way to use the tiniest pieces, even if I just made punch art for embellishments. In fact, Dodie was in the process of making a display of cute tags and cards I'd put together using itsy-bitsy scraps. We discussed adding a Thrifty Scrapbooking class to our current lineup. Our customers would be amazed at the ways I'd found to economize. "I don't mind them saving money," said Dodie, "because most of them will turn right around and find a way to spend it on other supplies."

She had that right.

By the time I headed home, I was exhausted.

The setting sun brought no relief from the high double-digit heat. I lowered the BMW's top, a maneuver that required brute strength, good balance, and a sense of humor, since this car was too old to have a push-button convertible roof. To drop the top, I stood in the middle of the back seat and gently folded the fabric into neat waves that would fit in the well while holding the well cover up with one hand. I balanced on tiptoes and decided I was one arm short. Whose bright idea was that, eh? A three-handed mechanic?

Ah, but the breeze all the way home was worth the effort. I didn't dare keep the top down on the hottest days because the sun was too intense. But this was the kind of evening convertibles were made for. The tree frogs, crickets, and cicadas sang love songs to me as I tooled along. I would miss my daughter terribly tonight as I did every night she stayed with her grandmother, but at least she would pass the evening in comfort.

Gracie met me at the back door with her long pink tongue hanging from her loose jowls. Saliva dripped off the white picket fence of her teeth. The inside of the bungalow was stifling. After a flick of the switch proved the power was still out, I retrieved a flashlight from my car and made my way to my bedroom.

A few minutes later, overnight bag in hand, kibble in a plastic bag, dog in passenger seat, and tent in trunk, I headed down Interstate 270 to the Yogi Bear's Jellystone Park, a campground over on Highway 44 near Eureka. The tree-shaded area had been my second home in the weeks after selling the house in Ladue and before taking occupancy on the bungalow. My Value Kard promised a tent site for twenty-one dollars and change. I could clean up the next morning in the communal showers, and Gracie was always welcome, as the place prided itself on being "pet friendly."

A night under the stars with a gentle breeze was far preferable to being cooped up in a hot, stuffy house. Sure, my tent wasn't a five-star hotel, but the campground was within my budget and this kept my dignity intact. With any luck, AmerenUE would have the power back on in the morning, and the house would cool down before Anya came home from school. In the meantime, as long as the mosquito spray worked and the neighbors in their RVs didn't play their boom boxes too loudly, I could pretend I was here by choice.

Just for one night, I decided I wouldn't think about George. I wouldn't worry over his murder or wonder how to solve the crime. I would pretend I was here with a man who loved me and only me. We'd stretch out on top of the cushy sleeping bag and smell the pine needles and name the constellations (which shouldn't take long unless he knew a lot more astronomy than I did). I'd show him Orion with Alnitak, Alnilam, and Mintaka, the three stars forming the giant's belt. I'd tell my companion about the mighty hunter and his faithful dog, Sirius. I'd pat my own canine sidekick and thank her for her fealty. He'd think I was pretty smart and maybe even irresistible as we snuggled close here in the last vestiges of Missouri forestland, under the maple leaves and the protective auspices of a noisy hoot owl.

As I drifted off to sleep, my fantasy lover revealed his face. He looked suspiciously like Chad Detweiler.

KIKI'S REVERSE LETTERING TECHNIQUE

You'll need sticker letters, an ink pad, and a sponge. Be sure the sticker letters are trimmed along their silhouette. You also need a bottle of Un-Du, a safe solvent that loosens the adhesive so you can pick up a letter after it's stuck and move it.

1. Write out the word or phrase you want to create. (If you skip this step, you're likely to misspell a word!)

2. Count the letters and spaces. Divide by two to determine the middle of your word/phrase. The midpoint may fall on a letter or a space. Make a tick mark on your rough version to help you keep track.

3. Check to see you have enough letters for your word/phrase.

4. Peel the letters from the backing one by one. Starting at the center of a plastic or metal ruler, stick the bottom edge (⅛" or so) of the middle letter to the middle of the ruler's edge (probably at 6" if you have a standard ruler). The sticky remainder of your letter will flop in the breeze. Be careful not to touch the top of the letter to any paper or surface!

5. Once you arrange your letters on the ruler as you want them to appear on your page, transfer them very carefully onto the paper. Start by pressing the tops of the letters to the paper. Move your way down the body of the letter until you peel the letters' bottoms off the ruler.

6. Burnish all the letters so none of the ink will run under the edges.

7. Dab an ink pad lightly with a sponge. (Test the sponge first on a piece of wastepaper to make sure it isn't too saturated with ink.) Now dab the ink on top of your letter stickers. Continue to dab until you get a pleasing intensity of ink. Your letter stickers should be covered!

8. Let the ink dry. Squirt on a little Un-Du. Slip the blade of a craft knife under the letters to peel them off. (You might be able to reuse these newly inked letters in another project by adhering them to wax paper for storage.)

SIXTEEN

"WHERE WERE YOU BETWEEN the hours of midnight and one last night, Mrs. Lowenstein?" Detweiler frowned at me.

All I could do was blush back at him. I'd been thinking all sorts of sexy thoughts last night with him in the starring role, and here he was in the flesh. I felt like I'd been caught reading a romance novel with a racy cover.

Detweiler stood uncomfortably close to me in a triangulated tough-guy pose. His Bic pen poised to write on a steno pad. With a jolt, I realized he was here because he had some problem with me. Gee, Kiki, I chided myself, did you really think the man came to ask you for a date? My dreams evaporated, and I hit the earth hard. Whatever the reason for this visit, he was not here to fulfill my fantasies. How stupid could I get?

"Mrs. Lowenstein? Hello? I need an answer. Where were you last night between the hours of midnight and one?"

"Hey," said Dodie. She'd been in her office, reading the morning paper, eating a gigantic blueberry muffin, and drinking a large caramel macchiato with whipped cream from Starbucks. I'd gulped down a carton of diet yogurt and a Diet Dr Pepper. My stomach rumbled in a queasy way.

Dodie raised her voice to Detweiler. "I need you interrogating my employee in my scrapbook store like I need another hole in my head. Get out of here. Scram."

"Okay," said Detweiler. "How about I take her downtown to the police station?"

And lose a half a day's wages? I didn't think so. Better to talk and work at the same time than to take the cut in pay. Surely this interview couldn't last long. "My husband's been dead for six months, Detective. What the heck difference can it possibly make where I was last night?" Now that he wasn't the man of my dreams, I remembered him in his alternate role as bearer of bad tidings. I pulled at my shirt and fanned myself with my collar. The store seemed unbearably warm.

"Just answer the question." Detweiler tugged at the neck of his shirt. Something likewise made him hot under the collar. Could it have anything to do with the way he was eyeballing me? I wondered. Well, he could just knock that off right now. Whatever was bugging him, I didn't care for his attitude. Or the effect he was having on me.

"Last night between midnight and one, I was in a tent at Yogi Bear's Jellystone Park over by Eureka. Not that it matters."

"Right. You look like a woman who camps out."

"I resent that!" What the heck was he implying?

"Right. Where were you? I don't have time for this."

"Neither do I." I continued to straighten paper on the shelves. The aftermath of every crop was disarray. No matter how hard I tried to put the whole place back in order before I left, there were always spots I missed.

"I'm losing patience here. I need an answer pronto. *Capisce?*"

"*Capisce*-sheesh. Speak English." If it wasn't Yiddish or elementary French, I was out of my element. Oh, and Hebrew. I knew a few words of that, too. But no Italian.

He growled, "I asked where you were last night."

"And I told you. The Jell-eee-stone Campground." I elongated my words.

Dodie drawled, "You got a hearing problem, bucko?"

"No, but Mrs. Lowenstein here has an attitude problem. Where. Were. You?" His breath tickled my neck. Goose bumps rose all over my body.

Over my shoulder, I said, "Okay, one more time with feeling, pal. I was in a tent at the Jellystone Campground off of Highway 44 by Eureka." This man was seriously ticking me off. He'd planted himself in the middle of the shelves forcing me to walk around him each time I put a piece of paper where it belonged.

Whack! Detweiler slapped his notebook against a nearby fixture. The noise made me jump. "Hello? Am I not getting through to you? This is serious. Do I need to haul you into the station for questioning?"

"You can't do that without just cause," volunteered Dodie. She was a big fan of true crime novels and police procedurals. "And you have to Mirandize her, bub."

"No kidding?" snarled Detweiler. "When did you get your badge? Because you're wrong. About the Miranda. This isn't an interview; it's an informal discussion."

Dodie shrugged elaborately. I could tell she was enjoying this. Dodie liked men and she liked trouble. Her input was making Officer Friendly more nasty by the minute. Being in the middle of a problem was her idea of heaven on earth.

But not mine. The fact I was being grilled by a good-looking man who probably knew how devastating his buff body was didn't make a bit of difference. Under other circumstances watching a manly man act all tough and macho might have made my motor purr. But not here and now. I was supposed to be working. And, need I mention, my fantasy encounter did not include a Bic pen and steno pads? Or my boss and messy shelves of scrapbook products?

I straightened, trying to ignore how my shirt gapped in the front. I probably needed to add a couple of snaps to the underside of the button placket. "Okay, smart guy. Look." I walked to the front counter. From underneath, I pulled my purse. I whipped out my wallet with my KOA Value Kard tucked among the trio of one dollar bills. "See? This entitles me to pitch my tent for twenty dollars and change. The electricity was off at my house so Gracie and I—"

"Gracie? Can she collaborate your story?"

"Sure, if you speak Danish."

Dodie laughed. "Good one, Kiki."

Detweiler grumbled an indistinguishable word.

"Here's the rundown, ace. I worked until five and picked up my daughter from my mother-in-law's house. When I got home, I discovered my electricity was out and my house was like an oven. At six, I took Anya back to her grandmother's to spend the night. I worked here until half past eleven. I ran home to pick up a change of clothes and Gracie. Then I headed for the campground. I've stayed there before. They've probably got a record because you have to check in at the ranger station."

"You slept in a tent?" Dodie's bushy eyebrows flew up like crows startled by a cat. "You could have bunked up at my house. There's lots of room now that my daughter is at Mizzou. Honest to goodness, where was your head?"

I started straightening the magazine rack. "Thanks for the offer, but I wouldn't dream of imposing. I've slept at Jellystone before. When my house in Ladue sold, before the place I'm living in was fixed up, I slept in the tent every night. I'd shower there and come on in. I kind of like being out under the stars. It's no big deal. You can call AmerenUE and see if they've turned on my power if you need to collaborate my story." I brushed back a curl that had fallen onto my forehead.

"That's corroborate, Kiki," said Dodie.

"Oh."

Detweiler tried not to smile. "That won't prove anything. You could have checked into the campground, driven to the Chester-field Mall, and made it back to spend the rest of the night there... under the stars." Detweiler was studying me with an intensity that made me flustered. His behavior was weird, really weird.

But also not my problem.

"I have no idea what you are talking about. I didn't go to the Chesterfield Mall. Why would I? It's not even near my house."

"There's a scrapbooking store out there. A big one."

"Yes, Archivers is there. It's gorgeous. I love that store."

"So do I," said Dodie, in a declaration of solidarity.

I continued, "But I work here. I get the employee discount here—and supplies for the demo pages I make are free. In case you haven't heard, I'm broke. Poor. Impoverished. Why do you think I sold my house in Ladue? And got a job here? For fun? No. Sorry. I do it for the do-re-mi. So I mainly shop here."

I hoped Dodie didn't catch the qualifier "mainly."

Most scrapbookers shop around for supplies. We aren't disloyal, but if you run out of photo splits in the middle of the night, and you have to have them, you can't always be picky. A necessity is a necessity, and that's a fact.

"What's this poor-mouth routine? Your husband must have had life insurance. George Lowenstein was a business man. A smart guy, or so I heard," Detweiler sounded confused.

"I wasn't his beneficiary." With my peripheral vision, I watched Dodie's eyes nearly pop out of her head. She figured I needed money, but I never told her what my husband owed Dimont or about George's life insurance. I assume she assumed what everybody else assumed, that I socked away a bundle for a rainy day. Realizing I'd just exposed one of my many personal problems to my employer really hacked me off. Great, I told myself. Bad enough Dodie knew I was desperate for employment. Now that she knew about the problem with George's life insurance, I was completely at her mercy.

I whirled on the detective. "Excuse me, but don't you have anything better to do? Or is this your idea of a good time? Picking on poor defenseless widows?"

Detweiler looked stunned. His handsome jaw dropped. He snapped it shut and glowered at me. He was at least a foot taller than I. "Hey, when did you get the personality transplant, lady? I don't remember you acting quite so sassy."

"You have a lot of nerve. When did I get the personality transplant, buster? Right after you and everyone else in the world ran all over me last fall. Right after I had the worst Thanksgiving, Hanukkah, and Valentine's Day of my life. Right after my husband died and left me indigent. Got it? That's when I got so sassy. What'd you think? I'd lie down, roll on my back, and bare my throat? George is gone, but I've got to go on. By myself. For my kid. Now, if you don't have anything better to do than harass me, why don't you let yourself out? There's the door." And with a sweep of my hand, I pointed to the front exit. I was on the verge of tears. The fast-track review of my circumstances made me feel pretty darn sorry for myself. I didn't dare add, "And I've been publicly ridiculed by my hubby's old girlfriend as well as being verbally slapped around by my mother-in-law."

I had to get hold of my emotions. Fast.

Detweiler turned those gorgeous eyes on me. They were angry, no doubt about it. "Actually I don't have anything better to do. I'm doing my job. This is my second assignment to the Major Case Task Force in the past year and each time, your name manages to turn up. I'm not leaving until you tell me what you know about the shooting last night." His arms remained stiff at his sides. He stared at me, daring me to look away.

"What shooting?" Dodie and I said in tandem. We could have doubled as the chorus in a Greek play.

"Don't play coy with me. The shooting last night at Chesterfield Mall." Neither Dodie nor I responded. We had no idea what the man was going on about. Chesterfield was a suburb several miles west of the city of St. Louis, while our store and my home were in the more centrally located suburb, Richmond Heights.

"Cut it out! Don't tell me you know nothing about it!" His voice was clip.

"It what?" I demanded. My voice rose higher and higher. "What are you talking about?"

"Roxanne Baker's murder!"

"Roxanne? Dead? You've got to be kidding me! How? When?"

"*Oy vey*," whispered Dodie.

"Like I said, she was killed last night in the mall parking lot."

"Whoa, so that was the body in the news," Dodie gulped. "They hadn't released the name this morning…"

I couldn't believe what I was hearing. "That's… that's awful. But we just saw her, when? Saturday? At the shower? Dead? Are you sure? And shot?"

I couldn't help thinking maybe she got what she deserved.

A wave of despair hit me. Now I'd never learn more about her relationship with George. Death had a curious way of ennobling people. Of washing away their flaws and elevating their reputations to a new purity. Sinners became saints once their bodies were lowered into the ground.

Now no one would tell me all the dirt on Roxanne. I suspected she might have been one of the two women my husband lunched with the day of his death. But how would I ever know?

Detweiler studied me.

"She wasn't a very nice person. She stomped in here and threatened to quit doing business with me if I didn't fire Kiki," Dodie volunteered.

My jaw dropped. "What?"

104

Dodie shrugged. "Soon after you came to work here. But I fixed her wagon."

For a moment, I thought Dodie was going to confess. So did Detweiler; I could see it in his eyes.

"Yeah, I fixed her good." Dodie's voice was casual.

I froze. What was she saying? Did my boss knock off my husband's ex-girlfriend?

"I tore up her frequent buyer card."

Detweiler made a strangled noise, a sound between a gurgle and a cough.

Dodie was totally serious. She pantomimed tearing a card in half, crossed her arms over her copious self and beamed smugly. As far as she was concerned, she'd shown Roxanne who was boss.

I turned to the detective and watched him struggle to regain his composure. "Who killed her? And why?"

"Do you have a suspect in custody?"

Boy, Dodie was really up on her law enforcement lingo.

Detweiler ignored her. Instead, he turned his attention back to me. "Where were you last night, Mrs. Lowenstein?" His voice was softer, less demanding than before. "Can your friend Gracie give you an alibi?"

"You can't be serious. No way was Kiki involved." Dodie wagged her head. "Yesterday she carried a spider out of the store rather than step on it."

"Answer my question. Where were you?"

"What? Me? You kidding?"

"You were overheard threatening her." Detweiler's pen touched his notebook. A lock of hair over his eyes gave him a rakish look.

I responded with a hard mental slap to my own face. This man had just accused me of murder and here I was salivating.

Proof positive I'd lost my cotton-picking mind. I gathered myself to my full height of five feet three inches. "No, I didn't kill her. Yes, people heard me threaten her. My exact words were, 'Eat bugs and die.'"

"Eat *bugs* and die?" Dodie and Detweiler spoke in tandem.

"Kiki, you know that's not how the saying goes. It's eat sh—"

"Stop," I popped my hand over Dodie's mouth.

"Oh, for crying out loud," she said after she peeled away my fingers. "You are such a girl scout." But she'd given me time to think.

"Did she have bugs in her mouth?"

"No," said Detweiler.

"There you have it. I didn't kill Roxanne Baker."

SEVENTEEN

DODIE DEFENDED ME STOUTLY. "That's right. Kiki couldn't have done it if there weren't any bugs."

I brushed off my hands. "And might I add, although I don't approve of violence, I'm not surprised. She was not a very nice person. And foul mouthed? Ugh."

I was trying to act nonchalant, but I was quaking in my Keds. I knew this looked pretty bad. I had every reason to want Toxic Roxie dead. I couldn't believe my rotten luck. I'd never told anybody to "eat bugs and die" before in my whole life. I wouldn't have thought to say it, but it was number three (in a revised form) on Mert's Snappy Come-Back List. Numbers one and two were "Go soak your head," and "Take a long hike off a short pier." I'd already used those in minor traffic confrontations. I was working my way down the list when Roxanne got under my skin.

Detweiler shook his head. "Mrs. Lowenstein, we have reason to believe Ms. Baker was your husband's mistress."

Dodie's eyes nearly burst out of her head.

I snarled, "Took you long enough. I figured that out all by myself, and I don't wear a big shiny badge. Good work, hot shot."

Dodie's mouth flapped open and shut.

"You had motive," Detweiler continued.

"Ha. So they were lovers before George and I met, big deal. She told me at the bridal shower that she'd dumped George right before … um … right before … um, he and I got together."

He studied me and I knew that he knew exactly what I meant. I was jabbering like a flock of parakeets at the St. Louis Zoo. My stomach hurt like crazy. The pressure was getting to me.

Detweiler nodded. "I understand."

My cheeks grew warm. His color heightened, too.

Dodie muttered, "I don't …"

We ignored her.

I looked away. "I didn't know they were still seeing each other."

"Come on. From the altercation at the bridal shower, you must have had a clue." He cleared his throat. "That was her scarf in his mouth."

"Why didn't you tell me about the scarf?"

Detweiler turned his head away and swore under his breath, then he glared at me. "That information is part of an ongoing investigation. Forget I said anything. What if you decided to do her in? Did you? Decide to shoot Ms. Baker because she was seeing your husband?"

"No. I. Did. Not. Kill. Roxanne Baker." I spat out the words. "Like I keep telling you: I worked here, went home, and spent the night at the campground."

"But you could have swung back by the mall before heading for the campground. Maybe you thought Ms. Baker killed Mr. Lowenstein. You decided to get revenge. Or maybe you didn't realize Mr. Lowenstein's death would leave you broke. Or maybe he left all his money to her. Made you mad." He leaned against a crop table and studied me.

"Look, I'm a single mom working retail hours, doing freelance scrapbook jobs, and dog sitting to make ends meet. I don't have the time or the energy to be mad."

"You wouldn't be the first person to muster up the energy to commit murder. Especially under the circumstances."

Dodie's head swiveled back and forth taking all this in.

"I would never do something like that. I'm not brave enough to take someone on. Even if they came after me first. The Bible says the meek will inherit the earth. Well, let's just say I'm waiting for my inheritance."

Detweiler kept pushing, "You didn't go to the mall last night and confront Roxanne Baker?"

"No. I did not. And how would I have killed her? With my trusty paper trimmer?" I waved a boxed example to make my point.

"Like I told you, she was shot." His posture changed. The tension in his shoulders relaxed. The Bic pen tapped his thigh in a thoughtful rhythm.

"Oh, puh-leeze. The only gun I own is a glue gun. I could have glued her mouth shut until she learned some manners. Or I could have stuck a red letter A on her forehead with sequins. But kill her? Uh-uh. No way. Now I've got work to do. Some of us have to earn a living."

I walked past Detweiler toward the back of the store. "Dodie, I'm going to check in the shipment from yesterday. I'd like to get the merchandise on the floor."

Detweiler called after me. "About that friend of yours, Gracie?"

He and Dodie followed me like ducklings on parade. Dodie walked on her toes, falling forward with each stiff step. Detweiler stomped along behind her, with his notebook in hand.

"You want Gracie? You got Gracie. Come on down, Mr. Detective." I waved him into the stockroom. Rounding a tall metal shelving unit, the policeman found himself face to face with Gracie.

"Wow!" Detweiler exclaimed. His whole face lit up.

Dodie and I exchanged expressions of surprise. Most people who meet Gracie cower or demand she be put on a leash. She's so quiet that Dodie and I occasionally forget she's back in the stockroom. Gracie usually snoozed her way through the day. She was such a good girl. So sweet. So happy to be loved.

"She yours?" Detweiler gave Dodie a big grin.

"You're trying to arrest the proud owner," Dodie responded. "That's the aforementioned Gracie, the Great Dane. I wouldn't have a dog like this. Slobbers too much. And gas? Man, can this girl let them rip. Old Gracie here can peel paint off the walls once she gets going."

"May I pet her?" He acted like a ten-year-old boy rather than a thirty-something man.

"Sure." I tucked a finger under Gracie's collar and led her closer to the detective.

"When did you get her? I mean, have you always had her?"

"No, George didn't want a dog. Gracie is a rescue pup. I just fell in love with her. Since Anya and I live alone, and the neighborhood is transitional, she's both a pet and a deterrent. But I've never heard her bark. Maybe she doesn't need to. Word gets around when you own a big dog."

Detweiler dropped to a squat and rubbed Gracie vigorously under her chin. "She's gorgeous. You didn't have her ears cropped?"

"No. She came this way. That's fine with me. I like them long. They only started cropping to protect dogs used as hunters. A wild boar could grab floppy ears and go for the jugular." I smoothed one of her ears that had turned pink-side-up. "Besides, I nearly fainted when I had my ears pierced. I couldn't do that to her." No way could I put my big girl through surgery.

"I like her this way," said Detweiler in a soft voice, running his hands gently over Gracie's head.

Suddenly, the stockroom seemed too warm. I fanned myself.

"And here I figured you for a leg man," drawled Dodie. We watched Detweiler bend down to Gracie's level. She batted her brown eyes at him and made a deep, satisfying rumbling noise of joy.

"This harlequin coloring is so cool. I mean, the fawn color is nice and so's the brindle, but give me a Boston or a harlequin any day. Isn't that black patch over one eye neat? And that black saddle on her back? Hey, aren't you one beautiful girl? Huh, baby?"

Gracie licked him in the face.

I didn't know whether to laugh or cry. This cop had gone absolutely gaga over my dog. Two minutes ago, he was all Mr. Tough Guy about how maybe I killed Roxanne Baker and now, he was practically rolling on the floor next to Gracie. Not that Gracie wasn't absolutely wonderful. She was, but . . .

"Hey, what happened to the police interrogation?" Dodie took the words right out of my mouth. She seemed disappointed.

Detweiler shrugged. "Sounds like Mrs. Lowenstein is in the clear. I'll have to check out her story. Shouldn't be hard."

Dodie continued, "You made a fast U-turn from bad cop to dog lover."

He laughed. "I'm a sucker for dogs. I grew up on a farm over in Riverton, near Springfield, Illinois. Dad got bitten by an old hound when he was a boy, so he hated dogs. Afraid of them, I figure. I always wanted one, but with my hours it wouldn't be fair. Besides I love big dogs, but they need a lot of room and—" At that point, he realized he'd been gushing like a love-sick school boy. He stood up abruptly, all business now.

Except that he knew, and we knew, he could never regain his tough-dude status. Thanks to Gracie. Good old sloppy Gracie with the thin thread of drool hanging from her lower lip had exposed the human being inside the cool professional.

I had to laugh. Dogs are like that. Cats, too. Animals bring out the best and worst in people. They don't judge. They only love. They are really clear about who they like and who they don't like. They can't pretend. Pets cut right through deceptions we throw up to protect ourselves.

I reached down to cuddle my Great Dane. "Isn't she wonderful? She's so sweet. You should see her with Anya. And she's very obedient ... except she does like to run. Got to watch that. She likes to take off. Aren't you a good girl, Gracie?"

Gracie gave another low moan of pleasure.

"Of course, she's a good girl," said Detweiler. "Anybody could see that. Anybody."

It seemed somehow like he wasn't just talking about the dog.

EIGHTEEN

DETWEILER HAD HIS HAND on the car door handle and was ready to head back to the station when I yelled to him. "Wait! Wait! Help!"

Detweiler had concluded his interview with a few more desultory questions. He promised to check with the ranger station at Jellystone to confirm my story. We figured they had security tapes. I knew there was no evidence linking me to Roxanne's murder. How could there be? His last comment was, "Don't leave town."

Right, like I had the money to run.

That last comment was said in a businesslike way, but his voice was decidedly friendlier now that he'd bonded with Gracie. He was heading back to the station when I ran after him.

I felt kind of silly running so hard, feet flying, arms pumping. I knew I was acting more like a ten year old in a school yard than a grown woman, but the urgency of the situation demanded it.

"I ... need ... I just ... got a call ... and—"

"Slow down. Catch your breath." He had a wonderful smile that crinkled the edges of his eyes.

"Someone broke into my house. Mert just called. She stopped by to put a coupon for dog food in my mail box. She saw ... she noticed ... my scrapbooking room window is open." I bent over, gasping for air. "I never leave it open. Never. There's too much paper that can blow around."

"Your car here? I'll follow you to your house."

A few minutes later, we pulled up in my driveway. Gracie and I hopped out, but Detweiler stopped me with, "Get back in your car and wait. Give me your house key and let me check it out first. I called for backup."

While he walked through my house, checking it for an intruder, I phoned Sheila and asked her to pick up Anya and take my daughter back to the house in Ladue after school.

"Someone's broken into your house? I'm not surprised. I told you that's no place to bring up a child. You wouldn't listen. Probably some crack addict who would have killed both of you in your sleep—and don't give me that bunk about your dog being a deterrent. We both know that fool of a hound would let Ted Bundy and John Wayne Gacy party at your place all night before she'd have the sense to bark. Stupid creature."

I sighed and hung up. As long as Anya was safe, Sheila could say whatever she wanted.

Detweiler stuck his head out the back door and motioned to me. "I've cancelled backup. They're sending someone to dust for prints. The house is clear. I need you to tell me what's out of place. Just don't touch anything."

Everything was the way I'd left it the night before with one exception: the hard drive to my computer was missing.

"Why would someone take the computer and leave the rest? I've got a lot of money in equipment here. That's a professional quality monitor, scanner, and printer, and ... it just doesn't make any sense."

"Something in your computer? What could be there that anyone would want?"

"Beats me. Just photos."

"Add anything recent?"

"I downloaded photos from the shower ... the shower where Roxanne Baker was."

"The party where you threatened her?"

I nodded. "You don't think ... I mean ... there couldn't be anything in the photos, could there?"

"I don't believe in coincidences. Not when there's been a murder. Tell me about the pictures."

I explained how Dodie pulled the memory cards, and how we downloaded the candid shots. I told him how I sent images to Snapfish and made copies. I retrieved the duplicate CDs from my bottom drawer, all the time feeling very self-conscious about having this man in my bedroom.

The tips of his ears turned pink, but he sounded very professional. "You sure went to a lot of trouble."

We walked out of my room. "I take my responsibility for other people's photos seriously. They are irreplaceable."

"Have you looked at these? The ones you loaded? Anything pop out at you?"

I explained that I hadn't looked at the images carefully, and why. Sure, I'd hoped to find something embarrassing in Roxanne's photos, simply because I didn't like the woman, but I hadn't gotten that far.

"So, someone who wanted to see the photos could find them on the website—"

"And they were on my computer as well. And on Mrs. Witherow's, but only temporarily. I mean, Dodie used that computer as a portal, not for storage. But I don't know how many people would really understand how we loaded them. You could also right click and copy the images. Okay, if you're a scrapbooker, you might be familiar with the site and what we're doing, and anyone with a digital camera might know—" I shut up. It was pretty clear that just about any moron could follow the trail of photos.

We couldn't go anywhere until the crime scene technician arrived. Evidently, my intruder pried open my spare bedroom window, crawled through, took the computer, and didn't disturb any other part of the house. Detweiler figured we were okay hanging out in the kitchen. He crossed his arms behind his head and rocked back in a chair. I said nothing. He didn't either. Apparently he was thinking.

I got up and poured us both a glass of ice tea. It was lukewarm. Luckily, when the power went out, I had nothing in my freezer but a loaf of frozen garlic bread and Girl Scout Thin Mints. A handful of salad in the chiller drawer looked edible. AmerenUE must have arrived early. The house was still uncomfortably warm but the A/C was struggling to cool it down.

Clearly, I hadn't lied about the power outage. Detweiler rolled up his shirt sleeves. Boy, did he have sexy forearms. I never even thought about forearms being sexy until I saw his. Detweiler didn't say anything for a long time. He just stared off into space. At last he said, "You haven't added anything else to your computer recently, right?"

"Nothing. Well, I couldn't because of the power being out."

"Hmm. There's another coincidence. Don't like that." Detweiler flipped open his cell phone and made a call to AmerenUE. He identified himself as a detective. In five minutes, he learned there had been no power outage in my neighborhood the night before.

"But the electricity definitely was out! It was hotter than a steam bath in here. You can ask my daughter. I picked her up from school, we came home, and immediately I took her to her grandmother's house."

In desperation, I turned around. My kitchen clock was eight hours behind.

Detweiler called AmerenUE again. He re-asserted his position and authority. This time he learned they had a record of my call for assistance. He asked to speak to the repairman who had been to my address earlier in the day. After a few delays, they patched him through.

"What did you find when you were here? That so? You're sure? And how was it done? No, no, I believe you. See anyone suspicious hanging around? Remember if a window was open at the side of the house? It was? Thank you." He slapped the phone closed. "Someone cut your electric line back at the box. If the suspect broke in last night, this could have been the same person. You see where this is going, right?"

"Someone wanted me out of the house?"

"Yeah. News of the unseasonable heat was all over television and radio. Obviously you couldn't stay here. Someone banked on the idea you'd find another place to go. But why take just your computer?"

The fact my home had been violated made me sick. I heard my stomach gurgle. Maybe Sheila was right about this neighborhood. Even so, whoever broke into the house had only taken one thing. "I guess it would be easier to grab the whole computer and check it out at your leisure rather than sit here and go file by file. I wonder …" I chewed on my thumbnail thoughtfully. "Dodie told all the women at the shower about the website and how I planned to work with the photos. But I can't see one of them breaking into my house."

"They could have hired someone."

"If this is really about photos from the shower, and if it's connected with Roxanne, why not try to remove pictures from the website as well? Wouldn't that make sense?"

"The photos are in three places, right? The computer, your backup CDs, and the website. More if someone copied them from the site." Detweiler retrieved a laptop from his car. He connected to the Internet. Sitting at my oak kitchen table and waiting for his computer to boot up, I watched him glance around and take in his surroundings.

"I didn't see much of your other house when I was there after your husband died, but I like this place better. It's more … cozy."

My "new" house is not very big, but it has a good flow to the rooms. It was a mess when I moved in. I ripped up the old carpet and sanded the hardwood flooring underneath. I stripped wallpaper before painting the kitchen walls a soft gray-green to bring out the golden hues of my oak kitchen table and chairs. I sanded the fronts of the kitchen cabinets and painted them white. I put up white shelves for my dishes. Small houseplants supplied a touch of greenery. I bought a couple of interesting orange crate labels from eBay and framed them to hang on the walls. A pair of old lace curtains from Goodwill framed the wide back window. Crimson and orange tie-backs picked up the bright colors in the fruit crate labels.

In many ways, this was more my home than the house in Ladue ever had been because that house had been decorated by a professional interior designer to George and Sheila's specifications.

Detweiler followed my directions to Snapfish. Using my password and the room code, he navigated to the shower photos. They were all in one "album" labeled Merrilee's Bridal Shower. I stood at his shoulder and directed his actions, while taking great care not to touch him.

"Why so many images? Did the shower go on that long?"

"No. Remember, the women didn't know we were going to do this. It was a special deal Dodie cooked up with Mrs. Witherow, because at most events we don't get photos of ourselves, only of other people. Dodie figured this would make it more personal for each guest. We only had a few minutes to borrow their memory cards and download the images."

"You didn't have time to edit what was already on the cards before you dumped them onto the computer, right?"

"Exactly."

The doorbell rang. Detweiler jumped up with Gracie at his side. He put one hand on her collar and ushered in a crime scene technician, then showed the man where to dust for prints. Gracie stood by Detweiler's side the whole time. The dog and the detective formed a natural pair.

"I'll need to take these CDs as evidence." Detweiler reached for my duplicates.

"You can't. If you take those, and if anything happens to the website, I won't be able to complete the albums. Those albums mean a lot of income to me. Please don't take them."

"There's been a murder, Mrs. Lowenstein." Detweiler was firm.

"For goodness sake, call me Kiki." I struggled to keep my voice even. "Look, I know there's been a murder. I'm not sure you need these, but I do. This extra income means I can pay my bills. Isn't there any way around you taking these?"

He thought a minute. "How's this—let's copy the disks. I'll take the originals while you keep the copies. And I'll need a list of all the guests at the shower."

"That works. And if you leave me copies, there's always the chance I'll see something you won't."

It was a compromise we could both live with.

He popped in a CD and started copying. Without my powerful hard drive, the process ran slowly. The crime scene technician finished his work in the scrapbook room, formerly a tiny spare bedroom, and called Detweiler in to talk. I strained to hear their conversation.

"Everything's been wiped down. No prints showed up. This wasn't done by a kid on drugs. The intruder knew what he wanted and didn't care about covering his tracks. He pried the window open and climbed on in. See the tool marks? It's a cheap latch. He probably checked from outside to see if this was the right room. The jerk didn't even wander around the house."

Detweiler called me into the room. "Sorry about the dust. It tends to get all over."

That was an understatement. I sighed and realized cleaning up would take at least a couple of hours.

The photos were still being loaded on disks when a key turned in the front door.

NINETEEN

"MOM? I'M HOME," ANYA said. I left the kitchen to greet her with a hug. The warmth of her body next to mine felt good. When we are apart, I try not to worry, but since George died, I find myself being more protective than usual.

"We've had a little excitement here, but everything's okay now." I gave her another squeeze and realized I could feel her shoulder blades through her T-shirt. Was it my imagination or was Anya losing weight?

Sheila followed two steps behind her granddaughter. A column of black, wearing tailored slacks and a matching silk blouse, she stood with her arms crossed tightly over her chest and her lip jutting out petulantly. Her lipstick had been freshly applied. "I brought her to pick up more clothes. She's spending the night at my house. It's not safe here. Get your things, Anya."

"No, Gran, really. It'll be okay. Gracie's here, and we'll be fine. Honest." My baby hung on to me, her arms wrapped around my torso. Soon she'd be taller than me, if she kept growing at the rate she was. I hugged her hard and kissed the top of her head.

"You aren't safe here. You're coming with me."

"Honest, Sheila, we're okay. The burglar was only after my computer and now that he's got it..." I spoke to eyes hard as polished pebbles.

"That's what you say. I have no reason to believe you."

"Excuse me? I couldn't help but overhear." Detweiler came in from the kitchen. "Mrs. Lowenstein? I'm Detective Chad Detweiler. I understand your concern, ma'am, but like your daughter-in-law says, the intruder was only after the computer. This wasn't a dope-addled kid or some random thief. I'll ask the local police to keep an eye out for your family here. Of course, it's up to you two, but I think the house is safe. Now if you'll excuse me, we're just finishing up in the kitchen." He turned to go but hesitated, stopping to smile warmly at my daughter. "Anya? We met the day your dad died. I'm Detective Detweiler." The big man extended his hand for a formal handshake. "I'm sorry for your loss."

Anya straightened from her position spooning close to my body and looked him in the eye before shaking his hand. I worried. How would my child respond to finding a cop in her home?

"Thank you." Her voice was soft but calm. "Nice to see you again, sir."

Love that kid.

"Ladies." With a polite nod of his head, Detweiler turned away.

"Thanks for the ride, Gran." Anya bounced over to give her grandmother a peck on the cheek, before taking off down the hallway to her bedroom.

"This is outrageous. If anything happens to my granddaughter, I'll never forgive you. In fact, if I hear of any more problems, and I'll get custody of her faster than you can say goodbye." Sheila hesitated. She stood there, arms wrapped tightly around her torso. Her mouth puckered and furled.

"Sheila," I said. "Come on. We're okay. Honest."

"Hrumph." She didn't move.

I waited.

"I suppose you heard about Roxanne Baker," Sheila's words rushed by like air whooshing from a punctured tire. "This is horrible news. Simply unimaginable."

I had wondered if Sheila knew about George and Roxanne. After all, according to Merrilee, their romance began back when they were in school at CALA. Sheila's pained expression—an expression of loss—made it incontrovertibly clear the two women had remained close.

"I didn't realize you two stayed in contact."

"I had hoped one day she'd be my daughter-in-law."

With that painful slap in the face, Sheila did an about-face and stormed off to her car.

Detweiler continued running the photos. Image files are much larger than document files. Copying the photos onto CDs seemed to be taking forever. He looked me over carefully when I returned to the kitchen. I could sense he was thinking about Sheila's threats and put-downs. My house is small enough that he had to have heard.

"You do need more security. An alarm system won't work because Gracie would probably set it off. It would be easy enough to add lights. A burglar would think twice about being in the spotlight."

I chewed my lip. I didn't have much money. However, this was important. "I think my lease says I have to notify the landlord first. I'll call him."

Mr. Wilson wasn't home. I left a message on his machine.

"I'm going to rustle something up for dinner. Probably spaghetti. You're welcome to eat with us. There'll be more than enough." I didn't sit down. I had to keep moving. I was determined not to let Sheila's comment about Roxanne ruin the rest of my evening. Didn't my mother-in-law even suspect that hussy of knowing who murdered her son? How could Sheila be so blind?

"Are you sure? I don't want to impose, but that'd be nice. I skipped lunch. Can I help?"

What a shocker. George never offered to pitch in.

"Uh, no, the oven needs to heat up. I'll put together a salad. The lettuce will be okay if I soak it in cool tap water. I have two tomatoes on my counter and a couple of carrots in the drawer." I assembled the veggies on my counter.

"Better yet, why don't I check out the lock on the window. After telling your mother-in-law you are safe, I probably should make sure you are." He stood and stretched.

There was an unopened bottle of salad dressing and a can of tomato paste in my cupboard. I filled a pot with water and set it on a burner. I didn't turn the stove on just yet.

"I appreciate you seeing to the latch. I better check on Anya before I start this."

My little girl was lying on her bed listening to the iPod her grandmother had gotten her for Hanukkah. Her foot jiggled to the music, her skinny legs taking up scant room in the bell of her skirt. I touched her gently on the shoulder and her eyes flew open. "Hey, kiddo, I'm making spaghetti. What else can I get you? Applesauce? Salad?"

She diverted her eyes. "Mom, I'm not hungry."

I didn't like the sound of this. "Honey, it's dinner time."

Her blue eyes roamed the ceiling. "I ate with Grandma."

I doubted that. I made her scoot over and I sat down. I wondered if she was more worried than she'd let on. "Are you okay?"

"Yep."

"What'd you eat with your grandmother?"

"I don't remember."

This clearly was a lie.

"Anya, is something wrong? You seem like you've lost weight. I haven't seen you eat a full meal in days. You only pick at your food."

She wouldn't face me.

"This isn't healthy, honey. Come on. What's going on?"

Anya pressed a finger against her lips. She didn't talk. Okay, two could play this game. I didn't move. I could wait.

She sighed. "Daddy's girlfriend died last night. She got shot. It was on the news."

I nearly fell off the bed. Take it easy, I told myself. You asked her to open up, and she did. Go slow.

"Daddy's girlfriend?" A parenting book I'd read suggested when you don't know what to say, repeat what you've heard. And I definitely didn't know what to say. I was stumped. "His girlfriend?" I tried again.

"Yeah."

126

That was helpful. Now what?

"Who are you talking about, honey?"

Anya pulled off the earphones and turned to me. I reached over and took her hand. Her eyes searched mine. "Mom, you knew about her, right? Daddy said you did."

My heart clogged my windpipe. I choked. What on earth had George told this child? "Honey, what exactly did your daddy… uh… say? About… um… his girlfriend… and me?"

She took in a long breath and let it go slowly. Her gaze was clear and direct. "He said she was sort of a secret. He told me not to say anything 'cause it might make you sad. And we didn't want to hurt your feelings."

"We? We who? You knew about his… girlfriend?"

She nodded.

"How?"

"Because we did stuff together. The three of us."

An invisible fist slugged me in the solar plexus. All the air left my body. I crumpled, then caught myself by grabbing the side of her mattress. I struggled to stay upright. I turned my head so she couldn't see my expression.

The muscles in my jaw spasmed, and my teeth clamped down hard. I wanted to scream. I wanted to bawl like a baby. I wanted to dig up George's body and drive a stake through his heart.

How dare he? How could he have involved our daughter in his tawdry secret life?

And to expose Anya to Roxanne? That monster and my baby? How could he? I wanted to throw back my head and scream until my lungs gave out.

But I couldn't.

Not now. Not yet. Not in front of Anya.

"Mom?" Her voice, tremulous and high-pitched, brought me back to the present.

"Yes?"

"You okay?"

"Uh," I stalled for time. "I'm surprised. Just, um, surprised. See, I didn't know about this arrangement. That you went places ... together." Gritting my teeth, I managed to add, "Tell me more."

She screwed up her mouth, considering. "Well, it started when I was little. Daddy and I'd go out and we'd run into Mrs. Baker. By accident. Accidentally on purpose, 'cause it happened all the time."

Mrs.? Mrs. Baker? What a laugh.

"And one day I said, 'Daddy, how come you and Mrs. Baker hold hands when you think I'm not looking?' And he told me ... "

"What? What did he tell you?" I struggled to keep my voice low and calm but I could hear the shrill edge.

Anya's brow creased. She turned worried eyes on me. "That she'd been his first girlfriend and that they'd always be special friends. He said it was like I'd always be special friends, like with Theresa, even though Theresa moved away in third grade and I never see her anymore."

"Special friends." From my lips, it sounded like a curse.

"Right."

"What did you think about that?"

"Are you mad, Mom?"

"No, honey." I broke a promise I made when she was born. I lied to her. I'd told myself I'd never do that. But I did. I lied. And I was getting good at lying, but this was no time to worry about it.

Her eyes filled with tears. I watched one spill and run down the side of her face. I hopped up and walked toward a box of tissues on her dresser. The chance to expend some energy did me good. It was all I could do to keep from running out of the room and screaming my head off at my dead husband. But instead I moved very deliberately, pulling the tissue gently from the box and walking it over to my child.

Anger bubbled inside me, but I put it aside. My daughter needed me. "It's okay, honey. You can tell me. What did you think about Mrs. Baker?" The last sentence came out more hushed and loaded than I wished.

"I didn't much like her."

Call me mean-spirited, but I was thrilled with her answer. "Did you see her often? I mean, did she join you and your daddy a lot?"

"Yeah. Well, no, not really. I got pretty tired of it. She would act real mushy toward Daddy, and I really didn't like that. Once I even said, 'Excuse me. No PDA,' and she didn't know what that meant so I told her how there's a rule at school about public displays of affection. She didn't like that one bit. So I asked Daddy if … if he was going to leave us … divorce you and marry her …"

"And he said?"

"He said he'd never leave us. Ever. But Mrs. Baker said at least until I got older."

"She did?"

"Yeah, I was scared. But Daddy got mad at her. Daddy said he'd never leave us. Ever. We were his family. Then Mrs. Baker got this mean look in her eyes and her mouth went all funny. I didn't care. I hugged Daddy, and I told him I loved him. He said it again. He promised he'd never leave me, never leave us, ever—but he did, didn't he?"

The floodgates burst and the pain of the last six months, along with the strain of keeping a secret for years, swept through my child. Anya gave up trying to hold back her tears and let it all go. Shivering, quaking sobs vibrated her slender frame. I pulled her close, held her to my chest, and rocked her the way I had when she was a baby. Her sweet, tiny head with its peach fuzz had grown into a nearly adult-sized head of silky blonde hair, but the same intense love for my baby filled me. I wanted to protect her. I wanted to make it all right.

And I knew I couldn't.

Now I had a motive for my husband's death: George told Roxanne he'd never leave us. That must have really frosted her cake.

But as I held my crying child, the person I wanted to kill wasn't Roxanne.

It was George.

TWENTY

WHEN I JUDGED ANYA to be cried out, I grabbed a washcloth, soaked it in cold water and wrung it nearly dry. I dabbed her eyes and forehead, wiped her nose, and gave her a kiss on the cheek.

"Ready to eat? I invited Detective Detweiler to join us. He's transferring photo files. That'll help him figure out who broke into our house." We leaned into each other, heads nearly touching, as we walked down the hall with linked arms.

A fragrance lured us into the kitchen. The scene that greeted us stopped us in our tracks.

In the middle of the table was a stainless steel mixing bowl of lettuce, topped with chopped tomatoes and carrots. Three places were set with plates, napkins, and salad forks. Instead of water glasses, there were coffee mugs of water.

Detweiler stood in front of the stove wearing an apron and stirring an interesting mixture of spaghetti and sauce. Fresh baked garlic bread was arranged on a plate in a series of neat slices.

131

Anya wiggled her mouth in an attempt not to smile and gave me a broad wink. She said to him, "Wow, you did a great job. I usually have to set the table. I've got all sorts of chores I'd be willing to share."

Detweiler flushed and pulled off the apron quickly. "Um, I couldn't find your glasses. I hope you don't mind me going ahead. I was kind of hungry and I figured you were busy." A kindness in his eyes told me that he'd heard at least part of my conversation with my daughter.

I shouldn't have been surprised, the walls are thin and I'd left her door open.

Well, welcome to my world, buster.

"Have you ever eaten Persian spaghetti?"

Anya shook her head.

"Prepare to be amazed," said Detweiler. "A friend in college taught me this. I doubt that it's authentic, but it sure does a great job of stretching a little pasta into a big, hearty meal."

We sat down and ate. As if to distract us, Detweiler talked about growing up on a farm. Anya wanted to hear about the animals. She was particularly interested in hearing about the pond on his parents' property. She was fascinated with bugs, frogs, snakes, fish, and all manner of critters. The kid was a budding vet or biologist. I liked hearing about Detweiler's family, especially his mother and two sisters, whom he identified as quilters *par excellence*. Detweiler asked Anya about school. She admitted she had another end-of-year test to study for. He told her not to worry, that police would be cruising past our house at regular intervals to check on us. I smiled to myself a lot during the meal. For dessert, I pulled the mainly defrosted package of Girl Scout Thin Mints from the freezer.

A knock at the front door interrupted us.

"Paris's mother left town unexpectedly. You got room for her?" Mert held a blonde Pomeranian with a jeweled collar. Paris was wearing a sundress and a straw hat with tiny flowers around the brim. Mert handed over the dog and her traveling wardrobe case with the jeweled letters that spelled out PARIS. "I'll get her food and crate," she said.

"Paris!" squealed Anya. "Hey, Mr. uh …"

Detweiler followed her into the living room saying, "Chad." He took one gander at Paris and froze. "What is that?"

Anya explained how Paris was our most frequent boarder. My daughter took the little fluffball from me gently. Paris loved Anya and wiggled with delight.

"What on earth is she wearing?"

"Paris has an entire wardrobe of pretty clothes and accessories. She has a yellow polka-dot bikini, a Burberry raincoat, and short-shorts," Anya chattered happily while holding the fashion victim under one arm. Gracie came over and sniffed Paris once before deciding this was your basic boring house guest.

"Why on earth? She's a dog, not a Barbie doll."

I laughed. "Yeah, well, don't tell her owner. You'll ruin the surprise."

Mert held her cell phone under her ear and was yakking her way up the sidewalk when Detweiler took the crate, a bag of food, and a monogrammed canister of yummies from her. Mert did a double-take, glancing at him, then at me, and almost dropping her phone. Watching the detective walk toward my kitchen, she sputtered,

"Great Gravel Gerty, have mercy. Who is he? Did Santa leave him under your Hanukkah bush and you forgot to tell me?"

Mert leaned closer to whisper, "And where can I get myself one jest like him? You been holding out on me. Yippee kai yai ay."

I loved her, but she could sure make me blush.

Mert and I stepped inside as Anya explained Paris's warped personality to Detweiler. "See, she loves to get yummies—" and Anya gave the fluffy pooch a small liver snap "—but she never, ever eats her treat right away. Instead, she buries it. Watch. Here's a yummy, sweetie."

Putting Paris and her treat on the sofa, Anya stood next to Detweiler to observe. The overdressed dog raced from one end of the sofa to the other, dug for all she was worth, and shoved her head between the arm cushion and the loose pillow, doing minor damage to her sunbonnet.

"Now, watch this." Anya straightened Paris's hat. The Pomeranian pranced to the far end of the sofa, leaving behind her buried treat. "I think I'll sit here," and Anya lowered herself onto the sofa cushion next to the hidden yummy.

"Yip, yip, yip, yap, yip!" Paris threw herself onto Anya's lap, turning in frantic circles.

"What's wrong Paris? Did you lose something?" Anya stood up and Paris began to dig at the sofa again, her small front paws moving at lightning speed. Poking her head between the cushions and whining, Paris was clearly beside herself, checking to see if her yummy had been disturbed.

"Don't tease her." I felt sorry for the silly creature. But then, I knew how it felt to act like a dope in front of an audience. Especially when food was involved.

Anya reached behind the pillow, retrieved the liver snap and handed it to Paris. The Pom took it gratefully and raced to the other end of the sofa so she could repeat the burial rites.

"That's something," said Detweiler.

Mert asked him about the break-in. I noticed her eyelashes fluttered double-time. I explained I'd called the landlord about security lights. "Good idea. Roger can install them tomorrow. He's only got one class at Meramec Community College. How 'bout I send him over to Home Depot? He'll bring you the receipt, and you can pay him back."

"I'll pay him for his time as well," I said.

"Nuts. Make him a couple loaves of your banana bread. He loves them, and I won't go through the bother. That'll be more'n enough payment. He'll be glad to do it for you."

"What would I do without you?" I gave her a hug. I meant what I said, and she knew it. She whispered in my ear and pointed toward the kitchen where Detweiler was back at his computer, "He's gorgeous. Man, he can play with my mouse any old day. Squeak, squeak! Hold me back. If love is a crime, lock me up."

I laughed. We made arrangements for her to retrieve Paris and said good night.

Detweiler and Anya cleared the table, while the photos loaded. I rinsed out the pots, except for pausing briefly to peep over his shoulder at the images.

He grabbed my arm. "I heard what your daughter said."

I froze. My skin tingled.

He let me go. His eyes were steady, deep, and thoughtful. They were the color of a Heineken bottle held to the sunlight.

"Sounds like Ms. Baker had motive. She couldn't have been happy hearing your husband tell her they had no future."

I nodded. "Right. She had motive. And there was that scarf. But how'd she do it? The autopsy said he had a heart attack."

He ran his hands over his face. "Probably poison. Because of Thanksgiving, the autopsy happened four days after Mr. Lowenstein died. Even if we knew what to look for, it would have been hard to find. But after four days? Really tough. Especially if it was organic toxins."

My eyes blurred with tears. I rinsed a plate and set it down carefully. I had to ask, "You still suspect me?"

"I still have a job to do. Sorry about the eavesdropping, but I'm glad I was here to listen in. You were surprised about your husband seeing Ms. Baker. Right?"

"I didn't want to believe he was cheating. Um, I had no proof. I figured I was imagining things." My hand made lazy circles with my dishrag. Round and round and round. "I guess I fooled myself. I asked him once and he ... he changed the subject. I didn't press it. I sort of figured there was ... might be ... someone else. He sure wasn't that ... uh ... interested in me."

"Why'd you stay with him?" His words held no malice, no hint of judgment, just curiosity.

"I thought it was best."

"Best for you?"

"For Anya."

The truth was I didn't think I had a right to expect more out of life. But that was none of his business. That was my baggage.

Time to change the subject. I pointed to the computer. "Which memory card are you on?"

"If they're labeled correctly, these are Ms. Baker's pictures."

I watched the photos load, studied them for a minute, then returned to washing salad bowls.

Creativity experts tell us water spurs our inspiration to new levels. Taking a shower or bath, even washing our hands, can unlock a portion of the brain devoted to ideas and imagination. When I get stuck on a page design, I get a glass of water. When I get totally scrap-blocked, I take a walk around a lake. That's the only way I can explain what happened next. My hands were in water when it came to me.

"Hey, wait a sec. Let me look at those photos." I didn't know what to call him. I felt awkward calling the detective by his first name. He'd given my daughter permission to call him Chad, but in my mind, the man sitting across from me would always be Detweiler. And I couldn't bring myself to say his name.

He brought up images from Roxanne's memory card. One by one he clicked and enlarged them.

I shook my head. "Not a single bridal shower picture among them. Let's go through them again."

There were a variety of photos: two of the engaged couple kissing, a beach, a structure of white poles, and Roxanne standing on white sand next to a man wearing sunglasses and a red baseball cap. Whoever he was, he wasn't George.

I pulled up a chair and sat at Detweiler's elbow. "Does that make sense to you? I mean, why bring your camera to a special event and not take pictures?"

He rubbed his chin thoughtfully. "Maybe the card was full."

"She's got a lot of poor quality duplicates on here."

"So?"

"Okay, look." I grabbed my digital camera and opened a photo. "Now look at this." I opened another photo. "Same subject; not as good composition."

His forehead wrinkled. "I don't get it."

I explained that scrapbookers love digital cameras because we take a lot of pictures. Let me repeat that: a *lot* of pictures. We're always hoping for the perfect angle, the best setting, the best pose, the sharpest focus. And we're willing to take tons of pictures to get what we want. Dedicated scrapbookers often snap pictures of the same subject in the same pose in both landscape and portrait composition.

"Why?"

"Landscape might work better in one layout but portrait might be better in another. You want flexibility. You want to choose the photo that works best on your page. So, like I said, we take lots of pictures. In fact, we take too many shots knowing we can delete the ones we don't like. After all, we aren't wasting film."

He threw up his hands in frustration. "I still don't get your point."

"Look carefully. Roxanne has duplicates she should have easily dumped to take more pictures. But she didn't."

"Which means?"

"Well..." I drummed my fingers on the table, a habit my mother abhorred. "Well...maybe she didn't intend to take pictures. Maybe she was using her camera as an album. What if she planned to show someone an image—or images? Maybe she didn't care about taking pictures of the shower."

Detweiler tensed. "If you're right, there might be an image here—" he tapped the screen "—that someone wants badly. So badly they broke into your house to get it."

My heart did a hop-skip-and-jump. Suddenly, I felt woozy. I stood up, got us both glasses of cold water, and took a sip. Was Sheila right? Was I endangering my child? Was I so quick to disagree with anything my mother-in-law said that I hadn't been fair? Calm down, I told myself. Think this through.

"Okay, someone has my computer. Now he thinks he has *all* the copies of the images. No reason to bother me again." I rubbed Gracie's head. Anya and Paris were watching television in the other room, but Gracie had taken a liking to the policeman and was nestled between our chairs. Her big head alternated resting on my thigh and then the detective's.

Detweiler spoke quietly, raising his fingers to count off his points. "Mr. Lowenstein might have been poisoned. Someone shot Ms. Baker. Your house was broken into. There's something weird going on with these photos. Maybe I spoke too soon about you being safe." He gave me a long, thoughtful look. "By the way, I nailed your window shut." He jerked his head toward my scrapbooking room. "That'll do for now."

He flipped open his phone and talked in a low voice. I could make out the gist of the conversation: he wanted the local cops to be especially watchful—and he explained why.

When he finished, I said, "I own a one-hundred-twenty-pound dog. I have a fenced-in back yard. We'll be fine." I talked big, but I was quaking in my boots. Our new theory had me worried.

"The local police will watch the house tonight. But at the very least, you need security lights. Anyone can get in through these windows, but with security lights, they'll think twice."

"Mert's son will pick them up and install them tomorrow. After I get permission from my landlord."

"Get those lights up right away."

I didn't argue with him about calling Mr. Wilson first. In my brief career as a renter, I'd learned my landlord wasn't always reasonable. Once again, being poor put me at risk in ways I'd never stopped to imagine.

We had only fifteen more pictures to copy. Detweiler's mouth settled into a scowl. "Hand me your cell phone. And does Anya have a cell phone? Get it for me."

I did as I was told. George had gotten Anya a kid's cell phone last year. At first I thought it an extravagance. But because the CALA campus sprawled over 100 acres, the phone facilitated tracking her down at after-school activities. In the wake of her father's death, the phone helped my daughter feel more secure. Sheila loved being able to speed-dial her grandchild. When she offered to take over the payments, I gladly acquiesced. She might have rescinded her offer if she'd realized how much I liked being able to call my daughter at her grandmother's house without my mother-in-law's interference.

Detweiler programmed his number into both our phones. Handing one back to Anya, he told her, "Anything happens that bothers you, anything at all, hit number nine and call me. Doesn't matter what time of day or night, okay?"

She studied him. "Are we in danger? Is something wrong?"

"No, Miss Anya," he said, "but what use is it knowing a police officer if you can't call him when you need him? Say a big bully picks on you on the playground, or you see an older kid drive too fast through the school parking lot, or you hear a noise at night and you get scared, I'm your man, all right?" And he concluded with a grin and a goofy thumb-to-the-chest gesture that made her laugh out loud.

"Hear that, Paris? We got police protection." Paris was wearing pink striped pajamas and fuzzy house slippers. The dog was better dressed for bed than I would be.

"Honey," I said. "As hot as it is, how about letting Paris sleep nude tonight?"

When girl and fashion-plate left the kitchen, Detweiler sank back in his chair and covered his face with both hands. "I could never be a parent. Here I'm trying to make sure she's okay, and instead I scared her."

I didn't tell him I thought he'd make a wonderful parent. I kept that to myself.

TWENTY-ONE

AFTER DETWEILER LEFT, THE house seemed strangely empty. All my fears came back to haunt me as I wiped black fingerprint powder from my scrapbooking room.

Were we safe? Should I have sent my daughter to Sheila's? Would the burglar return for the rest of my equipment? Was a killer watching my home and waiting?

Who killed George? Was it Roxanne? And who killed her? She hadn't been robbed. Detweiler told me her purse and jewelry had been undisturbed.

So Roxanne had been with George *before* he died. The scarf proved that. Or did it? What if someone had planted her scarf on George's body?

And maybe she'd been with him when he died. Did she kill my husband? If she killed George, why did someone kill her? To revenge his death? Or were there two killers out there? Two killers and a burglar?

My head started to hurt.

After I wiped down the room, I spent a restless hour. Finally, I let the dogs out for their goodnight piddle. A police car paused in front of my home.

Tonight we were safe. But for how long?

———

The next morning I dropped Anya at school and was in the store by quarter past eight. I brought Paris, her crate, and Gracie through the back door. I'm grateful Dodie lets me keep my canine babysitting charges at the store. She told me, "They're welcome to visit as long as they are well-behaved and crated. Except Gracie. She's free to have the run of the place."

But for the emotional security of our customers, Gracie mainly stayed in the back room.

I think Dodie secretly wants a pet but isn't ready to commit. I frequently find her in the back cuddling a lonely pooch. The woman is a study in contrasts, by turns hard-nosed businesswoman and sensitive employer. Although she expects a lot from me, she has made it perfectly clear she understands that Anya's needs come first.

Our relationship turned upside down when I moved from customer to employee. And yet Dodie has let me know that in many ways she values me more than ever. Back then, I was a minor source of revenue; now I am a revenue stream.

All in all, my decision to work for Dodie has been a good one, and I appreciate this job. Today I had lots to do. Every other Friday, we offer a Beginning Scrappers Crop, fondly called the Newbie-Do-Be-Do. I like to start early getting ready for them. For each beginners' crop, I create a new simple layout. Since working at Time in a Bottle, I've taught two beginning classes, this being the third. That means I have two other beginning layout kits I can sell to our newbies. Each kit includes all the paper they need, instructions, and a small color photo of the finished project. At the price, it's a bargain, but it makes money for Dodie. My starter kits help business in yet another way—beginning layouts encourage newbies to feel successful quickly, keeping them involved in the hobby.

I was paying close attention to the die-cut machine when the buzzer heralded a customer. The store doesn't really open until nine, but I flip over the sign as soon as I get settled. After all, you never know when a big sale will walk in.

I looked up to say hi to Merrilee Witherow.

Only, it wasn't Merrilee. It was Linda Kovaleski. She looked terrible. Her red-rimmed eyes were underlined by dark, puffy bags.

"Boy, for a moment I thought you were Merrilee."

"We have the same hairdresser," she said, flipping her tresses to show them off. They were a sunstreaked blonde that was probably as expensive as it looked. After the flip, she grabbed a piece of hair and twisted it cruelly.

"Can you believe it about Roxanne? Isn't it awful?" she talked like a woman on speed. "It's scary. There's a killer out there. None of us are safe." Her eyes kept roaming the ceiling, unable to focus, like a cell phone searching for service. I heard a tapping and glanced down to catch her foot in frenetic motion.

"Yes, it's horrible." This wasn't the place to get into theories of divine retribution. Truth be told, I wasn't as worried about the dead Roxanne as I was about the live whacko standing two feet from me. Linda's eyes ricocheted like pinballs, and her fingers moved at warp speed, turning and fiddling with her hair.

I asked, "Are you all right?"

"I've had a lot of caffeine. I didn't get much sleep last night. I can't stop thinking about Roxanne at the shower, you know? I wonder what happened? I mean she was alive and now—how could she be gone? Why would anyone hurt her?"

I bit back an answer.

"She was at the mall. Why there? She only shopped designer stores."

"I don't know what she was planning. Maybe we'll never know."

"She was this total scrapbook fanatic. I mean, it's odd that you and she ... uh, George and you and ..." The woman tailed off, momentarily stunned by her own bad taste, or so I hoped.

Her finger twirled like a helicopter propeller, ravaging her hair. "I mean, her scrapbooks were really important to her. Like, they were her life! She was always taking pictures. I'm worried about our photos from the shower. I heard about your computer being stolen."

"How'd you hear that?"

"Uh, I called Dodie at home first thing this morning. She gave us her business card with her phone number, remember? I was upset about Roxanne." Linda twisted a lock of hair, her finger chasing it round and round. "And I was worried about Roxie's camera. Was it on her ... her body? I mean, what about the shower photos?"

So that's what this was about. "It's okay. We're covered. She didn't take any photos at the shower."

"But your computer's gone. Our photos were in it."

"Right, but I also copied them onto CDs."

"And on this computer?"

"No. Customers use this computer. I can't store the photos here. I can't chance someone erasing them by mistake. And remember Snapfish?"

Linda's eyes measured the ceiling. Thinking, thinking, thinking. The answers are not up there, I was tempted to say.

She bit a corner of her mouth and got lipstick on her front teeth. "What do fish have to do with our pictures?"

I tried not to sigh. I didn't want to sigh. But I probably did.

I needed to recoup fast. I had no right to act unkindly toward her. There are plenty of things I don't understand: calculus, rocket science, and intelligent design. "Snapfish is a photo finishing and storage site. I probably didn't do a good job of explaining how it works. Why don't I walk you through the process?"

We sat side by side at the computer. I noticed her gorgeous French manicure and expensive perfume. Actually, what I noticed was money. Lots and lots of money.

Shades of my former life.

I opened the website, typed in my password and room code, and clicked on the album. Linda's eyes nearly bugged out of her head. She really was a computer novice.

"Those pictures are small. You can barely see anything." Her twisting ramped up. That poor strand of hair was turning and twirling for all it was worth. At this rate, she'd be bald before sundown.

"Right. We're viewing thumbnails. They're called that because of the size. Watch. I click and the image gets bigger."

She squinted. "You can't really tell a lot about what's going on, I mean, not really."

"That's part of my job. I can enlarge the photos. I can also adjust the brightness and contrast, fix red eye, and crop out distractions." As I spoke I brightened a picture of Merrilee and her mother opening a gift. I fixed the red eye and removed an annoying ficus at their side.

"Notice how taking away the house plant redirected our attention? We can focus on the bride and her mother."

"You sure can!" Linda leaped out of the chair, her purse held tightly to her body as if warding off a blow. "I've got to go." She walked straight out the door.

I sat at the computer and stared after her. Life had gotten so weird. Linda's bizarre visit proved that bedlam was the new norm. Was there a full moon out there or what? Certainly my life was in total disarray.

Then again, who was I to label her behavior strange? I fingered Detweiler's card tucked in my pants pocket. My husband had been dead less than a year and I had the hots for a man who'd accused me of murder. How sick was that?

Dodie walked in fifteen minutes after Linda's precipitous departure. Paris set up a barrage of warning barks, announcing she was on watchdog duty. After dressing herself for school, my daughter had outfitted Paris in a pair of denim capri pants and floral crop top. Dodie lifted the canine fashion model out of her crate. "Hey, gorgeous, how's tricks? Walked any runways lately?"

I told Dodie about Linda's visit.

"She called me at home. How would I know if the police found Roxanne's camera? How many times do we need to tell her the photos were loaded into your computer and Snapfish? Geez, talk about your ditzy blonde." Dodie paused. "No offense."

"None taken." Yes, I'm blonde, but that's because I believe in better living through chemistry. If my income didn't improve soon, my hair would return to its natural mainly-muddy brown.

I flipped open my cell and called Detweiler. That brought up a good question. Where was Roxanne's camera? We knew she hadn't taken photos at the shower. At least not before we loaded her memory card. Had she taken any pictures after? Did she have the camera with her when she died?

I left a message on Detweiler's voice mail.

Dodie worked the counter while I sorted photos. Most of them didn't relate to the shower. Culling through the rest, I looked for candid photos that reflected the celebratory spirit of the bridal shower. I immediately discarded any that were unflattering to the guests, although I hesitated before purging the picture of Roxanne with an ugly sneer on her face. With judicious cropping, I created portraits of Merrilee and each of her guests. One particularly striking photo taken by Linda showed Merrilee and her mother beaming at each other. No wonder the woman stressed out so much about the safety of her photos. Linda was a darn good photographer. She'd captured Mrs. Witherow lovingly cradling her daughter's chin in her hand. It was a portrait that would have made any professional proud.

Around lunchtime, I grabbed a strawberry low-fat yogurt from the mini-fridge in Dodie's office and chugged a Diet Dr Pepper. The dogs needed a potty-break and a walk. After fifteen minutes in the heat, we oozed our way gratefully into the air-conditioned cool of the back room. My short-sleeved cotton blouse would have wilted had I not soaked it with an entire potato field of starch before ironing. My short khaki skirt kept me cool everywhere but around the waistband. I splashed cool water on the inside of my wrists, returned to the sales floor, and shifted gears to work on the new layout for the newbie crop.

Try as I might, I couldn't decide what I wanted for that particular project. I kept shuffling papers and rejecting embellishments. I'd gotten nothing done but wasting time when my watch told me I'd better hustle to meet Anya after school.

I told the dogs. "Time to get our girl!"

Gracie hopped up and down, doing her heavy-duty imitation of a pogo stick. Her big tail thumped the nearby boxes. Paris yapped. She wasn't smart enough to know I'd suggested an R-I-D-E, but she figured if Gracie was excited, she might as well join in. Inside the car, Gracie perched her rump on the passenger seat and her front legs on the floor, so she looked exactly like a human with a blocky head. Paris raced back and forth in the tiny back seat.

My landlord, Mr. Wilson, rang my cell phone as I was driving to CALA.

"Heard the police were at your house."

"Yes, sir. I had a break in."

"That's never happened before at one of my properties."

I found that hard to believe. The term "slumlord" would have been a generous moniker for the man. But I didn't want to be disagreeable. "Yes, sir. I called because I have a friend who's installing security lights as we speak—"

"Your lease specifically forbids you from making any alterations to the property unless I approve."

So far his approval had extended to me turning a gross dump into a clean and attractive home. Wilson sure hadn't minded saying yes when it meant letting me put hours of my time into upgrading his property.

But my Nana always said you can catch more flies with honey than you can with vinegar.

"Yes, sir, I understand. I really do. And I'm so sorry this happened. I would have waited on the lights but it's really dark along the sides of the house and—"

"I don't care. I don't like the unsavory elements you've attracted."

"Pardon?"

"I'm giving you thirty days. I want you gone. And forget your deposit. That's mine now."

TWENTY-TWO

THURSDAY MORNING I WOKE up at dawn after a futile attempt to sleep. I'd tossed and turned for hours as the digital numbers slipped into place, one after the other, on the clock. I sat at my kitchen table, stared out the window, and watched the sun rise.

I had no idea where I'd find another security deposit. I'd sold everything we owned but some furniture, my old Beemer, and my diamond engagement ring that I'd asked Sheila to hold in her lockbox for Anya.

Even if I could scrape up the money, I doubted I could find a suitable place on such short notice. A rental property that took pets and had a fenced-in yard was hard to come by.

Despite the burglary, I wanted to live here. I'd put so much of myself into this place. Besides, how would I explain being evicted to Anya? How could I put her through yet another change?

I added upsetting Anya to my personal hit parade of worries. Topping the chart was housing, then came being broken into again, while replacing my computer brought up the rear. At least six people—not counting Mert, Dodie, and Detweiler—knew I had made CDs of the memory cards. How long would it take my home invader to discover he'd left those duplicates behind? I could take the copies to work and leave them there, but short of writing a note and taping it to my scrapbook room window, I had no way of telling the burglar I'd moved his cheese. My best recourse was to let as many people as possible know plenty of copies of the photos existed. Then there'd be no need to target me.

I turned to the matter of George's killer. Okay, Roxanne was dead, but an unsettling thought niggled at me. Two women left Antonio's with George the day he died. My husband's mysterious tablemates went to a lot of trouble to keep their identities secret. Roxanne was gone, but who was the other woman? Why hadn't she stepped forward? Was there more to their secret? Was she the shooter? What if Roxanne's scarf had been planted? Did the other lunch companion know who killed George? And how? And why?

Three people left Antonio's and hopped into a car together. Now two of them (assuming Roxanne was one of the two women) were dead. Detweiler said he didn't believe in coincidences. What was happening? Why had Roxanne been shot?

A ding-ding-ding went off in my head. Maybe George's killer also murdered Roxanne. But why? Did Roxanne take a secret with her to the grave?

I choked down two bites of toast before tackling yet another item on my personal worry list. I had to repay Roger for the security lights—and ask him to take them back down.

After dropping Anya at CALA, my body showed up for work, even though my brain was off in the stratosphere, circling Saturn.

Once again, I struggled to come up with a design for the newbie crop. The official title for my malaise is scrapper's block.

"Father's Day is right around the corner. How about you do a layout remembering George?" Dodie smiled kindly at me. "You could have Anya journal her memories."

The sincere expression on her face saddened me. If she only knew what a jerk my husband had been, taking our daughter along for trysts with his mistress, and swearing our child to silence. I'd gotten the rage out of my system last night and didn't want to revisit my fury by scrapbooking my husband.

No scrapbooker in her right mind would destroy a photo. Not only do we believe images spark the tinder that makes our memories blaze brightly, but we also secretly believe a picture holds a portion of the soul. How else can you explain the way the portrait of a loved one moves you? Photos are sacred to scrapbookers. I've heard stories of women risking their lives to save family keepsakes from flood, fire, earthquake, and paper-eating silverfish. Whereas in the early days of scrapbooking, crafters used scissors and templates to crop their photos into amusing shapes, now the tendency is to regard the photo with more reverence, only cutting away that which might divert our attention from the subject.

Yes, only a scrapbooker who had lost her grip on sanity would destroy a photo.

Which tells you exactly how crazed I had been the night before. I'd had a day and a half to think about George's perfidy. I couldn't believe he'd exposed our child to his affair with Roxanne Baker. The more I tried to rationalize his actions, the madder I got.

What else had George been hiding from me?

I got sick thinking about it.

I probably could have kept my cool, had it not been for the evening news.

Anya and I were sitting in front of our tiny television eating open-face tuna sandwiches broiled with a slice of American cheese on top.

Anya selected one of Paris's formal gowns from the tiny trunk. "I think this slinky green number sets off Paris's hair. What do you think, Mom?" A tiny evening purse had been sewn to the dress. Anya strapped silver slippers to the dog's back paws.

"She's lovely. Please put her down and wash your hands, sweetie."

Anya pushed her food around her plate. I encouraged her to eat, but she only swallowed a couple of bites. This was one of her all-time favorite meals. If she wasn't interested in tuna sandwiches, we were in deep trouble. Anya had never been a picky eater, but she definitely had her favorites.

Paris was watching Anya, too. Most fashion models are underweight, but there was nothing wrong with this fashion victim's appetite. Paris lurked under the coffee table, the better to gobble any scraps that fell to the floor. And that little hairball did not like to share. When Gracie eyed a crust of bread hungrily, Paris bared her teeth and growled. The big dog scampered to my side for protection, all the while making goo-goo eyes at my meal.

More and more of Anya's food was being pushed around and landing on the coffee table and floor. None of it traveled to her mouth.

"Aren't you hungry? What did you have for lunch today?"

She started to respond when a photo of Roxanne flashed on our tiny TV screen.

A solemn reporter explained authorities were pursuing leads in the shooting death of Roxanne Baker. A camera turned to Merrilee who told us Roxanne had been named after her mother, Opal Baker, a St. Louis socialite. The segment ended with a plea from the police for good citizens to come forward with any information about the murder of Opal Roxanne Baker.

I turned away from the set in disgust, but Anya's eyes never left the screen.

"First Daddy and now Mrs. Baker. They're together in heaven. Like they were here." She tossed her napkin onto the floor and stood up. "I should have never told him I didn't want her around!" With that, she grabbed Paris, ran to her room, and locked the door.

I let her have a private cry before I tapped on the door. She didn't respond. A dime rotated the keyhole of the lock and allowed me into her room. Anya had fallen asleep with her arms wrapped around a big stuffed Elmo that George had won for her at Dave & Buster's. Paris, still costumed in her long green dress, sat on the pillow next to Anya's head.

We were reduced to this: being watched over by a four-legged pygmy in an evening gown.

That's when I cracked.

———

I took an 8½-by-11-inch studio portrait of George out into the back yard. Armed with a butcher knife, I stabbed my husband—or his effigy—over and over, slicing his face to slivers of paper. I cursed him and cursed him and thought up new ways to condemn him to immortal misery. Like a fiend in a horror movie, I ripped my blade into his smiling visage. With each blow, I asked George, "How could you do this? How could you? To our daughter? To our child?" And finally, "To me?"

I don't know how long I was out there. I howled in pain; under a full moon, I might add. I quit when my arm was too tired to lift.

Wasn't there a limit to what one woman could bear? I could cast aside my disappointments, my hurts, and my embarrassment, but the tears of my daughter watered and nourished a gut-eating misery inside me. Exhausted by my outburst, I covered my face with my hands and cried until my stomach heaved. Paris watched me with a curious air of concern, moonlight glinting off her tiny purse. Gracie whined and tried to push her wet muzzle under my armpit, as she angled to distract me.

Or maybe she was trying to warn me.

I paused for a second and sniffed the air.

Uh-oh.

I was sitting in a pile of dog poop. In my frenzy I had smeared it all over my clothes. The mosquitoes were having a field day, dive-bombing me and shouting, "Buffet! All you can eat!" There I sat, sobbing, swearing, and stinking up my back yard. Scratch that. Mr. Wilson's backyard.

After all, I was being evicted.

Gracie bumped me again, bringing me back to the thin line, the hair-width border of reason. I picked myself up and walked back into the house to shower and go to bed. When I checked, Anya was still sleeping.

"What about it, Paris? Wanna sleep in the altogether?" I removed the dog's finery. Paris *au naturel* curled up on the foot of Anya's bed. I closed the door quietly, after saying a prayer for my daughter's protection. Gracie accompanied me to my bedroom. She made a loud Omph—like "glad that's over"—and settled onto the rug as I crawled under a thin cotton blanket.

When Dodie suggested I immortalize my husband on a scrapbook page, a review of my crazed nocturnal behavior passed through my mind. Given my meltdown of the previous evening, scrapbooking George for Father's Day was not a good idea. Instead, I created a page to honor his father, Harry. I titled it "Teacher, Father, Friend," and used manly shades of slate blue, almond, burnt orange, and black to support my theme. From what I'd seen of him, Harry had been a *mensch*, Yiddish for a person of strength and honor, and I regretted I hadn't known him better before he died.

After finishing the page for newbies, I copied the Essentials of Scrapbooking handout I'd written for beginners. As the last sheet shot out of the printer, Tisha Ballard tapped me on the shoulder.

"Did you hear about Roxanne?"

Frankly, I was tired of that greeting. I needed a sign for my forehead: "Ding-dong, the witch is dead. Get over it." But that might be going overboard, even for a sophomore at Tough Tamales U. I gritted my teeth and smiled (or tried to). "Hard to believe, isn't it?" A mental chorus of "liar, liar, pants on fire" threatened to blow my cover, but I hit the mute button and kept myself in check.

Tisha surprised me. "Actually, she deserved it."

My jaw dropped.

Tisha continued, "Yes, it's a shame, dying young and all, but Roxanne was horrible, wasn't she? Look at the scene she made at Merrilee's." Tisha fingered a diamond pendant hanging from a gold chain around her neck. "Her behavior was uncalled for. Unbelievably tacky. So she was from a wealthy Old St. Louis family. Big deal. You can't breed for class, can you?"

Hello, my new best friend. Finally another person saw Foxie Roxie as she truly was: low-rent, low-morals, low-life.

"Roxanne got what was coming to her." Tisha was on a roll.

Her plain-speaking encouraged me. "I wonder if she was involved in my husband's death."

Tisha nodded. "I wouldn't have put anything past her. When Roxanne didn't get what she wanted, she was vicious. Just vicious! And what she wanted was George. The fact he was married to you only made her want him more. It drove her nuts that she couldn't have him."

"I didn't know you felt this way." I was confused and it showed. "You were at Merrilee's shower."

"Only because Elizabeth Witherow and I work together on a charity board. Frankly, I don't have much use for Merrilee either. She and Roxanne are—were—both spoiled brats." Tisha brushed her hands together as if knocking off dirt. "But I'm not here to speak ill of the quick or the dead. Bill gave me a gift certificate for a private lesson."

She opened a set of envelopes. "While my dear husband attended a financing seminar over Christmas vacation, the kids and I went to Disney World. Any suggestions how to put these in an album? I've done a little scrapbooking, but not much."

I smiled. Dodie stocked tons of cool Disney embellishments and paper. This was going to be fun.

"I also have these." Tisha plopped down a large manila envelope. Four envelopes of photos were inside. "While Bill was at the housing trends conference at Palm Desert, I took the kids on a cruise."

"Palm Desert? I thought the conference was in Reno this year. See, I made a golf album so George could keep track of the courses he played. He was looking forward to Lake Ridge in Reno. It's a Robert Trent Jones course. Whatever that means."

She corrected me. "Bill specifically said the conference was in Palm Desert. He came back with a glorious tan. It rained every day of the cruise."

"Ugh."

Back to reality, grounded by the gravitational pull of motherhood, we talked over her options. An album can be simple and effective with a coordinated selection of papers and embellishments.

Tisha combed the display rack and selected a handful of dark-colored sheets of cardstock.

"You could use these," I said, being careful not to discourage her. "But when I think Disney or a cruise, I visualize bright and happy colors. When you go darker, the mood shifts."

Tisha blinked at me. Her eyes narrowed, and she hesitated. Finally she said, "Despite our husbands' partnership, we don't know each other very well. But you're reading me like I was a neon sign. Keep a secret? I haven't been happy for a long time. Bill and I are in counseling. I'm thinking of asking him to move out."

I must have looked chagrined.

She lifted her shoulders and let them drop. "It's okay. I've just had it with his bad-boy behavior. And I haven't felt like myself lately. I've been tired and my stomach's upset."

"I'll make you a nice cup of tea." I motioned to a chair by a work table. "How about you go sit down? While you sip tea, I'll organize the embellishments for your albums. You can talk if you want—or not—whatever suits you."

Plied with peppermint tea, Tisha relaxed. Soon she chattered a mile a minute. She was pretty sure that Bill had used his "business" trips as opportunities to "misbehave."

This was not a good idea. Tisha's family had loaned Bill the capital to buy half of Dimont Development—and he'd hit them up for more money to finance Babler Estates.

"My daddy is not going to stand for Bill two-timing me," said Tisha. "Weird, isn't it? No wonder George and Bill had such a good partnership. They both were a couple of cheats."

My face flamed red as I realized everyone in the world must have known about my husband's affair with Roxanne. Everyone but me. What is it they say about the wife being the last to know?

Whatever.

Now George was dead, and Wild Bill was about to get tamed.

My woolgathering made me miss a portion of what Tisha was saying.

"And he never even paid Daddy back." She launched into a full-blown rant. "That means half of Dimont is really mine, not Bill's. I could walk in tomorrow and close the doors. In fact, the only reason I haven't is because of you."

"Me?"

"If I closed the place, it wouldn't be fair to you."

"Fair to me?"

"Yes. There's that buy-sell agreement. Bill is supposed to pay you for George's half of Dimont."

I could have been hit in the head with a telephone pole; I was that stunned.

I didn't know what to say. But I had to say *something*. Back to the parenting book. I paraphrased Tisha's words: "Bill has to buy half the business from me." I stumbled over them. Did that mean what I thought it did?

Money?

Bill owed me money?

I was flat broke. I was being evicted. But Bill owed me for half of Dimont Development? Wow! What a shocker. I struggled to stay calm.

Tisha didn't notice. She just kept talking. "First the business has to be audited. That'll determine its worth. The audit will be done at the end of the current fiscal year, which is this coming August."

I focused on the scrapbook paper I was cutting. I didn't dare look up. "August."

Tisha chattered along. "That cash infusion last fall significantly improved the balance sheet."

"Significantly improved." As was my mood. I wasn't penniless!

"Remind me exactly how much cash that was." I kept my voice light.

But I nearly chopped off my finger when Tisha answered, "Four million."

Four million dollars?

"Daddy and Sheila both put in two million. George was really smart. He changed his life insurance. Made his mother beneficiary. If he hadn't, you'd owe her two million bucks."

TWENTY-THREE

I SHUDDERED. SORRY, GEORGE, I said to his ghost. Here I was angry with you for making Sheila your beneficiary, and you were thinking of me the whole time. I couldn't imagine owing my mother-in-law two million dollars.

I needed to know more. "Remind me how the buy-sell works."

"As I understand it, one partner takes out a life insurance policy on the other. When George died, his insurance policy supplied Bill with the money to buy George's half of the business. The paperwork on Babler Estates will be wrapped up sometime in the next two weeks. Then the business will be worth more than ever. Bill and I probably owe you a lot more than George was insured for."

"Right." Trying not to sound totally stupid, I said, "Babler Estates. That's the new group of houses being built ... uh ..."

"Out by Babler State Park," said Tisha. "Daddy figures it's at least a forty-million-dollar deal. At bare minimum. To be fair, you should get credit for part of that windfall because George helped put the deal together. I didn't mean to be avoiding you after the funeral, but until this is done, I'm in an awkward position because my husband owes you for your half of the business. And Daddy still needs to be repaid."

"Oh, no problem." What else could I say? I was sort of shell-shocked. Rats. What else didn't I know? How could I have been so stupid? Where had I been all these years? Standing in front of the refrigerator and stuffing my face?

I decided to change the subject before Tisha brought up the money George had "borrowed." Obviously it was small potatoes in comparison to the tens of millions involved in the housing project. Maybe Bill didn't mention George's indiscretion to his wife for the same reasons he told me he wanted to keep it quiet. If Tisha's daddy knew there'd been an "accounting" problem, he might want his two million dollars back right away.

My head was spinning like the cups in the Mad Tea Party ride at Disney World. The rich get richer and the poor get poorer, in part because the rich have access to good information. For example, if I'd been the daughter of a rich man, I might have known business partnerships include buy-sell arrangements. But my daddy had been a drunk, and the only buy-sells I knew of were rounds of beer at the bar.

I had one more question for my new best friend. "Tisha, have you ever heard of a company called 'orb'? Or maybe it's O.R.B.?"

She shook her head. "No, do you know what kind of business it is?" Seeing my negative reply, she continued, "Sorry. I can't help you."

For the duration of Tisha's visit, we talked about our children.

"We really should get the girls together," suggested Tisha. "I'd like Britney to have a friend who's grounded. In touch with reality.

I love CALA, but sheesh, too much wealth and privilege at an early age can't be good for these kids."

As we worked on Tisha's pages, I puzzled over how to proceed. If she was correct—and I had every reason to think she was—I didn't want the business evaluated right away. But I did need to ask Bill for a copy of the partnership agreement.

I wondered what other secrets that document might reveal.

I rang up Tisha's purchases. I showed her the page kit for the beginner's crop, and she signed up to come back the next night. She also asked me to set aside a complete set of the newbie page kits. I told her I'd have them ready for her at the crop. As she walked out the door, I congratulated myself on having made extra of the Father's Day layouts. Then a nasty, small voice reminded me that while I was very good at making a buck twenty for Dodie, I hadn't been smart enough to make sure I was repaid for my husband's portion of a multi-million-dollar company.

Bill wasn't in when I phoned. I left a message with the receptionist. I no sooner hung up than Merrilee walked in. This time it really was the bride-to-be, and not her doppelgänger, Linda.

"I can't believe Roxanne is dead. It's too, too horrible. She was always so vibrant and alive, and I can't ... I can't ..." and Merrilee started to cry. Only her snuffling and hiccuping weren't as dainty as crying. It was more on the side of blubbering, actually. I grabbed a tissue box from under the counter and offered her a Diet Coke from the back.

The trip to the refrigerator supplied time to gather my wits so I wouldn't start screaming. Despite my good news, I was still sick of that murderous home-wrecker. Here I'd thought I'd never have to hear Roxanne's name again. Instead, she was invading every second of my life. If it wasn't my mother-in-law mourning her or my kid crying about her at home, it was customers at my workplace going on about her. I wanted to run and hide, but the best I could do was dole out Diet Cokes as though they were mood-altering drugs.

Get a grip, I told myself. And find out whatever you can to prove Roxanne murdered your husband.

I popped the top so Merrilee wouldn't ruin her nails. She slurped the cola and started in on a trip down Memory Lane, starring dearly departed Roxanne. For what seemed like an eternity, I nodded my head and made interested noises. Finally, I interrupted to suggest Merrilee make a memorial album for her friend.

"Could you help me? I mean, I know the two of you had your differences."

Right. Like she was mean and rude and slept with other people's husbands and I didn't? Yes, we certainly had our differences.

I tried to think of a suitable platitude. Finally I blurted, "We're all God's children." I stopped myself from adding, "As was Satan."

Instead I said, "Of course, I'll help you with a memorial album." All the while thinking, I should charge her extra for my pain and suffering.

Merrilee blew her nose. For a dainty nose, it made a big blasting honk worthy of a Canada goose. She sniveled. "I don't care what Roxanne told us. You're not such a bad person after all."

"Gee, thanks." A pain shot through my head as I fought the urge to roll my eyes. "Um, what did she tell you about me? Or George?"

"She loved him so much. He was everything to her."

"I heard it was over between them."

"She was so upset about him wanting to end their relationship. They were childhood sweethearts, and he wanted to break it off. Isn't that sad?"

Uh, not really. I nearly pierced my own tongue biting down. I needed a muzzle to keep from screaming. Was this woman really this dumb?

"Poor darling Roxie had so much heartache in her life. So many disappointments. She wasn't crowned Queen of Love and Beauty like her mother was. Her grades weren't good enough for an Ivy League college. And she lost all those millions in the dot.com crash."

"Poor baby." I quickly mumbled, "Bless her heart," which every Southerner knows is a code for, "What a moron!" Then I asked, "What did she live on?"

"Oh, like I told you. We all loaned her money, a lot of money. She told me she'd made a big investment, and I'd get it all back." This was punctuated by another loud honk. "I don't know if I'll ever see it again. And I didn't get a promissory note so I can't write it off. That really stinks. I took a real hit on this. My accountant is sooooo upset."

So that was what all this caterwauling was about. Money, not friendship. I could barely contain myself. What was wrong with these people?

Merrilee was too self-involved to notice any change of expression on my face. After all, I wasn't even human. I was a servant, and therefore, part of the décor. How could I possibly have feelings? And if I did, who cared?

"Roxanne was always larger than life, you know?" Merrilee blew her nose. A big booger stuck to the tip of it, but I didn't tell her. Nana used to say, "Pretty is as pretty does," and this new accessory seemed just right.

"Roxie was perfect. Really, really perfect. You saw how she dressed and how beautiful she was. What a figure. And that hair. Gorgeous. Only thing was, she couldn't have kids."

Roxanne couldn't have kids?

With one turn of the phrase, all the colored glass settled in the kaleidoscope, and the pattern revealed itself. While Merrilee yammered on, I picked up the layout featuring Harry Lowenstein. I studied George's father's face with fresh insight.

From the farthest recess of my mind, I recalled the rabbi at our wedding saying that in the Jewish culture, a man isn't a man until he marries and fathers a child. I remembered Harry davening, mumbling his Hebrew morning prayers. I thought back to the joy in the old man's eyes as he talked about the granddaughter he wouldn't live to see because cancer would claim him first.

A door opened, revealing a pathway lit with understanding. On one side I saw George and a barren Roxanne and on the other Harry and a frustrated Sheila. I walked a narrow road between those couples and carried Anya in my arms. I saw the forces that shaped my married life. Forces I couldn't reckon with because I hadn't known they existed. As I made my journey, the solemn voice of my daughter reminded me, "Daddy said we were a family, and he'd never, ever leave us."

My unplanned pregnancy had intersected with George's father's need to leave a legacy. What conflict my husband must have felt! On one hand was a woman he loved (or at least lusted after) who could never have children. On the other was a woman he barely knew but had gotten pregnant. In the end, he chose easing his dying father's mind over making himself happy. The joy George felt when he held our baby in his arms had been real. It was the joy of continuation, of preserving his father's memory, and of being a father himself.

George meant what he said to Anya. He never planned to leave us. He had managed to compartmentalize his relationship with Roxanne, dividing his thoughts as though his mind was a duplex. We lived in one half; she lived in the other.

And what must it have been like for Roxanne? To have that "perfect" body betray her? To watch my daughter and her father and to know a portion of George would always be off limits to her?

It must have made Roxanne mad enough to kill. But if that was the case, then who killed her? And why? And what did the photos we'd downloaded from the shower have to do with any of this?

Suddenly, I thought about Sheila bribing the housekeeper at the Ritz-Carlton and the waiter at Antonio's. Maybe she had more moxie than I credited her for. Could she have killed Roxanne? Had Roxanne gone from favored candidate for daughter-in-law to dead woman walking when Sheila discovered the debutante had murdered her son?

"Hey? Kiki? Hello?" Merrilee waved a soiled Kleenex in front of my face.

"Sorry. My mind wandered."

"I want an album for Roxanne." Merrilee snuffled loudly. "I want you to do all that scrapbook stuff for me. There will be a celebration of her life at Antonio's on The Hill. I want to show off the album at the gathering."

Antonio's! Now that Roxanne was gone, maybe one of the wait staff would be willing to talk.

"Of course." I made the bride-to-be a copy of my special handout, and we moved to the album display.

I had one more question for Merrilee. "Did Roxanne have a favorite waiter at Antonio's?"

KIKI'S MEMORIAL ALBUM IDEAS

1. Begin with a title page. Showcase a favorite portrait of the loved one and the subject's full name, date of birth, and date of death.

2. Collect as many photos as you can. Ask other mourners to contribute. Once you have those pictures, edit them judiciously. You'll want to leave plenty of space for written remembrances.

3. Remember: Your job is to fill in the spaces between the dash, the symbol that separates our birth date from our date of death. If your subject lived from 1934 to 2006, think about his or her lifetime in the context of the times, those seventy-two years of history. Our lives are shaped by the world around us and events we live through.

4. Prepare a list of significant events during your subject's lifetime and add them to the album.

5. Compile a list of people who knew the deceased. Send them the following letter:

> Dear Friend,
>   I am creating a memorial album for _____, and I'd appreciate your help. Please share any special memories you have. When and how did you meet? What did you have in common? What did you like or admire about him/her? What did you like to do to-

gether? Where did you enjoy going? How would you describe this person? What will you always remember about him/her? What message would you like future generations to read regarding this person?

My goal for completion of this album is (date). Of course, I'd also appreciate any photos you can share.

Sincerely,

(Your Name)

6. Add pressed flowers from floral offerings, memorial programs, obituaries, and pressed flowers from floral offerings to your pages. Slip them inside a protective pocket.

7. Consider how complex you want your album to be. The simpler the album, the easier it will be to make multiple copies for friends and family.

TWENTY-FOUR

MERRILEE HAD NO MORE than walked out the door when Detweiler returned my call. "We're still looking for Roxanne Baker's camera."

"That's a good idea," I said. "Who knows what's on it? Do you think her murder is connected to George's? Or my break-in?" I tried to sound calm, but my heart was racing. I didn't tell him I planned to visit a certain waitress at Antonio's. It was none of his business. Detweiler had given up on finding my husband's killer and was now totally focused on tracking down the person who killed Roxanne.

"Unfortunately, I can't get any more done today because I'm leaving town this afternoon. I have to testify up in Springfield, Illinois, on Monday. Real pain in the butt. I'll be staying at my parents' house, but you probably can't get me by cell phone. The towers are pretty spotty on the other side of the river."

I assured him I didn't anticipate any need to call. "The security lights are up."

"Good. Be careful. Keep your doors locked. Patrols are still scheduled to watch your house, but don't let your guard down. Those lights are a good first step."

Typical man-talk. Detweiler was now comfortable enough with me to be a real Mr. Bossy Boots. I didn't tell him the security lights were due to come down, and I was going to have to find a new home. I could only handle one complication at a time. And it was his fault I was being evicted. Wasn't he the hotshot who demanded I put the lights up before I got permission?

He told me to give Gracie a pat, tell Anya hello, and then he hung up. The warmth of his voice flooded me with complex sensations. I was trying not to like him. I was working at it really hard. But I was falling fast and I knew it. My phone rang again.

"Mrs. Lowenstein? Bridget Kammer here. I'm the school nurse at CALA. I don't want to alarm you, and your daughter is fine. Do you have a moment?"

"Is something wrong?" I worried when anyone from Anya's school called. I bet every mother did. A phone call from the school nurse was especially unsettling.

"Not exactly. I'm calling because Anya looks a little thin to me. She seems to be losing weight. Does it look that way to you?"

"Yes. In fact, I told her a few days ago I was concerned."

"How did she respond?"

I thought back. "She said she wasn't hungry. I've encouraged her to listen to her body. I don't want to push food on her like my mother did on me."

"That's to be commended. You are absolutely right. Our bodies will tell us what we need and how much, if we will only listen. Can you remember when she last had a full meal?"

"Actually, now that you mention it … no. But she's at school and her grandmother's as well as home, so I guess I assumed …" My voice faded. A tidal wave of guilt swept over me.

"Hmmm. I made a special point of watching her at lunch. She took a salad and an apple from the cafeteria. As far as I could see, she only ate two bites of each. Did she eat any breakfast?"

"No, I poured a bowl of cereal. I offered her a granola bar." I was becoming increasingly frantic. How had I let this slip past me?

"Hmm. Is she in the habit of eating breakfast?"

"No. I've never been able to get her to eat much in the morning."

"And I assume she doesn't eat a big dinner."

"No. Especially lately. Of course, the nights when she's at her grandmother's, I don't know what she eats."

"I see."

Was she thinking or judging or both? I felt like my world was caving in. I said, "Mrs. Kammer, what are you telling me? What do you think is going on?"

The other woman sighed. "I wish I knew. I don't want to alarm you. We have to watch these young girls so carefully. Eating disorders can sneak up on us. We've had other girls in Anya's class diagnosed with both anorexia and bulimia. Unfortunately, girls are very impressionable at this age. As a culture, we send mixed messages. Movie stars are severely underweight, but we put them on a pedestal. All the magazines talk about six-packs but don't explain you have to get down below your suggested body weight for them to show. Conversely, on television we see one image after another of food. In restaurants our portions are enormous. It's terribly confusing."

"It's even hard to sort out as an adult," I added. I thought about all those years when I found myself staring mindlessly at the boob tube and snarfing potato chips or candy. I would be surprised each time I reached the bottom of the bag. Where did the food go? I'd been "unconscious" as I ate it!

"When one student stops eating, another child who's at risk may join in. They get notions, ideas about thinness. Often it's a passing lark, but I really do try to keep on top of any changes I see. I know Anya's father died right before Thanksgiving. How is she adjusting?"

My breath caught in my throat. "We have good days and bad."

Mrs. Kammer sounded kind. "Stress can cause all sorts of … well, coping mechanisms. Adjusting to the loss of a parent takes time. Any disruption to a family routine can be unsettling, even in the best of circumstances. Have you had any other lifestyle changes?"

"We moved, and I started a new job."

"Goodness. You certainly have had your hands full. Why don't I try to talk with Anya? Let's see if she'll open up to me. Afterward, I'll call you, and we'll discuss how to tackle this if there seems to be a problem."

I was speechless. My heart was competing with my Adam's apple for limited space.

"Meanwhile, I suggest you hold off on any more changes if you can. Give Anya the chance to catch her balance emotionally. It's important she feel a sense of security and stability."

No way was I going to tell this woman we'd just been evicted. That'd cinch my chances of being Rotten Mother of the Year for sure.

Drat. I thought to myself, this really stinks. Anya needs stability and I can't provide it.

Things couldn't get much worse.

Or could they?

On one hand, I felt all yippee-skippee about the buy-sell agreement. On the other, I knew better than to count on the money. After all, look what happened when I was so confident I was the beneficiary of George's life insurance. Since his death, my life was just so uncertain. Hadn't I learned the hard way not to let my guard down?

If the buy-sell gave me enough money to find somewhere else to live, I'd be set.

I closed my phone and stood rooted to the spot. During Friday crop nights, Anya goes home with Sheila and spends the night. The two of them enjoy their special evenings together, by lighting Shabbat candles, snuggling, and eating the roasted chicken and kugel Linnea is famous for.

After that disturbing conversation with the school nurse, I needed assurance Anya was all right. CALA wouldn't let out for another fifteen minutes. I decided to turn to the one other person who shared my concern for Anya's welfare. I dialed Sheila. I tried to sound bright and cheery. "Hello, Sheila, are you on the way to pick up Anya?"

"Of course I am. Don't be silly. Where else would I be? Have I ever let her down? Or shown up late?"

"No. No you haven't. And I appreciate it," I trailed off. I wasn't sure how best to approach this. Sheila could be prickly. "Sheila, Anya seems rather thin to me lately. I'm concerned she's losing weight. Would you please encourage her to eat a good meal? And a big breakfast? I know she loves Linnea's cooking—"

"Of course she loves Linnea's cooking. That's why she was getting pudgy."

"Pudgy?" I couldn't believe my ears.

"Darn right. I put a stop to it. I told her that with her mother's weight problems, she needed to cut back now or no one would ever love her."

I saw red. Steam came out of my ears.

Dodie walked by carrying a clipboard. She took one look at my face and mouthed, "Something wrong?"

I could only blink twice in reply. I needed to choose my words carefully. Getting upset with Sheila wouldn't help the situation. I needed her cooperation, and Anya needed her love. I willed myself to calm down. I stammered, "Sheila, I know you care about Anya's well-being. I know you want what's best for her, but she's only eleven. She's never been overweight. She is underweight. The pediatrician said so at her last visit. We need to encourage her to eat, not scare her away from food."

Dodie's jaw dropped. A head shake of incredulity told me that even as a casual listener she, too, was horrified. If her stunned look was a reflection of mine, I must have been wearing a fright mask.

"Confused? I'm not confused. Childhood obesity is a national epidemic. I simply won't allow my granddaughter, my flesh and blood, to pack on the pounds."

"But she hasn't packed on the pounds. She's underweight! Didn't you hear me? For her age and size, Anya is underweight. I repeat: at her last check up the pediatrician said she was slightly below average weight. Since then, she's lost a few pounds and gotten taller. Encouraging her to eat less is not healthy. Please tell me you'll have Linnea fix her a sensible meal. Please, Sheila."

"We're having salad for dinner."

"Just a salad? But she hasn't had anything today but a couple bites of apple and some lettuce!"

"And she's not going to. You can never be too rich or too thin. She needs to start thinking that way now."

Something broke loose inside. I think it was the last remnant of my self-control. I'd had it with this woman. "Too rich or too thin? Are you nuts? She's eleven years old. Now either you see to it she gets a good meal and quit this nonsense or—"

She hung up on me.

I stood staring in horror at the phone, my mouth flapping like a flag on a windy day. She'd gone too far. She'd imposed her out-of-whack, bizarre, elitist thinking on my child.

"I've got to go. I've got to stop her. I've got—"

"You've got to settle down." Dodie put a meaty hand on my shoulder. "She won't listen to you now. You are both irrational. Calm down." Dodie turned me to face her. "Think this through. Give it a rest for now. That lightweight birdbrain isn't capable of hearing logic when her feathers are ruffled. Leave it to good old Dodie. I'll take care of this. Listen and learn."

She pulled her cell phone from her back pocket and hit the speed dial. I shifted my weight from one foot to the other while wringing my hands. I heard the ringing stop and a voice say, "Domino's Pizza. Pickup or delivery?"

Dodie said, "Delivery. I'm going to give you my credit card number. I want you to take this to a friend's house in about forty-five minutes, got it? A big hand-tossed cheese pizza. An order of chicken fingers. A liter of lemon-lime soda. Some of those garlic sticks and dipping sauce, okay? Throw in those cinnamon thingies for dessert. Now here's the address." She handed the phone to me. "Tell him where Sheila lives."

I did. She took the phone back, gave the man her credit card number, and ordered three more pizzas for the store. With a look of triumph, Dodie snapped her phone closed.

"Get the door, Sheila, it's Domino's!"

TWENTY-FIVE

THE FATHER'S DAY PAGE was a big hit. We had a full house with newcomers. Since newbies need a lot of time and attention, I try to keep our class number under a dozen. In any group, you get visual learners who catch on quickly, and folks who need their hands held, literally speaking. Occasionally, I'll get a person who really, truly can't manipulate the paper or the tools. It's a struggle not to yank the stuff right out of her mitts and do it myself. But I'm learning. See, it's not about how good the teacher is. It's about how good the student feels. And nobody feels good when you do things for them. Besides, the best way to learn is by making mistakes. I know because I've made plenty of them. I've inadvertently cut photos in the wrong place. I've dropped pieces of paper and had them stick to the sole of my shoe, which left me to re-cut them. I've spilled glue on my layouts. I've gotten water on photos. And those are just the highlights. Whoo-wee, do I know how to make a mess of a page.

But here's my biggest tip: it's just paper. Unless you are working with irreplaceable family pictures, you can always start over.

A lot of mistakes lead you to new techniques or unexpected opportunities to be creative. I hate to tell you how many of my best pages happened when I had to work around a problem. Necessity is the mother of invention, but boo-boos are the parents of out-of-the-box thinking. Nothing like a real goof-up to stretch your mind, to lead you where no papercrafter has ever gone before.

True to her word, Tisha came to the Newbie-Do-Be-Do. She finished the Father's Day page quickly and started on her Disney World pages. I showed her how she could use the Father's Day page design with her Disney paper and get an entirely different look. I explained how she could flip the design, or rotate it, and change the look yet again.

Scrapbookers often tell me they run out of ideas or get blocked creatively. What they don't realize is every page they make does not have to be a new layout. All you need is to make a few changes, and voilà! It's like when I was growing up. I'd buy a dress pattern and sew it over and over using different material. Not only did I save money by reusing the pattern, but I got faster and faster because I knew what I was doing. It's the same with scrapbooking.

My goal as a scrapbook teacher is to give people permission to be creative. When you think about it, if you aren't creative, you aren't alive. Your body re-creates itself every seven years. When that stops, you're dead. Creativity is the fountain of youth, keeping your brain engaged and your spirits elevated. Without a creative outlet to absorb all my mental energy in the months after George died, I would have fallen into the dark crevasse of depression and not made it out.

Mert stopped by the crop to pick up Paris. The pick-up and drop-off service is one of the many reasons Mert's dog-sitting business is growing. I dressed Paris in her pink nightie and slippers and sent along a note card fashioned from leftover paper. It explained to the Pomeranian's "Mama" that Paris had been the guest of honor at a pajama party. This was the sort of silliness that made Going to the Dogs more memorable than other local kennels.

I gave my students a ten-minute break so they could finish up the pizza and use the restroom while I talked to Mert.

"So that no-good Roxanne has gone to meet her maker."

I nodded.

"They'll be partying like all git-out down in H-E-double-you-know-where. You reckon you'll ever get the straight scoop about what she had to do with George's death?"

"I don't know. I've got the name of her favorite waitress over at Antonio's. I'm going there as soon as I can to ask who ate lunch with him the day he died."

"Where's that hunky cop friend of your'n?"

I told her about Detweiler's visit to Illinois.

"You be careful going home, hear? Thank goodness Roger got them lights up over at your place."

I couldn't bear to tell Mert about needing to have the outside lights taken down. Instead, I asked her to thank Roger and promised to bake banana bread over the weekend.

"I'll tell him." She lowered her voice. "Hey, you don't suppose Roxanne's being shot has anything to do with your house getting robbed?"

"I think she might have wanted to show somebody the images on her camera. Maybe there's a picture there that shouldn't be." I sighed. "But if so, I can't tell which one it is."

Mert nodded and gave me one more warning before taking her leave. "Keep your wits about you, okay? Stay out of trouble. Call me if you need anything."

I phoned Anya while Dodie showed the ladies the other newbie page kits. My daughter answered on the first ring with a giggle. "Mom, I can't believe the Domino's guy was standing on the doorstep when Gran and I pulled up. It was awesome. I wasn't going to eat, but it all smelled so good. Even Gran had a couple of pieces. You're the best. I love you. You rock."

I told her she had Dodie to thank, and she did exactly that, bringing a blush of pleasure to the woman's face. With a huge grin on her face, Dodie handed the phone back to me. I gave Anya a goodnight kiss over the phone and told her I loved her.

"Do you have soccer practice tomorrow? Your grandmother will drop you off. I'll be there at five to pick you up, honey."

After I hung up, I said, "Dodie, you are something. You really saved the day."

She waved a hand in the air dismissively. "Shoot. It was nothing. Tell you the truth, I kinda enjoyed putting one over on old Sheila. She's such a pain in the—," and she paused. "What on earth?"

TWENTY-SIX

Dodie pointed to the front of the store. A uniformed police-man was knocking on the glass. Behind him stood a man and a woman. They were bathed in the bright security light as moths and bugs swam up and down the night air currents. Dodie strode past me and unlocked the door. "What's up, officer?"

"Richmond Heights police, ma'am, we're looking for a Kiki Lowenstein. Is she here?" said the uniformed cop. Both his hands rested on his heavy black belt.

I stepped forward, keeping my voice down as I said, "That's me." I didn't want to alert the ladies in the crop area to a problem. The most likely reason for the police visit was that my car had been vandalized. Having a ragtop in this part of town wasn't a great idea. There was no need to get everyone upset and remind them the fringes of this neighborhood were dicey. Our parking lot was well-lit, but stuff happens, right?

But I did a double-take. The two plainclothes people showed us detective badges from Chesterfield. That was odd. Why would two Chesterfield detectives drive all the way down Highway 40 to our little store? It didn't make sense.

"You're Kiki Lowenstein?" The woman was a solid gal who looked like an ex-Marine. She had a certain toughness to her face and a commanding presence to her stance.

"Yes, I am. What's wrong?" I'd just gotten off the phone with my daughter, or I would have been even more worried. Knowing Anya was safe gave me a false sense of bravado. Gracie was still in the back room. I'd taken her for a long walk before the crop started. Since she and I were both out of the house, this visit could only mean my car or my house had been broken into. The provenance of the police still didn't make sense, but who knew about jurisdiction? "Is my car okay? Has my house been broken into again?"

The male detective and Lady Marine exchanged indecipherable glances. "Your car's fine as far as we know. Your house was broken into?" asked the man.

"Yes, my house was burglarized a few days ago. Did you find my computer?"

"Computer?"

"Yes, it was stolen. If you found it, that would be really good news. I can't afford a replacement."

Lady Marine did a slow-mo, "Mrs. Lowenstein, you are under arrest for the murder of Roxanne Baker." She frisked me faster than I could blink.

Next thing I knew, I was wearing handcuffs.

Evidently the Chesterfield jail was full because the two detectives drove me to the St. Louis County Jail in Clayton.

The man took my elbow gently and guided me, waiting to be sure I had my balance as I climbed out of the unmarked car. His partner, Lady Marine, came up to his shoulder and radiated all the personal charm of a junkyard dog with a bad case of worms.

We stepped onto the elevator. "Turn around. Face the back," said Lady Marine. I did as I was told, my knees quaking. What were they planning to do while my back was turned? Make out?

The elevator stopped and we got off in a short hallway where I was relieved of my purse, watch, and the shoelaces to my Keds. The clerk behind the low counter took an inventory of my belongings and had me sign a document. Lady Marine handled my Canon digital with distaste. I guessed she wasn't a scrapbooker.

"No photos," she grunted.

So much for scrapbooking my adventure. Then again, as *St. Louis Post-Dispatch* columnist Bill McClellan once quipped, "Nobody looks good in a mug shot."

The detectives walked me through a variety of questions, the first one being, "Have you ever been here before?" Finally we got to the fingerprinting. I expected that to be familiar since I often use rubber stamps and ink on my pages. I was wrong. St. Louis County has gone to electronic fingerprinting.

Lady Marine led me into a room about thirty feet long by twenty feet wide. Bathrooms were on one side and holding cells on the other. A large metal ring attached to the wall was the obvious place for police to restrain manacled prisoners. I glanced up at the silver circle and shuddered.

I was lucky. Lady Marine unlocked me. My wrists felt chafed and sore. I vowed never to wear bracelets again as long as I lived.

A part of me completely dissociated from the entire experience. I put all my efforts into mental drivel while being processed for my stint in jail. It was the only way I could maintain a semblance of composure—to see this as a giant scrapbook adventure.

"What evidence could you possibly have?" I asked. "I didn't do it. And out there somewhere is someone who did."

Lady Marine didn't respond, but I guessed she was thinking, "That's what they all say."

"Are you charging me? Do I need an attorney?"

"We can hold you for twenty-four hours without charging you."

A county corrections officer took over.

"See that red line?" He pointed to a painted line running around the interior of the room.

"Yes, sir."

"Don't cross it. Long as you behave, you can stay here in open seating. You have a problem, raise your hand and I'll come talk with you."

I didn't dare ask him to share his definition of "behave." I was pretty sure it meant "shut up and sit tight."

"Open seating?" I repeated. This sounded strangely like first available seating in a restaurant or even the cattle call that loaded passengers onto Southwest Airlines flights. I must have misheard the man. His head was nearly bald with his burr haircut. To compensate, he sported a bumper crop of gray hair sprouting from his ear canals, giving the impression he wore a fuzzy pair of earmuffs. Probably very handy in the winter.

"As long as you behave yourself, you don't have to go in a cell," he repeated with a marked absence of emotion. He didn't much care whether I behaved or not. Either way, he could handle the situation.

Open seating meant I could find a spot on one of the many benches scattered around the room. The area reminded me of a Greyhound Bus station I once "visited" in my college days. Talk about your huddled masses yearning to be free. The smell of sweat, fear, and unwashed bodies assaulted my nose. A man with a three-day growth of beard sat on a nearby bench and chanted quietly, "I didn't do it. I didn't do it." A scary woman with eye shadow the color of an Easter egg paced back and forth muttering, "That son of a sea cow. When I get a hold of him, he'll pay." The back of her skirt swept the floor behind her. Long, sparkling earrings dangled amid a mass of upswept hair. Her attire was more suitable for a cocktail party than a prison break, but maybe she, too, had been caught off guard by her visit.

A couple of people slept fitfully, their heads thrown back and mouths gaping as they snoozed. I didn't know why they were here, and I prayed I wouldn't find out. One smelled distinctly of pee. A line of people waited for the phones, and I noticed none of my fellow inmates had any shoelaces or belts, which left one man to struggle mightily with his sweatpants.

Trying not to make eye contact, I wandered to an empty bench. Worst case scenario, I told myself, twenty-four hours and I'd be free. At least Anya didn't have to know about this. She was with Sheila. On my way to the detectives' car, Dodie had promised to take Gracie and give my mother-in-law a call. I also asked Dodie to call Detweiler and gave her his number. So far, though, the cavalry wasn't kicking up dust as they galloped over the hill.

Did I really believe he'd come rescue me? Obviously, I'd watched a few too many westerns.

Well, he'd warned me he might be out of range.

Then it struck me: could he have known about this? I flashed back to him saying, "I have a job to do."

The timing of his out-of-town visit sure was suspicious. I knew cops used intimidation to get people to talk. Was it possible Detweiler didn't believe me? Was he working with the Chesterfield detectives to secure my confession? Otherwise, how could the Chesterfield police have so conveniently overlooked the fact I had an alibi for the night Roxanne was killed?

That was it. It had to be.

Detweiler set me up.

Chalk up another failure in my dismal track record with men.

The adrenaline of being arrested began to wear off. My eyes grew heavy. I felt weary. The armrests of my bench made it impossible to get comfortable. After a while, I listed to one side. As I tucked my head down, I caught a whiff of body odor. Mine.

The benches were notoriously unforgiving. First my arm went numb, then my hip. I tried the other side with equally painful results.

Hours passed. I busied myself creating scrapbook pages in my mind. It was the only way to keep my brain off my surroundings.

A corrections officer passed out brown paper bags. Mine opened to a squished, garlicky bologna and cheese. The sandwich was very dry. I ate a few bites, and the masticated food stuck to my teeth. I drank from the water fountain and tried again to get comfortable on my bench.

Surely, any moment, Sheila would take pity on me and hire an attorney. Having her daughter-in-law in the county slammer wasn't the type of gossip she'd want bandied about by her friends at the Bellerive Country Club. I thought about calling Mert, but I figured Dodie would tell her the news. I didn't want to stand in line by the phones or draw any attention to myself. I was too scared. That little red line didn't seem like much of a deterrent to me.

Then it dawned on me that if Sheila didn't send an attorney, Mert wouldn't be able to. She didn't have the money. Maybe Dodie would loan it to my friend.

Could there be enough trumped-up evidence for the police to charge me? I remembered an old Alfred Hitchcock movie where Henry Fonda played an innocent man accused of a crime. What was the film's name? *The Wrong Man*? I'd heard it was a true story. I groaned. Great. I was starring in my own version of *The Wrong Woman*.

I tried to conjure up a reason why I was suddenly a suspect again. I didn't own a gun. There wasn't a trail of money leading to my door. I had an alibi, sort of. Surely by now the police had a record of my stay at Jellystone. I had threatened Roxanne, but couldn't they cut me slack? One little smart-alecky remark, and boom, here I was in jail?

In my life small mistakes cost me dearly.

But Anya wasn't a mistake.

What if Sheila told her where I was? Surely she wouldn't do that. What would Anya think of her mother, the jail bird? Would she hate me? Be embarrassed? Never speak to me again?

Maybe Mert was sick of me, too. Maybe Dodie was tired of having a problem employee. Maybe my boss decided not to call my best friend.

I saw my father's face. I heard him call me a loser. I thought of my mother. I saw her laugh as my father called me names. No wonder my mother didn't want anything to do with me. Just look how I turned out: broke and in jail. My sister Amanda would have a field day at my expense. She'd never let me forget this. We'd never gotten along. Catherine, my other sister, was God knows where. I couldn't blame her for not leaving me a forwarding address.

I thought and thought and thought. I dug up every bad and sad thing in my life. I chased those miseries around like a blue jay takes after a sparrow.

Finally, my mind tired of thinking. I gave in to depression, a formless miasma of pain. I started to cry. Only a little. The tears trickled over the bridge of my nose. When I was a kid, crying only made my dad get meaner. I'd learned the hard way to be the quietest crier imaginable. And that's what I did.

I cried. Very, very quietly. But I cried.

TWENTY-SEVEN

"Okay, lady, let's go." A corrections officer tapped me on the shoulder. I guess I must have fallen asleep.

"Go where?"

"You're being released. Follow me. Your attorney's here. You're free."

"My attorney?" That was a new one on me. When did I get an attorney?

My body ached from my uncomfortable perch on the bench. I moved slowly. It took a while for his words to sink in.

"What does free mean?"

He scowled at me. "Huh?"

"'Free' as in I didn't do it, and you know I didn't do it? Or 'free' as in you think I did it, but you can't prove it? Which kind of 'free' am I?" I stumbled along behind the man, walking away from my fellow prisoners, keeping my arms hugged tightly against my body as if to avoid contagion. Bleak faces followed my release, and I was careful not to engage the eyes of others not lucky enough to be leaving.

This wasn't the type of place you went to make new friends.

We stopped for me to sign forms reclaiming my personal property. A bored clerk with eyes glazed-over handed me a large manila envelope containing my purse, camera, watch, and shoelaces. I left the jail area, rode in the elevator facing front this time, and stepped cautiously into the inverted bowl of the rotunda, my feet dragging along the terrazzo tile. The gleaming rays of sun poured in through tall glass windows. My mood improved with every inch I traveled toward the door. I was out of the "open seating" and free from my fellow criminals. Soon I'd be home with my child and my dog.

"There she is!" Dodie grabbed me. The big woman enfolded me into an all-consuming embrace, burying my head in her massive chest. When she let go, I stood swaying in the aftershock, fighting to regain my physical and emotional balance. I was surprised. I really didn't think she cared that much about me one way or the other.

I'd been wrong. She examined me with motherly affection. "You okay?"

"Yes. Sort of."

Standing beside my boss was Bonnie Gossage, the young mother who brought little Felix to our recent crop. She gave me a "don't say a word" jerk of her chin. She needn't have worried. I was speechless.

"My client and I will be in touch with you. We may wish to bring charges against the citizen who perjured herself and caused my client this outrageous hardship." As she addressed the corrections officer, Bonnie's lips settled into a firm line. Her eyes were shrewd and lively as a brown wren's. Despite the fact her navy jacket strained to cover her breasts and one side of her skirt hung longer than the other, she looked remarkably professional. Dangling from one hand was a battered leather tote.

Previously she'd used it as a diaper bag.

I raised one quizzical eyebrow.

Bonnie said, "A woman claimed she saw you driving away from the scene of Roxanne Baker's murder in a gold Lexus SUV."

"But I don't own a gold Lexus SUV."

"I know," said Bonnie as she gestured to the officer, "and now they do, too."

"I mean, I did own one, but I sold it months ago."

"Right. Somebody with clout wanted you out of the way pretty badly." Bonnie took me by the elbow. She added, "Whoever did this waited until late yesterday, hoping you'd be held overnight. Which you were. She maliciously manipulated the legal system."

"Ms. Gossage," said the corrections officer who'd accompanied me. "We're just as interested as you in finding out who called in that false report. Sorry for your trouble, Mrs. Lowenstein." He looked at me kindly, if curiously. He seemed to be puzzling out why I'd warrant all this fuss. I'm sure I didn't look worthy of the effort to rescue me. Frankly, my tail was tucked so far under my legs, I could scarcely walk.

The officer stopped to sniff the air. "What's that smell? Sour milk?"

"It's probably me. I could use a shower." My sweat-drenched clothes clung to my body. My armpits were sticky. My mouth was dry, and I was sure my breath could stop a camel at fifty paces.

But I wasn't the one the officer was sniffing. A cottage-cheese trail of spit up ran down the backside of Bonnie's left shoulder. Felix had baptized his mother on her way to rescue me.

"We'll be going now," Bonnie said. "You've got my card." Under her breath, she muttered, "Good thing I didn't leave all of them at the office when I went on maternity leave."

"Still can't decide whether to go back to work or not?" Dodie asked.

We'd been dying to know Bonnie's decision. Dodie took advantage of the opening to ask, although the timing seemed pretty odd to me.

"I'm going part-time next month. I love being a mother, but my brain may turn to rice cereal if I hear "Wheels on the Bus" one more time."

I hot-footed it to the door, nearly leaving the other two women behind. Between Felix's spit-up and my b.o., I couldn't wait to get a breath of fresh air.

"Bonnie, I can't thank you enough. I don't know how I'll repay you but—"

"I need help with my wedding album. You can work it off. And I'd like to get Felix's baby album done before I get pregnant again."

"No problem. I'm in your debt."

"You're planning on another baby?" Dodie smiled.

"Don't tell Jeremy, okay? The less my husband knows about birthing babies, the better. He's still in shock over this one. Trust me, it wasn't a miraculous birth, but to hear him tell it, I did this all on my own. Now, I've got to hustle. It's time for Felix's mid-morning meal."

"Ms. Gossage! Ms. Gossage!" The corrections officer was hailing us, running in our wake, flapping paperwork. "Forgot to give you these."

Bonnie's eyes danced hula hoops in her head. "Oh, sugar," she muttered. She pulled her jacket tight over her chest and half-walked, half-trotted back toward the man.

Dodie stayed with me. I was eagerly eyeing the sunshine streaming though the glass. All I wanted was out! Every muscle in my body twitched in anticipation. Bonnie grabbed the papers and hustled her way back toward us.

Never had a doorway to the outside world seemed as lovely as this one. I entered the door feeling lightheaded with ecstasy. I pushed hard, hit the open air with gusto, and nearly tumbled to the sidewalk.

"I'm sprung!" I called back to Bonnie and Dodie. "I am free!"

"Huh uh." Dodie planted herself in front of me and grabbed my hand. "I want to scrapbook this. Stand here." She positioned me in front of the brick wall.

In keeping with the occasion, my expression was murderous. Okay, all right, I'll say it: sometimes we scrapbookers go too far.

"Hey, hey, hey, guys." Bonnie sounded frantic, as she waved us on. We walked three abreast along the congested streets of downtown Clayton. People parted to let us through as if we were a military unit. Bonnie led the way, heels first, arms pumping. "Speed it up, kids. Sorry, but it's time for Felix's mid-morning feeding. Either I get moving or I'm likely to spring a leak."

At a crosswalk, a mother with a baby carriage paused to adjust the canopy. As she did, her baby let loose with a mewling cry.

"Oh, sugar," said Bonnie. Two wet circles blossomed on the front of her blouse. "My milk let down. Anybody got any tissues?"

TWENTY-EIGHT

"I GUESS I FLUNKED Mert's Tough Tamales University trial by fire, huh? I couldn't help myself. I whimpered most of the night." We'd seen Bonnie to her car after stopping at a St. Louis Bread Co. and swiping handfuls of paper napkins. By the time she finished stuffing her bra, she'd added another cup size.

Dodie looked at me in wonder and snorted. "Huh. Being locked up overnight should get you extra credit. Mert was beside herself that she couldn't afford to hire a lawyer. I was about to do just that when we remembered Bonnie used to practice in downtown St. Louis. Only problem was we had to wait 'til Jeremy came home to take over with Felix. Mert said to tell you she'll be by this evening to see with her own eyes that you're right as rain. She had a full schedule of house cleaning."

"I'm fine. Really I am. I appreciate everything you all have done for me. When I get home, I'm taking every striped item of clothing I own and making a bonfire."

"I can't blame you." Dodie hopped easily into the driver's seat of her Expedition. For me, it was a hike. I needed a step stool.

Her big hands covered the steering wheel easily, but I sunk into the passenger's seat like a kid in my mom's car, barely able to see over the dash. Dodie had dressed for my jail break in a tailored black dress, pearls, and black pumps. It was too hot for hose, but she looked nice. As I realized she'd gussied up to put in a good appearance for me a lump formed in my throat.

She treated me to breakfast at Hardee's. I ordered my all-time favorite biscuits and gravy with an orange juice. Life was looking up. We ate in the car, and afterward she drove me home to shower and change.

"No sense in you taking the day off. The store's been busy and Gracie's there waiting for you. You can catch up on your sleep tomorrow since it's Sunday."

"How is Anya?"

Dodie scratched a spot on her leg. "Fine, I think. I told Sheila what happened and asked her to keep her mouth shut. She said she would pick up Anya from soccer. Sounded good to me, because we weren't sure how long all this would take. Sheila asked why they took you in. Gloating like. Told her they'd made a mistake. She can sure be a stinker. I suppose I should've called an attorney last night, but I didn't want to run up a bill."

I waved her apology away. "I appreciate it. Again, all I can say is thank you. It was really kind of you to ask Bonnie to help and to take care of my dog and my child for me."

I silently marveled at the breadth of the sisterhood that is scrapbooking. Women who scrapbook are extraordinary. We come from all walks of life and all levels of education. What brings us together is the desire to create a visual record of our lives. Our scrapbooks pay homage to our priorities—family and friends. Kids grow up quickly. Our strong and dependable parents grow weak and needy before our eyes. Our beloved pets grow feeble and break our hearts as they die. Nothing lasts forever, but our work can immortalize those we love for generations to come.

Sure, not every group of scrappers includes an attorney, but it's a real mistake to underestimate the skills and talents of women who scrapbook. Not to mention their generosity of spirit. How kind it was of Bonnie to come to my rescue! How nice it was of Dodie to help me meet my responsibilities! How wonderful it was of Mert to worry so about me! I was humbled by their willingness to help. I wasn't sure how many of my old neighbors in Ladue would have come to my aid. Not many, I'd guess.

"Boy, that Sheila. I don't understand her. I asked her last night if she was going to find an attorney for you, and she laughed. Laughed! Said you were responsible for your own actions. I pointed out you're family, and she said—"

"That Anya and George are—were—her family. I'm not, right?"

"You got it. That is just wrong."

"She's never liked me. At least she's been honest about it. And she's still not over George's death. Now she has Roxanne's murder to add to her list of sorrows."

"Rabbi Sarah's been after her to join the grief work group," said Dodie, never taking her eyes from the road. "Need more air?"

"I'm fine." The cool air blowing from the vents was refreshing, especially after the open seating smell that seemed to cling to me. "Rabbi Sarah? You go to the same temple as Sheila?"

Dodie shifted her bulky frame. "Yes. I have for years. We go to the Central City Temple. Rabbi Sarah's an angel. When our son died, Horace and I started attending her grief group. That's how come I know the rabbi's asked your mother-in-law to join us."

"You lost a son?"

Dodie swallowed, her eyes followed other cars on the road, but I could see the moisture gather along her lower lids. She wiped her face with the back of a rough hand. "Nathan, of blessed memory. Gone these five years. Swimming accident. He was twenty. That's how I got started scrapbooking. I wanted to remember every little detail of Nathan ... his life ... every small thought ... I couldn't bear ... to forget."

She stopped talking. She couldn't go on.

We pulled into my driveway.

I put a hand on Dodie's shoulder. "I didn't know. I'm so sorry. I can't imagine."

She nodded. Again, she reached up to wipe her face. In a gruff voice she said, "Want me to wait here?"

Of course I invited her in. I settled her at the kitchen table.

"This is real nice, Kiki. I can tell you've worked hard on the place."

I sighed, thinking about having to move. "Thanks. I'll be right back after I clean up. Help yourself to whatever's in the cabinets. There's instant tea in the canister next to the sink."

I showered quickly, thinking how much I'd learned about Dodie in the last hour. That made me wonder what I didn't know about the other people around me. I resolved to see more of my friends' scrapbooks. Typically I saw whatever pages they were currently working on, but not their old albums. Today had been a revelation.

I wasn't sure that I'd treat Dodie differently from now on, but I knew I'd never see her quite the same.

The clean scent of shampoo made me delirious with pleasure. I scrubbed myself with body wash again and again. After a heavy dose of deodorant, I threw on a fitted pink tee with khaki pants and slipped a pink gingham belt through the loops. A touch of mousse in my curls kept the frizzies under control. I added brown sandals and stopped to cover the circles under my eyes with concealer. A dab of mascara, a tiny bit of blush, and lip gloss, and I was good to go.

Dodie handed me a glass of ice tea and sipped her own. I opened the manila envelope holding my things and tossed the wallet and camera back into my purse. I checked my phone and saw a message from my daughter.

"Mom, Gran won't tell me what's up. She's being really sneaky. She said you were in big trouble. I asked what that meant. I told her I had a right to know. Please call me when you get this message. I'm worried. I love you."

I called but got her answering system. I left a message that I was fine, and we'd talk when I picked her up after school. Wanting to end on a positive note, I suggested that she be thinking about what she'd like to do on Sunday since we had the whole day for whatever we wanted.

"Bonnie didn't find out who lied about me?" I asked Dodie as we climbed back into her car.

"No. Just that a woman called the Chesterfield station. Must have been a hoity-toity with clout. The detectives didn't even check her story. When Bonnie heard about the SUV, she hit the roof. Heck, we all know you drive that old Beemer. I figure the snitch must have been another parent or an old neighbor. Who else would know what you used to drive? Someone who doesn't know you sold the Lexus. Or maybe a person who just doesn't pay much attention. Thank goodness. If she'd have said you were driving the BMW, it would have been harder to prove her wrong. All they had to do was call the Missouri DMV, and presto—you're sprung." Dodie scratched a spot behind her knee. "You've got to wonder why, eh? First, someone breaks into your house. Then someone gets you thrown in jail. What's going on? What's so special about you?"

"Not much." That was all I was sure of. It had been a long time since I was the center of so much attention. Twelve years in fact.

I was too tired to think. I hadn't slept much the night before. My fellow prisoners proved a noisy lot. I'd jerk to consciousness to a loud snoring. Or I'd startle awake to someone talking loudly. The corrections officer would remind him or her to behave. I'd quake in my Keds. Finally, I'd drift off. But I kept one eye open and cat-napped more than I slept.

When I did sleep, I dreamed. Bad dreams. Sad and heavy. They pressed on my heart.

Dodie scratched her elbow. "Maybe someone is trying to keep you from doing your job. Maybe you're a threat."

I shrugged. "Detweiler told me to be careful. He didn't like the coincidence of Roxanne's shooting and my home invasion. But this doesn't make sense. I still can't see why my computer mattered to anybody. Anybody but me. I don't know how I'll replace it."

"But there has to be a reason," muttered Dodie. "And a connection. He's right. The timing is too neat. And you are at risk. I'm worried about you, sunshine." She studied me carefully, then returned to picking at her eyebrows.

Dodie was worried about me. Me the person? Or me the employee? I couldn't tell. I decided to spill my guts. I told her what I'd learned from Anya.

"That poor baby! I can't believe George did that." She let loose with a stream of Yiddish curses. She finished with, "And if he were alive, I'd wish him the best of Ten Plagues, plus a hernia."

When she ran out of steam, I said, "Roxanne wanted George to leave me. He told her he wouldn't. She was angry. I wonder if she killed him."

"Killed him? I thought he died of a heart attack."

I outlined Detweiler's theory that George might have been poisoned.

"Murdered? *Oy*. Poor, poor Sheila. You think Roxanne acted alone?"

"She and another woman had lunch with my husband right before he died. The other woman has managed to stay anonymous."

Dodie nodded and revised her question. "So you figure Roxanne was in cahoots with someone, both of them killed George, and now her partner in crime bumped her off? How does the burglary fit? Was the thief after the shower pictures? What was in those photos? I've viewed them. I didn't see anything out of the ordinary."

"Beats me." I turned my head to watch Manchester Road speed past. This section was home to a hodgepodge of businesses: the gumbo shop, an antique store, a florist, and a bookstore. A fishing equipment shop offered "Free Fly Casting Lessons." I planned one day to take them up on the offer, just for fun. My mind skipped around in a desultory fashion.

"But somebody lied to the police. That's pretty big stuff. And they did it to put you in jail. If you went to the pokey to keep you from doing your job, what is it about your job that's got someone worried? You're only scrapbooking. I mean, it's not like you're digging into family secrets."

"It has to be the pictures," I interrupted. "Everything leads back to them. First someone steals my computer, and what's on it? Pictures. What do Roxanne and I have in common?"

"George?" Dodie offered.

I glowered. "Pictures. We both liked to scrapbook, and we both took a lot of pictures."

Dodie shifted in her seat. Her new position gave her unrestricted access to scratching her elbow. "I'm thinking we've got that Purloined Letter thing happening here. We're looking at the clue, but just can't see it. There's something in those pictures. And we've got a lot of them. We downloaded, what?"

I shook my head. "I counted a hundred and eighty-two. But not all of them are important. All that matters are the pictures taken by a dead woman. Has to be. See the connection?" I traced an imaginary triangle with my fingers: "George to Roxanne, Roxanne to photos, and photos to my computer."

I continued, "When my house was broken into, I made a list for Detweiler of all the shower guests. But now I realize: anybody could have heard what we did. It was no secret. We thought copying their cards was such a big deal. Such a cute idea. And see where it got us?"

Dodie dug at a spot under her arm. "Back up there, sunshine. You're overreacting. Think about it. Only Merrilee's pals knew about the downloads immediately." She continued to claw at her skin. "Although … I did leave messages on answering machines. Reminders. A hubby or roommate could have overheard."

"And the guests could have told their friends. That's a pretty chatty group. News travels fast when you have lots of free time to spend yakking."

"So one of them broke into your house," Dodie said. "Or paid somebody to break in, since none of those women would risk ruining a manicure."

My gut tightened with fear. Who had been in my house? It had been empty last night. Had anything else been taken? Or ruined? The thought sickened me.

"What about Roxanne's camera?" Dodie wondered.

"Far as I know, it's missing. I plan to ask Detweiler about it when he gets back to town. Maybe it turned up over the weekend."

"That might give us a clue to why she was murdered."

Us? I smiled to myself. Dodie was on the case. Good. I needed help. Not from Detweiler, either.

Maybe he was making a fool of me. Maybe he had given the Chesterfield detectives the "go ahead" to haul me in. Sitting in that fishbowl of a jail, watching all those misfits mill around me, I pledged to make some changes in my life. I couldn't trust anyone. Especially not any man. I'd nearly fallen for Detweiler after he made nice over my dog and my kid. What was it he'd said to Anya about having a cop as a friend?

Huh.

Some friend. Where was he when I huddled on that cold bench? How far did his protection extend?

Not far enough.

No way was I going to let my emotions run away with me again. Lord knew, I was the world's worst judge of character. Especially when it came to men.

I needed to toughen up and strike back.

Like the mug said, "No More Mrs. Nice Guy." I planned to earn my degree from the School of Hard Knocks.

Time to prepare for my final exam.

TWENTY-NINE

GRACIE SURE WAS HAPPY to see me. She stood on her hind legs, planted her paws on my chest and licked my face greedily. I lingered in the storeroom long enough to bask in doggy affection.

"Did you miss me, girl?"

Dodie beamed. "She was a model citizen. Horace even said so. Miss Gracie is welcome to spend the night at our house any time."

After my brief incarceration, I was delighted to get back to the Witherow bridal shower albums. Being engrossed in my work would take my mind off my disastrous evening. Dodie thought my jail time worth immortalizing on a scrapbook page, but I wanted nothing better than to forget it.

All the shower guests except Roxanne—Markie, Sally, Linda, Merrilee, Tisha, and Mrs. Witherow—had indicated which photos they wanted. I merged their requests into a master list. I opened the photos in Snapfish one at a time and loaded them into Photo-

Shop Elements. PS Elements had all the tools necessary to crop the pictures, adjust brightness levels, and take out red eye.

Prettifying photos was time-consuming work that required every bit of my attention. Enhancing always included a myriad of small chores like using the clone tool to remove plants sprouting out of people's heads. Once I even gave a woman a boob job. Poor dear. The photo had made the ravages of time painfully obvious, so I lifted and separated, taking ten years off her age.

I'm not a PhotoShop expert, but I am learning. My ability to adjust contrast, to fix brightness, and to erase unwanted images turns formerly unusable photos into family keepsakes. Let's face it: life isn't a series of posed shots. We can't always shoot in perfect lighting conditions or great settings. PhotoShop can make a big difference in the quality of the finished picture. What people are paying me for is a memory. Why not make it a good one?

"See anything hinky?" Dodie plopped beside me to watch. She hadn't had the chance to look over what we downloaded.

"Hinky?"

"I read it in one of my crime novels. Means suspicious."

"All I see are women chatting, eating tiny bites of cake, working on scrapbook pages, opening gifts, and giving each other air-smooches."

"How many photos have you worked on?"

"Twenty. The guests chose sixty all total."

Dodie stared at the screen with me. "And you've checked them?"

"I examined them as I transferred them from the website to PhotoShop. I mean, I haven't fixed all of them, but I did see them enlarged."

"And nothing was there?"

"Nothing I could see. But I don't want to spend more time looking right now. You aren't paying me to solve a murder."

"In case you haven't noticed, I'm also not real keen on bailing you out of jail either. Although it will make for a great scrapbook page."

She handed over the photo of me in front of the St. Louis Criminal Justice Building. She'd printed it off while I was working on the shower pictures. I didn't know whether to laugh or cry.

"Can't decide on a page title," Dodie said. "My choices are 'Kiki, the Jailbird' or 'When Good Scrappers Go Bad.'"

I groaned.

Dodie tucked the picture away and turned her attention to the screen. "While I enjoy the scenery when Officer Friendly is here, I have a business to run. For right now, I think you better concentrate on finishing the bridal shower albums." She rubbed her chin. Being a hairy woman, she had a bit of razor stubble. "Want a diet cola? Caffeine helps you think."

"Works for me. Any Diet Dr Pepper?"

She brought me a can. "On the house. You probably need a break. I want to rethink these candid photos." She pointed to the small images on the screen. "Let's go over the images from Roxanne's memory card."

Merrilee and Jeff kissing. Tropical scenery. Roxanne and a mystery guy in sunglasses and a ball cap. Beaches. Sand. Palm trees. Vacation photos, I guessed. I put my can in the recycling bin, stood up and stretched. "One of these must be important to the killer, but I can't see how. Unless ... unless it's not because they show something . . . but they prove something? But what? How could vacation photos trigger a murder?"

"You haven't seen the pictures Horace took of my backside in my thong."

Nor did I want to.

"Maybe we're wasting our time. Who knows what went on in Roxanne's head. She wasn't the sharpest craft knife in the Cropper Hopper." Dodie went through the photos again quickly. She turned to me in surprise. "And Roxanne didn't take a single photo at the shower?"

"I think she brought the camera along to show off a picture. She never intended to take photos. She left the picture taking to the others."

"That's weird, but . . ." Dodie sighed. "It's possible. If that's the case, we need to find out who Roxanne showed her pictures to."

I hadn't thought of that. Dodie was right.

"I could ask the guests. They'll be coming in to pick up their albums. Either someone will spill the beans or her reaction will tell us what we need to know. I better pull up all of Roxanne's and adjust the contrast."

"That's Merrilee and her fiancé," Dodie said, pointing to the two shots of people kissing. "She's coming at one. How about you print these for her? That'll be a nice 'thank you' for signing that big contract."

"Good idea." The caffeine had perked me up, but I was still too tired to think clearly.

Dodie studied the monitor a little longer. She tilted her head thoughtfully. "I have a couple of vacation scrapbook magazines in the back. I wonder if we can match up that photo of the lighthouse. Might tell us where it was taken."

———

After my night on the concrete bench and sitting in front of the computer for hours, my lower back started to hurt. I stretched and called Dimont Development. My visit to the county jail delivered a cruel reminder that money is power. My penury had forced me to the bottom of the food chain. I'd been lucky Bonnie was willing to come to my aid. But I couldn't always count on finding a scrapbooker who'd trade her professional services for my work. If Tisha was right about the buy-sell agreement, I should get money from George's share of Dimont.

According to a perky recorded voice, the office was closed until Monday. That figured. I'd forgotten it was Saturday. I decided not to leave a message. I was curious as to why Bill hadn't returned my previous call. I also wondered why he never mentioned the buy-sell. I decided to swing by Dimont on Monday on my way to pick up Anya from school.

Dodie was waiting on a customer while two more were wandering around the store. Glad for the reason to walk the kinks out, I approached one of the women. She wanted to use foam rubber stamps on her pages, but the acrylic paint she used as ink was too goopy.

"All my letters wind up blotches. My pages could double for Rorschach tests. Why are the letters on all my other friends' pages neat and tidy?"

"Ever visit Kaldi's?" I asked. I loved that local chain. In 1994, their first coffeehouse opened in a neighborhood not too far from our store. They hand-pulled every one of their drinks—and you could taste the difference.

"Uh, yes. Why?"

I demonstrated how a wooden coffee stirrer from Kaldi's could be dipped into acrylic paint and wiped over the raised foam image. "Use the thinnest smear of liquid. Most likely your letters are blobs because you have too much paint on the stamps. The other possibility is wobble."

"Wobble?" She grabbed her backside.

"Not that kind of wobble. I'm talking about rocking or moving the stamp when you press it against the surface. Pretend your stamp is kissing the paper. Touch it down once lightly. By the way, if you need to leave your project midway through, you can pop the paint-covered stamps into your freezer. When you return, thaw them, and you'll be good to go."

The customer's eyes flew open like cheap window blinds. "Wow. That's a great tip. Do you teach here? I bet I could learn a lot from you."

"We all learn from each other. We do have a class schedule though, and I am the instructor."

A little after noon, my cell phone vibrated. As I flipped it open, my stomach growled. I never seemed to grab lunch until I was hungry enough to eat white paste. I said hello and heard my sister Amanda's voice.

"Kiki, how could you?"

"How could I what?" Had word of my visit to the jail traveled across the nation?

"Forget Mom's birthday. Yesterday."

"What's today's date?" I had truly lost track of the month.

Amanda countered with, "You know darn good and well what today's date is. Even Catherine called! Now listen here. You still owe it to Mom to remember her birthday."

"Mandy, I'm sorry. I forgot! I didn't mean to. I was busy and—"

"Of course you were. We all are busy." That last word was a hiss. "You aren't more important than the rest of us, Kiki. All mother's friends remembered her birthday."

Yes, I thought, but that's because their only other sources of excitement are laxatives and bingo.

"I'm sorry, Mandy. I had a prob—"

"That's right, you had a problem. Don't even try that. What a crock. I don't want to hear it. There's no excuse. The world doesn't revolve around you. Mom spent all yesterday moping around. Last night she was so upset she didn't want to go to her genealogical society meeting. She was that distraught. You better call her and apologize right this instant."

I winced. A part of me wanted to protest, "Hello? Self-centered? I was in jail, Mandy." But the majority ruled, and my common sense said, "Don't go there."

Mandy and Mom had this fantasy about my married life. Neither had ever visited, but they'd seen pictures. As a result, they took turns making mean cracks about how rich I was. George's death didn't change their minds. They figured he was worth more dead than alive. None of my family showed up for the funeral. Mandy couldn't get off work. I didn't know how to contact my other sister, Catherine. Mom said traveling was too hard for her.

I never told them about the missing half a million dollars. They knew I sold the house, but as far as they knew my new place was a step up from Ladue. Whenever their lives got tough, they fortified themselves with the belief I'd gotten the luck of the draw. They were firm believers that life was intrinsically unfair, that I'd gotten the big piece of the wishbone, leaving them to squabble over the short end.

I did like I always do. I gave in. I took the beating and asked for more. "Amanda, you are right. How could I have been so selfish? I'm sorry. I appreciate you calling. I'll hang up and phone Mom. If you talk to her before I do, please tell her how bad I feel."

I closed the phone. I needed to get lunch. Being hungry didn't help my spirits.

If I called my mother now, while I was in a bad mood, I'd only add to my problems. I added "make a groveling call" to my procrastination list, along with telling Mert I needed the security lights removed.

THIRTY

TIME IN A BOTTLE sat at a right angle to busy Brentwood Avenue. At one end of the street was the Galleria with all its fancy shops. The retail district immediately to the south gobbled up whatever leftover customers the Galleria couldn't satisfy. Each block away from the mall, the pickings became more scarce. Our block was a mix of retailers and service businesses. A couple of blocks away was a convenience store/gas station. I ran in and grabbed the last of their turkey sandwiches and a Diet Dr Pepper. Then I drove back to the store. Dodie had purchased an older home zoned business, gutted it, and added a parking lot in the rear. She and Horace put in a border of flowers around the asphalt. But it was too early for the petunias to take off, and the nicotania had a while to go before they bloomed.

Still, I liked looking at the greenery. I savored every bite of my food.

Reluctantly, I tossed my trash and went back to work. When five o'clock rolled round, I was nearly weak-kneed with relief. I bid Dodie goodbye and drove to Antonio's to try to find someone who'd seen my husband the day he died.

Antonio's sat on a corner in The Hill. Large gold letters spelled out the restaurant name on each of the two large windows that met at right angles on the intersecting streets. Parking was on the street and at the rear of the brick building. From the sidewalk, the place looked unassuming.

Behind the front door was an elegant world. The bar and hostess station served as a staging area for hungry patrons. A serene young woman wearing a tasteful black cocktail dress escorted me past the floor-to-ceiling wine racks serving as dividers. She gestured and I slid into a booth. Before she left, she offered me a menu. I scanned it for food I could afford.

My budget could handle a Diet Coke.

"Welcome to Antonio's, madame." A dough-faced man in black slacks, crisp white button-down shirt, and a tapestry vest bowed to me. He gave me a sincere smile. "It is my honor to serve you this evening. May I interest you in an appetizer? Could I tell you about our specials? The chef has a lovely lobster bisque that's not on the menu."

"Just a Diet Coke, please. And is Olivia working tonight?"

His face fell. "Yes, of course. I'll get her for you."

I felt like a heel. Fortunately, the dinner crowd hadn't shown up, so I wasn't taking up a table that might mean a big tip.

A tall woman with sleek auburn hair held back by a black velvet headband hustled to the table. Although she was neatly dressed and held herself regally, she looked as though she'd been rode hard and put away wet. "May I help you? The chef has a wonderful selection of specials."

Oh, gosh, but this was embarrassing. "I . . . I didn't come to eat."

She tilted her head and studied me. "No?"

"I'm sorry, I'm really sorry, and I don't want to take a lot of your time, but George Lowenstein was my husband," I blurted. I was so tired. My energy was flagging, and I gave in to desperation.

Her eyes registered concern. The hostess glided behind my waitress, while leading two couples on their long tour to a table.

"I apologize, but I have to know what happened the day he died. I know he ate here with two women. Now Roxanne Baker is dead and—" I caught sight of her necklace. Hanging from a thin gold chain were four little figures formed from faux gemstones, a popular Mother's Day gift. Suddenly, I knew how to approach Olivia. Her jewelry told the world she was a mother of four.

"I have a young daughter and I'm scared. Please, could you please help me? I need to know who George was with the day he died." I paused and shared my most worrisome thought, the thought that made my blood run cold, "I'm afraid whoever killed George and Roxanne will come after me next!"

Her eyes darted around the dining area. "Meet me at the delivery door. In the back. I'll be there soon as I can."

Kicking myself for splurging on lunch, I put a five-dollar bill on the table. It was all I had.

At the back of the building, two doors faced the gravel lot. One was clearly marked "Employees only." The other had an aluminum screen frame, a stoop, and a faded but neatly lettered sign that read "Deliveries." I parked my bottom on the concrete step and waited.

Thirty minutes passed. Had Olivia fobbed me off? I sighed. My stomach rumbled. Gracie waited in the car. Time here meant time away from Anya, my child who deserved an explanation about my disappearance the night before.

A screech of rubbing metal announced the door was opening. Olivia handed over a plastic bag with "Antonio's" on the outside and two large Styrofoam containers nestled inside. The smell of tomatoes, garlic, and olive oil bathed my senses in glory.

"I can't afford—"

She waved me silent. "Mr. Lowenstein was plenty generous to me over the years. He was a real gentleman, and I miss him. Mind if I smoke?"

Perching on the edge of the step next to me, Olivia touched the flame of a Bic lighter to her Virginia Slims. "Sorry it took so long. Had to give the boss a reason for sneaking out."

"I was told you were Roxanne Baker's favorite waitress."

"Favorite? Huh. I put up with her. Mr. Lowenstein gave me extra to keep an eye out. I loaded her into taxis when she was drunk, and he wasn't around." Olivia inhaled deeply. She shook her head and crushed the butt under her sturdy shoe. A lone waft of smoke curled around her face. "What he saw in her, I'll never know, but she had him on a short leash, for sure."

"Who paid you to keep quiet about the women George ate lunch with the day he died?"

"Ha!" Her eyes went wide. "Paid me? Paid Al is more like it. He's my boss. Al told me to shut up or hit the road. I've got four kids to support. I'm already working two jobs to get by, and this one pays pretty good." She reached into a pocket and handed me a folded slip of paper. "Now take this and leave before I change my mind."

THIRTY-ONE

SHEILA ANSWERED THE DOORBELL by cracking the door an inch and saying, "Oh, it's you. I'm surprised to see you. I figured they'd keep you longer. At least a year or two. I told Anya you couldn't make it. Usually there's a trial when you commit murder."

She blocked the entrance with her Aigner loafer. Anya stood behind her, looking from one of us to the other. Her eyes were filled with misery. She'd been crying and was one blink from starting up again.

"Cut it out, Sheila. They had no reason to hold me. You knew I'd be here. I've always called when something's come up."

"Something's come up? Like getting arrested and going to jail? Hmm?"

I was too tired for this. I wanted to get my daughter and go home. Anya was hanging on to every one of Sheila's words. Her eyes blinked rapidly and her hands twisted together. She was wearing a new pair of shorts and a matching shirt. Her hair had been trimmed and her nails were painted. I was glad that Sheila was able to give my daughter some of the luxuries I couldn't afford.

"I was falsely accused."

"I don't know that."

"Well, you know more than you let on. You paid a housekeeper and a restaurant manager to keep their mouths shut."

"I did not! How dare you! You never deserved to be my son's wife!"

"Sheila, don't do this. You are hurting your grandchild." I pointed past her to where my child stood, tears streaming down her face. Her nose was red and raw.

Sheila stopped to glance at Anya. When she turned back to me, a feral expression crossed my mother-in-law's face. Her fingers gripped the door and door frame, her knuckles white with the pressure. She spat out, "My grandchild needs protection from you. You're a common criminal."

"That's not true and you know it. Someone lied to make a problem for me."

"You are the problem. You've always been the problem. You tricked my son. You cheated him out of a good life, and now you want your child to pay for your mistakes. I won't let that happen."

Sheila stood between me and my daughter.

I needed to get a grip. The temperature had dropped rapidly since leaving work, and the air was thick with moisture that made it hard to breathe, let alone think. The sky was full of mischief. A greenish cast of light forecast possible tornados. I needed to get us home and into the basement for safety. Gracie's pink tongue lolled out the rolled-down window. She couldn't wait in the car much longer.

"Anya, please get your belongings," I called past Sheila.

"She'll do no such thing! She's staying here!" Sheila screamed. Her face contorted with rage. The words were barely out of her mouth when her expression changed. "Oh-oh!"

A black-and-white blur streaked past me. Gracie had climbed through the car window. She raced up the lawn. The big dog skidded to a stop between Sheila and me. A ridge of fur on her back stood at attention.

"Woof!" Her bassoon bark reverberated through the marble foyer. "Woof!"

"Eeek!" My mother-in-law turned and ran.

I grabbed Gracie's collar. I swear, that dog looked up at me and smiled as if to say, "See? I can bark if it's really, really important." Her tail began to wag slowly as if this was all a great joke.

Anya looked from Gracie to me in amazement. "I'll go get my things."

———

We didn't talk on the ride home. Gracie lounged in the back seat as if nothing had happened.

At the house, I opened the Styrofoam containers from Antonio's to discover a huge wedge of lasagna, a salad with balsamic dressing, tender spears of asparagus, and a thick chunk of garlic bread. I heated the food on plates while listening to the tornado warning on the radio. Anya and I loaded backpacks with water bottles, flashlights and blankets, put kitchen towels on trays, and carried our food to the basement. Brushing away cobwebs, we descended the rickety steps. Our vision adjusted slowly to the dank and dark. Anya picked over her dinner as the buzzing alerts of weather updates interrupted local radio shows.

Gracie whimpered softly at first, and later with real alarm as the drum roll of thunder shook the house. A loud boom caused her to shriek, an ungodly noise between a bark and a scream of pain. Both of Anya's arms were wrapped around the Great Dane when she jumped up and howled.

"What's wrong with her, Mom?"

"Remember, she's a rescue dog. Maybe her previous owners left her outside during a storm, and she has bad memories."

My big girl became more and more agitated, turning in tight circles and crying. A spank of thunder rocked the house. Gracie lifted her head and sobbed, running to cower in the farthest corner of our underground safe space.

Anya and I moved our things closer to her. The sight of our poor girl-dog, so frightened and miserable, made us feel helpless.

"I'll be back." I dashed out of the basement, following the beam of my flashlight. Up in the bathroom, I found an open box of Benadryl left over from my run-in with the bees. I'd heard dogs had a metabolic rate four times that of humans. Gracie and I weighed roughly the same. One Benadryl put me to sleep for eight hours. I calculated that four—plus one to grow on—would get her through the storm.

From a cabinet, I grabbed a jar of peanut butter and scooped out a tablespoonful. I closed the kitchen door behind me and moved carefully down the narrow, wooden stairs to our hideaway in the basement.

Prying Gracie's mouth open was a trick. The moment she relaxed her jaws, I slapped the thick paste and the pills as far back as

I could. I stroked her throat until she swallowed. My timing was terrific. A lull in the storm followed.

I set up Scrabble. Anya and I played without conversation. My kid beat me soundly.

Shortly after midnight, authorities announced an all-clear. AmerenUE promised electricity would be restored shortly. By then, Anya and Gracie were snoozing side by side on the pile of blankets. I decided not to wake them. I wadded up a kitchen towel under my head and fell asleep on a small carpet sample left by previous tenants.

My uncomfortable position didn't allow for deep sleep. I was rolling over when I heard a noise in the floorboards. The storm had ended, but the night wasn't quiet. A soft creak-creak-creak told me we had a visitor. Cautious footfalls picked their way across the kitchen floor directly above us. Feet moved to the back hall.

I dialed 911 and told them we had an intruder. Gracie slumbered in a drug-induced fog. Anya snored lightly. Silently I picked up an empty box left over from our move and positioned it in front of the dog and child, to block them from view of the stairway.

I perked up my ears, trying to follow any movement. A light scuffling told me someone was standing on the other side of the basement door. The flashlight with its C batteries made a heavy baton when I turned it upside down. My eyes were adjusted to the dark. I could discern a shadow moving across the threshold, flickering between the door and the floor. I crept to the foot of the stairs.

Above me, the door handle jiggled and turned. I squatted on my heels, butt touching the damp concrete. The musty scent of old wood and damp nearly overpowered me. The basement door protested as it opened. A dark silhouette hesitated. I rose and tested the heft of the flashlight in my palm. I revived a mental picture of Mark McGwire at bat. I crouched, modeling my stance after Albert Pujol's.

I was ready to protect my child, my dog, and my home. Every cell in my body crackled with coiled energy.

My heart thumped. My breathing was shallow. My lips stuck to my dry teeth.

A big foot in a basketball shoe lowered itself to the top stair.

I waited.

A second shoe tapped the edge of the wood, then felt its way along. I could make out the shape of bulky ankle-high leather.

The foot reached down, touched a toe to the next step and tested it for security.

A warm blast of moist air redolent of dog tickled its way across my neck. I nearly toppled into Gracie. She stood at my shoulder, her jowls even with my face. Her gaze was on the feet on the stairway. Drool slid down my arm. I moved to grab her collar, to hold her back, to protect her.

But Gracie was too fast for me. She launched herself at the form on the steps. Bump, bump, bump. She took the stairs four at a time, a moving hulk of dark and light. Her body sent a breeze of dog-scented air cascading through the stuffy odor of the basement.

Thump. Gracie landed.

"ARGGGGHHH!" A voice rent the dark in two. I turned on the flashlight and trained it toward the noise. All I could see was a black-and-white tail switching above a set of prone athletic shoes. I raced up the stairs.

Where were my neighbors? Surely everyone on the block heard that crash.

"Noooo!"

I raised the flashlight over my head, ready to swing hard.

"Help! Help!" A meek voice rose from the kitchen floor.

I stumbled at the top stair, nearly falling over the big pair of feet. The overhead light fixture hummed. Lights flickered then stayed on.

I stood, holding the flashlight like a weapon, staring down into a ski mask. All I could see was the whites of my intruder's eyes.

"Mom?"

"Stay in the basement, Anya! Stay there!"

"GRRRRR." Gracie's tail slugged my leg. Her huge paws were planted on the armpits and groin of the man she'd flattened.

"Police! Open up!" A banging at the front door added to the pandemonium.

"Come around back!" I yelled. I crouched next to the figure in the ski cap and showed him the butt-end of the flashlight. "Move and I'll bash your head in! Hear me?"

"Yeeesss." He swallowed, his Adam's apple bobbing. "Don't let her bite me, please, please."

"Open up!" The banging started at the back door.

"Don't you move or she'll have you for a snack. Got it?" I shouted over the din.

"Yessss. Please! Please! Don't let her bite me!"

"Bite? She's going to eat you!"

"Grrrr." Gracie was a bit mollified now. Her face never moved more than an inch from her quarry's. A silver thread of slobber dripped from her maw to the ski mask.

"Mom?" Anya's voice grew louder, more insistent.

"Stay in the basement, Anya!"

I yanked the back door open. Two cops stood at attention with guns in hand. I managed to gasp, "He's on the floor. My dog's got him."

———

"Where would you like to go today? It's raining outside, so I think we'd better skip Babler Park." The bulk of the storms had moved on, but their legacy of rain drummed angrily on our windows. The winds had caused havoc and disaster to the south of us. Two people had died in their mobile home, and another in a flash flood. I immediately said a prayer of thanks for keeping us safe from the bad weather and our intruder.

Huh. Some bad guy. He was nothing more than a local high school student. "Cal Kleeber is his name," said one of the police officers. "Stupid kid. Got paid a case of beer for breaking into your place and grabbing CDs." The cop handed over Enya, Manhattan Transfer's Christmas album, and a Frank Sinatra disk. "They get dumber every year."

Finding out who hired the boy was a waste of time.

"Could be anyone from Jennifer Lopez to Jennifer Aniston. She wore big sunglasses and her hair was tucked under a hat. He never saw her car. Was supposed to meet her back at the liquor store. Of course, she's long gone," sighed the policeman. "No lie, and he's an altar boy at St. Aloysius parish. Father Bechstein is going to have a cow."

I didn't explain that the boy had gotten the CD part wrong, poor dope.

I watched Anya push pancake pieces around her plate. She'd taken a teensy trial bite of the bacon before setting it aside. Seeing that our "burglar" was a pimply faced sixteen year old with more thirst for Budweiser than good sense had gone a long way toward calming her down after the incident.

And learning he'd peed his pants made Anya darn near hysterical.

"Gracie wouldn't hurt a fly!" she'd giggled.

Now I had to get us back to normal. "Honey, you have to eat. You aren't overweight. Remember the pediatrician said you needed to gain a few pounds?"

I made a mental note that five Benadryl tablets only put Gracie to sleep for two hours. Our big, furry hero groaned at my daughter's feet and closed her eyes. She'd had a busy night.

Anya looked at me dubiously. Okay, I had no credibility when it came to what a female should weigh. Even so, I was her mother, and I needed to marshal whatever powers I had to get my kid to eat.

"We're not going anywhere until you have at least have a couple of bites."

"Mom, don't make me eat, okay?" Under her eyes was smudged purple. Her bottom lip trembled. We were both exhausted.

I sighed. We still hadn't discussed my night in jail. I couldn't even get her to look me in the eye.

"Anya, we have to—"

A knock at the door interrupted me.

"Couldn't make it here last night with the storms an' all. Wanted to be sure you're okay." Mert's face was drawn and tired. She wore a black T-shirt short enough to display a rhinestone charm in her belly button. Stretched across her bust and outlined in sequins was the word "Queen." Her white short-shorts barely covered her rear end. She gave me the once-over before extending her arms for a hug. I thanked her for helping Dodie to remember Bonnie was an attorney. Then I told her about the past evening's excitement.

"No kidding? But the security lights are up!"

"And the electricity was off."

"Rats," said Mert.

"That's not my biggest problem," I added. "It's Anya. Sheila told her I was in jail. Now she won't talk to me."

"Jest leave us alone." Mert's truck keys dangled before my eyes. "Go get yourself a cup of coffee at Kaldi's and come back in an hour."

"No. I can't. This is my responsibility. I'm her mother."

"Go on and get. She won't listen to you right now, but she'll listen to me. Don't give me any lip about your re-spon-si-bil-i-tee. You think you're the only one who loves that kid?" Mert's mouth was set hard. "Listen. Sometimes you got to let others carry the load for you. You hear me? Now go."

THIRTY-TWO

I CLIMBED INTO THE candy-apple red Toyota pickup. Frankie, the dead ferret whose skin Mert had draped over the rearview mirror, winked at me with tawny glass eyes. "Oh, shut up," I said to the animal, "what are you looking at? You eat your young." The tiny American flag taped on the dash waved jauntily as I shifted gears and pulled away from the curb. I felt guilty, and I felt relieved.

Shouldn't I be handling this? Shouldn't I be the one my child turned to? Was this proof I couldn't cut it as a mother?

Then again, maybe Mert was a better choice for talking to Anya. Maybe Anya would open up to her. They'd known each other for years. I was so tired, so spent. I drove to Kaldi's, put an espresso macchiato on my charge card, and sat on the truck running board to sip it. As I did, I prayed.

It was a pitiful ecumenical choice—caffeine and Toyota instead of Holy Communion and church—but if God really is everywhere, why wouldn't he be at Kaldi's? And if his eye is on the sparrow, why wouldn't he be watching me and knowing I needed him?

I asked for help. I think he heard me.

An hour to the minute, I pulled up in my driveway.

Anya and Mert tumbled out of the front door. My daughter gave me a shy smile. "Let's go see WE. Mert's never seen her."

"Sure, honey," I said. "That sounds great."

———

WE is a two-headed female albino rat snake which was purchased from a breeder in Illinois a few weeks after her birth. When she came to the World Aquarium, no one expected her to live more than a couple of months. But WE is unusual; both WE's two heads connect to her stomach.

After showing her off for six years, the aquarium decided to sell her on eBay for $150,000. The bids never got close to that price, but the publicity did make WE St. Louis's most famous reptile.

The world has since learned that WE may actually be fraternal twin snakes—male and female—sharing the same body. The aquarium plans to introduce WE to a he in the hopes of spawning wee WEs or mini-WEs.

I had sympathy for the poor snake. I'd been married to a two-faced rascal myself. I'd read the note Olivia had given me, and it was tucked safely inside my wallet until I could follow up on the misbehavior that had led to my husband's death.

I love all living creatures, but snakes are definitely at the bottom of my list. And WE, well, she gives me the creeps. Her color, her quadruple glassy eyes, her twin flickering tongues make the hairs stand up on my arms. But Anya is fascinated by WE. We—Anya and I, that is—can't visit that bifurcated animal often enough to suit my daughter.

As usual Anya marched up the stairs immediately beyond the City Museum foyer, past all the sparkling mosaics and glittering inlaid stones that attract other kids. She went straight to the World Aquarium on the second floor, turning right and making a beeline for WE's glass case.

Mert followed her gamely, but the moment she saw the four-foot-long reptile, her knees buckled. "Do Lord," she whimpered. "This is like a horror movie I once't saw at the drive-in. Couldn't handle it then, neither." I led her to a nearby bench. Actually, what they need is a fainting couch. I'm sure Mert's not the only visitor who's felt woozy after viewing the squirming ivory body with its pair of reddish triangular heads and four beady eyes.

"Honey, why don't we show Mert the rest of the City Museum?" I suggested. "I bet she'd like the Everyday Circus and the crafts area."

"Or the jets on the roof," Anya said.

"Or the architectural relics."

Mert whined, "Anything that ain't moving on its belly. Please!"

———

That night I tucked Anya into bed.

"We need to talk."

She looked down at the tented mounds that were her feet. "Yeah. I guess so."

"I didn't—"

"I know. I always knew." She sighed. "I just get tired of hearing Grandma tell me how bad you are. After a while, I start to feel confused." Her cool hand slipped into mine as she continued, "And I know you and Gracie will protect me, and that you would never hurt anybody. Honest, Mom. But sometimes I miss our old life, and then…"

"Then it's easy to blame me?" I kissed her fingers and gave them a squeeze.

"Yeah." Her eyebrows peaked in a dubious question mark. "How come I do that? And how did you know?"

"It's natural to want to find someone to blame when things go wrong." I swallowed the lump in my throat and added, "And since parents are supposed to make everything better for their kids, it makes sense that I'd be the one to blame."

She rose up to hug me hard. Her hair smelled of baby shampoo. "But I know I shouldn't."

I whispered to her hair as I held her. "Part of growing up, sweetie, is finding out that parents aren't perfect. We're just people. Bigger. Older. Sometimes smarter. Sometimes not. So try not to blame me for everything, okay? Please, sweetheart, try not to."

———

Monday morning Anya seemed fine. I took her to school and walked into the store determined to finish my computer alterations to the photos. Maybe today I would discover whether the downloaded images held the answer to Roxanne's murder. I fingered the note Olivia had handed me at Antonio's. The sooner I finished the bridal shower albums, the sooner I'd be able to interrogate the mystery woman my husband had eaten lunch with the day he died.

Around one thirty, Detweiler popped through the front door. In his dark suit, white shirt, and tie, he was a man on a mission. Each step slapped the floor hard. He pulled a chair up next to me. He half-threw himself into the seat. "I heard about the break-in and your trip to jail. I can't believe it," he rubbed his face with both hands. "I was only gone two days!"

"What happened the other night was no big deal."

"No big deal!"

"Not really. But I did want to talk to you about my trip to the slammer." I hit SAVE and twisted to face him. "I think you told them to take me in. You wanted to see if I would crack." I kept my voice even. My eyes never left his face.

"What?" He was mad. Sparks flew from the hard set of his chin. He grabbed my elbow. "I don't play games. Get it? Not now. Not ever. Especially not with you. I know what you've been through. You deserve better." He leaned toward me, his face nearly touching mine. "I can't believe you'd think that."

I pulled away. "Why wouldn't I? Why should I trust you? Or anybody? You have to admit the timing was pretty convenient."

"Yeah, I do. And I'm worried. There's something going on, and I want to get to the bottom of it. But I wasn't involved. I would never hurt you. Never."

My eyes got watery. I pulled my arm away from his grasp and faced the screen again, sniffling a little. I wasn't going to let him off that easy. "But you had my alibi. You knew I was at Jellystone."

"No," he shook his head. "I knew you said you were at Jelly-stone—and I put that in the file—but the security videos won't be available for viewing until this afternoon. That's how they justified taking you in."

Okay, so that was his story. Could I trust him? More importantly, did I want to trust anybody ever again? No, no, and no.

He said, "When I left town, you were in the clear. Someone with a whole lot of clout put pressure on the Chesterfield P.D. and did an end run. Trust me, I am not happy about this. And I will get to the bottom of it. The system works, but … people can be …" he hesitated "… can do the wrong thing."

"Wrong thing, huh? That's what you call throwing innocent people in jail? Making me sleep all night on a bench surrounded by goodness-knows-who? Or what?"

"What? All night?" He jumped up and paced, his hands jammed into his suit pants pockets. "Why didn't you call someone to get you out?"

"There wasn't anyone to call."

"Family?"

"No one nearby." I didn't add we were on the outs anyway. Rats, I still hadn't called my mother. I slapped my forehead.

"Your mother-in-law?"

"Sheila. Right. She thinks I'm guilty."

"Of what?"

"Of everything."

"She didn't send help?"

"Nope."

"She's family and she didn't help you? With all her money?"

"No," I rubbed my face. "I'm on my own. Except for friends." I pushed back from my work to study him. His jaw was set at an angle and his eyebrows met in the center of his forehead. A vein pulsed along his forehead. He was seriously ticked off.

"The open seating area is no place for someone like you. We get clowns waiting to be arraigned. Weirdos coming down from dope. Folks off their meds. You name it. You shouldn't have been there. They could have at least put you in a cell."

"A cell?"

"To keep you safe." He slapped his fist into a palm. "They should have called me in Springfield. Geez, there are times when I hate this town—and my job."

I smiled to myself. He was being protective, and that felt good. Then immediately, I stopped myself. Was I nuts? I was doing it again. Falling for him. Could I trust him? Maybe this was all an act. Maybe he hadn't been out of cell phone range.

He must have read my mind. "I didn't get your phone message until this morning. I drove straight here after testifying. I was out of cell range until I hit the Mississippi." His earnest expression made me go all soft and gushy. His face was very close to mine. Very, very close. A pleasant tingle, a feeling I'd forgotten, began.

"Okay." There was a catch in my voice. Talking to him, seeing him looking strong and capable, seemed to give me permission to break down.

But I didn't. I couldn't. I had my child to think about. I turned back to the monitor. "This has been hard on Anya. She doesn't know what to think."

His big hands clenched in fists. "Now we know. Someone is convinced you know something important. Otherwise she wouldn't have gone to so much trouble to put you in jail."

THIRTY-THREE

"I STILL THINK ALL this is related," said Detweiler. "I'm just not sure how. Have you had any time to work on the photos?"

"I'm doing that now."

"By the way, I went to the pond yesterday at my parents' farm and scooped up a few tadpoles. I figured Anya might enjoy watching them turn into frogs."

Other women get flowers. Or diamonds. I got tadpoles. And I liked it. "That was very thoughtful of you. Thanks. I know she'll be thrilled. I hear Gracie's tail thumping all the way out here. You better go pat her. If she gets to swinging it too hard, she's liable to do some damage." As he walked to the storeroom, I noticed how strong his shoulders looked, how beautifully his suit hung on his body. He was a dangerously good-looking man.

Careful, Kiki, I warned myself. The last time you felt this way, you wound up pregnant and part of a love triangle. I turned my attention to the computer screen.

Detweiler came back grinning. "Man, she's a great dog. Sloppy, but great." He wiped his hands with a cloth handkerchief.

"Hence the name."

"Great Dane. I got it. You all right with slimy critters in the house? Tadpoles don't bother you?"

I grinned, recalling our visit to WE. "I'm fine with tadpoles and frogs. Anya will be in seventh heaven. She loves any sort of creepy crawly thing."

He pulled his chair closer to mine. "I'm not kidding when I say I'm worried. I'll follow up on your latest break-in. Any idea who might have called in a favor to get you locked up?"

I shook my head. "Whoever she was, she thought I still owned the Lexus. Lucky for me. Proved she was lying."

He stretched his long legs and rocked back in the chair. As he'd done in my kitchen, he linked his hands behind his head and studied the ceiling.

"Could you hazard a guess? Who knew you once owned a Lexus?"

I shrugged. "Anyone who knew me before George died."

Dodie hustled over to us. She put two meaty fists on her hips. "Hey, buddy, you planning to make these visits a habit?"

Detweiler and I both turned red.

"You missed all the action, pal. A jail break and a break-in. It's been a real exciting couple of days. You're lucky she's even speaking to you. Kiki tends to look on the bright side." She gave a menacing leer, "Whereas I tend to hold grudges. Whose side are you on anyway? You're sure not much use. At least not so far. Anyway, we're on the case. Just call me Sherlock."

Dodie winked at me. "Watson and I had a thought about those photos." She explained our idea about matching Roxanne's vacation pictures to shots in scrapbook magazines. "Maybe that'll give us a bead on the locale. They usually print commentary with a place name next to the scrapbook pages."

"That's a great idea," Detweiler told Dodie. "Kiki, would you be willing to look over Ms. Baker's albums? Think you could tell anything from them?" He seemed hopeful.

"I might. I'm not sure what."

"Forensic scrapbooking," said Dodie. "Now I've heard everything."

"How about we go to Ms. Baker's apartment so you can see them? The place has been locked up since the murder. Our people glanced through the albums but didn't come up with anything. You might interpret them differently."

"What would I be looking for?"

Detweiler shook his head. "I don't know. All I know is if there's anything weird in them, you'd be the person who'd notice."

"I can't help you until later. First I have to run by Dimont Development. And I have to pick up Anya from school. Since we're on the subject, did you find Roxanne's camera?"

The detective shook his head again. "No luck. At least not yet. It wasn't in her car, or her purse, or at her apartment."

If she was a keen scrapbooker, she probably had her camera with her at all times. That led me to suggest, "Maybe her killer has it."

Detweiler rose and stared down at me. "Or your home invader. The first one."

"Maybe," said Dodie, "maybe those are one and the same. Kiki, you better be careful."

THIRTY-FOUR

DIMONT DEVELOPMENT INC. HADN'T changed much since my last visit. A new receptionist sat behind a nameplate that read, "Beth Hoover." Young and flashy, Beth was standing behind her desk with a phone tucked under one ear. Her skirt was a mere suggestion of fabric. Her blouse was low cut, exposing a black lace bra. Everything about Beth confirmed she was strictly decorative.

I took a seat and waited. The sitting area appeared to be unchanged from the last time I visited, except that now a framed photo of George with his date of birth and date of death took a place of honor on the wall. The magazines on the coffee tables were dated six months ago. That surprised me. When George was partner, he insisted on displaying current magazines. "I think it shows we're current, too," he always said.

I thought he was right. He was right about a lot of things. And wrong about even more.

The place needed a good cleaning. A thin film of dust covered the silk plants. A hairball the size of a Yorkie sat under one of the end tables. A coffee stain marred the top issue of *The Economist*.

Obviously Beth didn't do anything manual except manicures.

"May I help you?" She didn't look up from her nails.

I pointed to George's portrait. "I'm Kiki Lowenstein." I extended my hand. "George was my husband."

"Wet polish." Beth avoided my handshake. "I didn't work here when he did. In fact, most of us are new. A lot of customers have mentioned how well-liked Mr. Lowenstein was."

"George was a kind person. I miss him. Actually, I'm here to see Bill Ballard. Is he in?"

The corners of her mouth turned down in a girlish pout. "Aw, too bad. You missed him by ten minutes. He's supposed to be here all day tomorrow. Can I tell him you'll stop by?"

"Actually, please tell him I'd like a copy of his buy-sell agreement with George. How about I write that down for you?"

———

Back at the store I loaded Gracie into the passenger seat. With her ears flapping in the soft breeze, and the world beginning to turn solidly green, my spirits lifted. Trees were wearing party dresses of gossamer leaves. Azalea bushes made their debut in chiffon pinks and purples. All around us, the dance of spring swirled and twirled. The gloom of winter was behind us. A surge of confidence accompanied my every move. I was thinking a lot about Detweiler, and that made me feel good all over, too.

The school pick-up line at CALA runs past the parking lot, around a concrete median, and alongside the honking-big new gymnasium. Gracie watched children climb into cars, her tail wagging with anticipation of seeing our little girl. My heart was thumping along with hers. I was looking forward to a quiet evening with my daughter. I planned to take her to St. Louis Bread Co. where I'd wait in the car with the dog while she ordered two green teas and two turkey sandwiches on asiago bread. After we picked up our food, we'd go to Queeny Park and find a picnic table. I was sorely in need of a breather from work. I wanted to talk to her about the break-in and the jail incident, to make sure she wasn't scared or worried. I wanted to quiz her about her eating habits. Mainly, I wanted to hug her and recharge my mom batteries.

Gracie and I kept our eyes on the school doors eager for our first glimpse of Anya. A phalanx of luxury cars lined up behind us.

At last I saw Anya. Her pale face bobbed this way and that, searching for me. I sat up in my seat and waved. The line moved. I pulled forward. I half-stood and waved again. She started toward me calling out, "Mom! Gracie!" Gracie stood and yodeled with joy, her fat tail whopping me in the face as she wagged her whole body with happiness.

"Mrs. Lowenstein?" A woman in a tired gray suit stepped to the side of my car. Her face was careworn. She carried a scuffed and misshapen canvas substitute for a briefcase. She flashed an ID. "Letitia Smith. Children's Division Case Worker, Department of Social Services."

"Yes?" I kept an eye on Anya as she ran to the passenger side, hugged Gracie, and moved to throw her book bag into the back.

Ms. Smith put one hand on Anya's arm. "Sorry, honey. You won't be going home with your mother today."

"Pardon me?" Ever polite, my Anya tried to withdraw from the woman's grasp.

Ms. Smith waved toward a Mercedes in the back of the line. Sheila hopped out. My mother-in-law beamed triumphantly at me. In her navy St. John's pants suit with matching navy pumps, she was the picture of a wealthy Ladue matron.

"Wait a minute," I said. "My daughter is coming home with me. There must be some mistake."

"I'm sorry, Mrs. Lowenstein. Anya has to go with her grand-mother. We are investigating a report. Anya can't go home with you until there's been an assessment. For the time being, you are not to have any contact with your daughter. A hearing will be scheduled—"

"What?" I was close to shouting. "You're saying my mother-in-law is taking my child away?"

"No. Not exactly. Anya will be staying with her grandmother until there's a hearing."

"Come along, darling." Sheila wore a smug look on her face as she tugged at Anya's arm.

"Gran, what are you doing? I want to go home with Mom." Anya pulled away violently. She tried to open the passenger-side door of my car. Gracie leaned forward to lick her.

"Good Gracie," cooed Anya, and she put her arms around her dog.

"That animal tried to attack me yesterday," Sheila said.

Ms. Smith stepped away, her eyes wide with concern.

"Gracie wouldn't hurt a flea." On the other hand, Gracie was feeling her oats after tackling our home invader.

"Restrain your dog." Ms. Smith's eyes were big as coasters in her head.

I grabbed Gracie's collar.

"Anya, I know this is hard," Ms. Smith's flat voice betrayed the fact she was accustomed to situations like this. "But you can't go home with your mother right now."

I rolled up the passenger window, let go of the dog, got out of the car and ran to the passenger side. Ms. Smith stood between me and my child. Anya reached for me. I reached for her, but Ms. Smith raised her arms to form a barrier.

"I want my mother!" Anya tried to push Ms. Smith out of the way. My daughter's lip trembled. The silver half-crescent of tears formed in her eyes. "Mom," her voice broke into tiny glass pieces. Pieces so sharp they pierced my soul. "Mom, please. Please. I want to be with you. Take me home, please!" The last word ripped from her chest and behind it came a sob.

"Anya. Anya, baby," I grabbed for her.

Ms. Smith blocked me. Short of hurting the woman, I couldn't get to my child.

Gracie scratched at the window. She gave a low, grumbling warning.

"Mom..." Anya's plea was fading. As was her confidence in me.

Gracie growled louder.

"That animal's a menace. Now come with me, darling," Sheila said. Using Ms. Smith as a barrier to keep me from my daughter, Sheila snaked out an arm and grabbed Anya.

Anya tried to shake free. Sheila held on. Anya gave it one last-ditch effort, her whole body fighting Sheila's grip. "Mom," she whimpered as tears spilled down her face.

A car door slammed. The noise jolted me; I realized where we were. The entertainment we were providing. The entire CALA car-pool gawked at us. Heads craned out of cars to stare. Mothers gathered on the sidewalk and exchanged horrified whispers. A clutch of girls I recognized as Anya's classmates giggled and pointed.

This could only get worse. By tomorrow this drama would be all over school. The more upset Anya became, the faster the story would travel. I could imagine the girls text-messaging each other. The mothers would pick up where their daughters left off.

I had to think of Anya. I had to think long term.

"Let me see your paperwork," I said. I kept my voice low and restrained.

Ms. Smith handed over a sheaf of papers. My eyes were too misty to focus, but I could tell I held an official document. My hand shook, the letters swam around, an official seal jumped out at me.

I gave the sheets back to Ms. Smith. My face relayed my defeat. "Okay," I managed. I sniffed hard to hold back tears.

"Your mother's finally being reasonable," said Sheila to Anya. "Come along, darling." When Anya refused to move, Sheila snapped, "Enough of this nonsense. Get in my car. We're going home."

Anya's posture stiffened. Her grandmother never used that tone of voice with her. My child's face twisted into an angry mask. "It's not my home. It's your house. Not mine."

Sheila had gone too far.

Anya stared at me. "Mom?" This time it was a plea.

I had to be strong. "We'll get this all straightened out. You're just going to your gran's. That's all. It's nothing new. Someone made a mistake. I'll find out what's happening and you'll come home tomorrow."

"You promise?"

"I promise." My heart hurt. Tears threatened. I wanted to strike out. To wipe the smirk off Sheila's face. Instead, I told myself to think of Anya. "Anya, honey, I don't want you to be embarrassed in front of your friends," and I cast a glance around us silently indicating the many students climbing into their parents' cars. "I love you. For now it's best you go."

Sheila seemed so pleased with herself. She gave my child a little push. "Get in my car, Anya, darling."

"Get your hands off of me," Anya snapped. She hoisted her backpack over her shoulder. She gave her grandmother a look of pure hatred.

Whatever Sheila had hoped to gain by this stunt, she'd lost more than she knew.

My mother-in-law stepped back in shock. She turned to me as if asking for help.

But I had none to give her.

I clenched my teeth until they hurt and wanted to say, "This isn't over, Sheila. I'll never forgive you and neither will Anya."

But I remembered the last time I threatened someone.

Roxanne's gloating visage mocked me from a dark recess of my mind. I waited until Sheila's car doors slammed. I waved goodbye to the Mercedes as though nothing had happened. A cold fury replaced my heartbreak. I asked Ms. Smith, "When is the assessment? Anya will want to know."

A sadness crept into Ms. Smith's face as she studied me. "You can't have any contact with your daughter. It's all in the paperwork. Not until the hearing."

"When's the hearing?"

"Next Monday." She handed me a thick envelope. "It's all inside."

THIRTY-FIVE

I COULD BARELY DRIVE. I don't know how I got home. I vaguely recall holding on to Gracie's collar and letting her guide me through the back door. I collapsed sobbing, my head on a chair seat, my rear end on the linoleum floor. I cried and cried and cried.

My phone rang. I pulled it from my back pocket. I was desperate to hear from my daughter and forgot for a moment that we weren't allowed contact. "Hello?" I stuttered.

"Kiki?"

I sniveled into the phone. A wet, hiccupping sound, totally unintelligible.

Mert said, "Kiki? You all right? What's wrong?"

I was incoherent. As much as I wanted to tell my best friend what happened, I couldn't form sentences. I spit out, "Anya," and "case worker" and "Sheila." I started retching. All Mert heard was gagging noises. But that was enough.

"I'll be right there."

Minutes later she barreled through the kitchen, almost tripping over Gracie as she hovered over me nervously, licking my face. I handed Mert the envelope and sank back down on the floor wailing. All the tears in the past six months flooded out of me at once. I couldn't speak for sobbing.

My face was wet, my throat hurt from keening noises, and I didn't care. The depth of my sorrow pulled me so far from life, so far from the belief anything would ever be right again, that I wanted to give up. My arms ached for my child. A pressure on my chest forced me to breathe in short pants. Whatever pain Sheila had hoped to inflict, she'd succeeded.

Mert walked me to the living room. After planting me on the sofa, she left with a "Be right back." I fell over on my side, unable to muster the energy to sit upright. Gracie sat in front of me whining, wagging her tail in sympathy. She pawed at me, trying to comfort me—her big footpads rough and demanding.

I didn't respond.

Mert brought a cold washcloth and a glass of ice water. "Drink it."

I did. She sat beside me, wiped my face and rocked me, while patting my back as though I were a baby.

"Go ahead. Git it all out. You poor thing. You've jest had a real hard time of it, ain't you?"

After a while, I started to wear down. My sobs faded to dry little blurps. I fell asleep on Mert's shoulder, exhausted.

I awakened to a knock at the door. Mert left me to answer it. Hushed voices jockeyed back and forth.

The back side of a cool hand brushed my cheek. "Kiki? Can we talk?"

It was Detweiler. He reached out and pulled me to him. He smelled of spice and cologne and man. Held in the cradle of his arms, I cried into his shirt. It was as if I'd always belonged there. The soft dub-dub of his heart was a familiar metronome.

I didn't even care how bad my appearance was. My eyes were swollen and red. My face was chapped with tears. I looked up at him. "She took-took-Anya!" I started sobbing all over again.

He set me back on the sofa.

Mert offered me a glass. "Here, kiddo. Take a snort."

I swallowed. The liquid scalded my throat.

"Bourbon," said Detweiler. "From a friend in the Alcohol, Tobacco, and Firearms division."

"A snort's always good for what ails you." Mert pressed more on me. She was on one side and Detweiler was on the other, propping me up. "We gotta powwow and get us a plan, babycakes. No way are we letting that witch keep your kid."

Detweiler had an idea. "Let me take the tadpoles to Anya. I have to explain how to care for them. If she puts straight tap water into the jar, they'll die."

Mert added, "I'd like to put straight tap water into Sheila's jar. She keeps it up, and there's gonna be one more murder for you to investigate."

"Your mother-in-law will have to let me in." Detweiler's plan was a good one. Anya would know he was my emissary. Talking to him would help her feel more hopeful about the situation. His presence might also remind Sheila that I wasn't entirely without supporters.

"I'll call Bonnie and ask her for advice about Family Court," Mert said. "Maybe she can come over to Time in a Bottle tomorrow. We should talk this through. You need a plan. Sheila just can't up and steal your kid."

"Actually, Anya shouldn't be staying with her grandmother for any extended length of time." I told them about Sheila encouraging Anya not to eat. "Even Mrs. Kammer, the school nurse, was concerned about how Anya's weight has dropped."

"No! You can't say a word about that." Mert's face turned bleak. "Promise you won't."

"Why not?" Detweiler asked. "If I were a judge or a caseworker and I heard a grandparent was keeping a skinny kid from eating, I'd have that kid out of the house in a hot New York second. Sounds like a great idea."

"No! You don't understand." Mert wrung her hands. Her eyes were wide with fear. "You don't get how this works. If DSS hears Sheila's unfit to care for Anya, they'll put her in a foster home."

Detweiler scratched his head. "So?"

"Please," Mert's voice cracked. "You cain't understand. Listen…" And she swallowed hard, tried to talk, and couldn't. Now it was Mert's turn to cry, a big tear slipping down her cheek. "She could be … foster homes aren't always safe … and please don't."

I was stunned. I'd seen my friend in every sort of situation, and never had I seen her distraught. What secret in her past caused this violent reaction? I vowed that someday I'd find out. I passed Mert the rest of my bourbon. She tipped her head back and downed the liquid in one swallow.

Detweiler's eyes turned thoughtful. "Okay. Maybe it's best Anya stay with Mrs. Lowenstein."

Mert shook herself. The bourbon must have helped. "Anya won't starve to death in a week. I'll take her pizza and that peanut butter fudge she likes."

My friend's face was pale beneath her heavy makeup. One eye began to twitch. To see strong, tough Mert reduced to such misery convinced me. Much as I'd like to take my child from Sheila just to prove to the woman she wasn't invincible, I had Anya's welfare to consider.

"All right."

Mert continued, "We need to get letters. People have to write on your behalf. I wish we knew what Sheila went and told DSS."

I turned to Detweiler. "How about I ride along while you drop off the tadpoles? I'll stay in the car. From there, we can go to Roxanne's, if you still want. I want to look at those scrapbooks. I'm tired of living like this. If solving Roxanne's murder gets my life back to normal, I'm on it."

———

"We had a chance to speak while her grandmother left the room to get a placemat for under the jar. Anya says Mrs. Lowenstein reported you for your visit to the county jail. If that's the case, it should be easy enough to get your daughter back." Detweiler reached over and took my hand. "Try not to worry too much. Family Court will get this cleared up."

The warmth of his flesh felt comforting. I wished I could share his optimism.

"How did Anya look?"

"She was pretty calm but she'd obviously been crying. You could tell she was mad as all-get-out at Mrs. Lowenstein. Your mother-in-law seemed shook up. Mrs. Lowenstein made a tactical error—and she knows it."

Detweiler's phone rang. He spoke quickly, then snapped it shut. "Good news. As of five minutes ago, you have a solid alibi for the night Roxanne Baker died. The ranger station has you registering at eleven twenty-five and leaving the next morning. A convenience store worker noticed you driving away from the scrapbook store at quarter to eleven. Good thing that old Beemer is so recognizable. There's no way you could have squeezed in a trip to the Chesterfield Mall."

I hadn't realized I'd been holding my breath. A big whoosh of air escaped my lips. "Thank goodness."

The evening had fallen and darkness enveloped us. As usual, St. Louis weather had swung from one end of the thermometer to the other in the snap of fingers. The temperature was cool enough to make me shiver. Detweiler let go of my hand and turned up the heat in the car.

"Want me to stop and grab my jacket from the trunk?" His offer flooded me with emotion. Wouldn't it be lovely to feel cherished? George had always been kind and thoughtful in a perfunctory way, but to feel you were the most important person in another person's life, well, wouldn't that be wonderful? I could only imagine. And I didn't want to imagine. I didn't want to put myself in a position where I could be hurt. Yes, Detweiler was nice to me and my child, but what did I know about the man? Nothing. And what had I to lose?

Everything.

I told myself it was one thing to accept his help and another to let down my guard.

Neither of us talked on the way to Roxanne's. I tried not to worry about my daughter, but I couldn't help myself. Maybe this was Sheila's misguided effort to replace George. Not that I cared.

Right at the moment, I hated Sheila.

THIRTY-SIX

Roxanne's apartment was an expensive loft in downtown St. Louis. The parking attendant started to give Detweiler a hard time about not having a guest or resident sticker, but a flash of the badge and the man was nice as pie. The attendant buzzed a doorman and escorted us into a vestibule. A security camera with an unblinking lens like a fly's eye recorded us. Detweiler flashed his badge again, and we moved through a set of doors like an air lock into a fancy foyer.

The elaborate rigamarole started me thinking about the two times my—Mr. Wilson's—little house had been violated. This is what money bought: security. I experienced a new surge of determination to get to the bottom of the buy-sell agreement with Bill Ballard. Sheila had used my brief visit to jail to her advantage. But if I'd had the kind of clout she did, I'd be working with a lawyer instead of talking to my former cleaning lady about how to get my kid back.

A nattily uniformed concierge stepped from behind a desk to ask our business. Detweiler flashed his badge and explained we were heading to Roxanne Baker's apartment. The dapper man shook his head, causing the gold braids on his shoulders to sway, and murmured, "A shame, such a shame."

Hardly, I thought. But I kept that to myself.

The concierge made us sign in, escorted Detweiler and me to a bank of elevators, and pushed a floor button to send us on our way. Classical music accompanied us to the top of the building where doors opened quietly to a deeply carpeted hallway lit by elaborate Art Deco sconces. Obviously placed security cameras monitored every step of our journey.

Stale air and old perfume made Roxanne's apartment smell and feel stuffy. Detweiler rotated a glowing dial to bring up the lights, revealing that we were poised at the edge of a beautifully decorated sunken living room. He handed me a pair of latex gloves.

"Merrilee told me Roxanne had money troubles, but this place must have cost a fortune. And these," I walked over to examine the side tables carefully, "are either antiques or expensive reproductions."

I crossed the room to get a better look at a painting. "This isn't a print. I can make out the brush strokes." I knelt to examine the rug. "Our decorator showed us a carpet like this in a rug showroom. We're talking serious money."

Detweiler spoke softly. "Do you think Mr. Lowenstein paid for all this? Her bank account shows regular income from a corporation. We're trying to track it down."

"George might have. I've heard he took care of her." I paused to survey the room. "But Merrilee Witherow said she and other friends loaned Roxanne money. Maybe she didn't pay them back. That could be a motive for killing her. Frustration."

Detweiler said, "This place is paid up through next month. Since your husband's been dead for more than six months, Ms. Baker must have had another source of income. We've been working on what that might have been. None of the answers are very … pretty."

"Merrilee Witherow told me Roxanne'd taken up with another married man. But she didn't have a name. Roxanne kept his identity a secret."

We followed a wide hallway into a spare bedroom. A walnut sleigh bed against one wall doubled as a seating area, making the room perfect for company, but leaving enough space for a wide armoire nestled between two large built-in shelf units. When opened, the armoire revealed a scrapbooker's dream workspace.

"Wow," I said. "I've seen these in magazines, but never in real life. This is one fancy piece of furniture." I flipped through paper supplies in horizontal shelves. "All of this is new. Purchased this season."

"How can you tell?"

"Manufacturers bring out new designs on a regular basis. I recognize these patterns and colors. None of this is more than six months old."

The bookshelves were extra-deep. "This was custom built. Twelve-by-twelve albums require more space than regular bookcases. Notice how these fit perfectly? She must have ninety albums here. This must have cost a fortune."

I pulled an album from the top shelf. The legend on the spine dated twenty years ago. Sure enough, Roxanne and a pimply faced

George mugged for an unseen camera person. I flipped through the pages quickly. A dull ache began in my throat. Whatever else I might think about these two, it was patently clear they'd loved each other for years before I stumbled onto the scene. Roxanne's journaling was skimpy, as is often the case, but her words testified to how important George was to her.

I almost felt sorry for Roxanne. Almost.

Detweiler sat next to me on the edge of the sleigh bed. To the sound of a clock ticking in the next room, we went through every album page by page. I didn't expect them to tell me anything new. I simply wanted a feel for the woman and her life. Her friends had been right; she'd been addicted to scrapbooking.

Near the bottom of the shelves, I found an album labeled "All About Me."

"This should answer a lot of questions," I said. "When scrapbooking started, we focused on our families. Recently we've realized we need to tell our own stories. This will be an illustrated autobiography."

I flipped to the title page. Roxanne had capitalized each first letter of her full name: O-pal R-oxanne B-aker.

"Well, that's one question answered. My husband supported her. He's been writing checks to 'orb' every month for years." I pointed to each letter of her name in turn: O-R-B.

Detweiler nodded. "I'll check out her bank statements, but I think you're right. Sorry."

"Here I worried he was being blackmailed. After that stunt with borrowing money from Dimont, I didn't know what to think. But this … this is pretty clear."

I pulled the most recent album from the bottom shelf.

"Here we go." I pointed to the photos of the tropical scene. "We loaded this onto Snapfish the day of the bridal shower. That means she printed out copies but left the images on her camera."

"That supports your theory she wanted to show the photos to someone at the shower. Unfortunately these still don't tell us much," said Detweiler.

"Or do they?" I wondered. Okay, kiddo, I told myself. You know this. You're good at this. Concentrate.

Over the years, Roxanne's scrapbooking style had changed. Like most of us, she started with cute layouts and quickly moved to more sophisticated pages. But I noticed another difference. Most of the layouts kept to the style she'd shown throughout her scrapbooking career: solid backgrounds with small patterned paper add-ons, sticker letter titles, pre-made embellishments, and journaling below her photos.

And yet … there was a different feel to her recent layouts. I tried to analyze what had changed. There was a subtle shift in mood. There were no playful photos of friends, no exuberant comments rife with hyperbole. These pages weren't about her fun-loving life. Or her wild weekends with friends. No, she hadn't even focused on her romance with George on these final layouts.

Instead, a feeling of distance prevailed. These pages were almost businesslike. Workmanlike. As though she'd made them out of habit. The layouts showed no spark of spontaneity—no sense of enjoyment.

The vacation photos called for bright backgrounds and embellishments. But the colors she used were somber, not at all in keeping with the tropical images. She had matted photos and slapped them down on background paper. No journaling explained what we were seeing.

Could she have been pining for George?

The photo we had of Roxanne with the guy in the baseball cap was featured in one of her more recent pages. Conspicuously missing was any page title.

I pointed out the discrepancy to Detweiler, and he made a note in his steno pad. Tapping the picture with his pen, he said, "We need to track that guy down."

I nodded. "I bet this was the guy Merrilee was talking about. The married one."

Since I'd been through all Roxanne's albums, I decided to take a closer look at her supplies.

Inside a drawer labeled "Adhesives" sat an empty bottle of Un-Du. I pulled a tissue from my purse and picked it up. Why, I wondered, would she have put it back empty? All her other supplies were full and stored with obvious precision. Why would Roxanne neglect to buy more of this essential product? And why would she store an empty bottle? No scrapbooker could forget that particular product's name! You used Un-Du to undo anything stuck to your pages.

The answer came to me: because Roxanne didn't put it back. Someone else did.

"This is important," I said. I explained why the bottle represented a drastic variation from what I perceived as her habits.

Detweiler offered me an evidence bag.

Okay, I thought to myself, someone used up her Un-Du. Why? How? Doing what? I remembered the missing page title. I pulled the "ballcap guy on the beach" layout from its plastic page protec-

258

tor and ran a finger over the area where I would have expected a page title to be. A slightly tacky film met my fingertip.

Holding the page beneath a workspace lamp, I detected vestiges of adhesive. I set the page down and examined Roxanne's supplies.

"What is it?" Detweiler stood beside me and watched.

"Someone used up the Un-Du removing the page title from this layout."

"You're talking Greek."

"A page title is like a book title for your scrapbook page. The empty space here—" and I touched the layout I'd extracted from the page protector "—would be perfect for a title. But as you can see, the space is empty. And therefore, the design doesn't really work. Which is odd, because she was a big fan of symmetrical page designs. This product—"and I pointed to the Un-Du "—allows you to remove anything you've glued down without ripping your paper."

He was still puzzled.

"Feel this." I rubbed his gloved finger over the two empty spaces.

"Sticky."

"Right. Someone took the page title off this page. Someone who knew something about scrapbooking."

I crawled onto the floor, moved an empty trash can, and peered into the kneehole of the armoire. Stray pieces of paper stuck to the wooden panel on the back. "Got 'em." I peeled off a series of torn die-cut letters. I backed out of the desk. Not my best angle, but under the circumstances, what else could I do?

Working gently, I smoothed the letters flat.

"Whoever tossed these in the trash didn't realize Un-Du leaves the adhesive intact," I explained. "He or she thought they'd been thrown away."

"A-M-Y-N-A." I unfolded one other curved portion of a letter. "What's your guess? Is this a Q or an O or a C or a G or a zero?"

Detweiler studied the letters. He wrote them down. After a couple of arrangements, he said, "Cayman. She must have been hiding money."

THIRTY-SEVEN

DETWEILER WALKED THROUGH MY house, making sure I was safe. He offered to stay or call Mert, but I wanted to be alone. I thanked him and locked the door behind him. Gracie followed me into Anya's empty room, her tail hanging low as my spirits. I grabbed Anya's old stuffed Elmo, sank down onto her bed, buried my face in her pillow, and sniffed in the strawberry shampoo she always used.

"My baby," I whispered. I'd lied to her again. Not intentionally. I thought she'd be coming home tomorrow. I was wrong. "Aw, Anya, I'm such a bad mother." Whatever made me think I could take care of a child? I was an idiot. A dope. A loser. "I'm sorry, honey. I'm so, so sorry."

The tears came. I cried until I fell into a deep, dreamless sleep. I awoke with the sun in my eyes and Gracie pawing my arm.

My first thought was of Anya.

After toast for me and kibble for Gracie, I showered and paired navy slacks, slightly faded from multiple washings, with a soft blue boat-neck tee. My makeup only took seconds, although the under-eye concealer had to be put on twice to cover my dark circles. I stared myself straight in the eye and said, "Be brave. No breaking down. You've got work to do."

One, I needed to talk with the woman who'd had lunch with George the day he died. I realized belatedly that I should have told Detweiler what I'd learned. Well, chalk that up to my inexperience running an investigation. And, I'd had other things on my mind.

Two, I needed to see if I could learn the identity of the married man Roxanne had taken up with. She hadn't shared his name with Merrilee, but maybe she'd told one of her other friends.

Three, I needed to clarify with the shower guests that everything Dodie and I had downloaded was now—and had been for some time—available for public consumption. (Hello! No more reasons to break into my house!)

Four, I needed to meet my friends at two thirty to figure out how I would get my daughter back.

Numbers one, two, and three hinged on finalizing the photos for the Witherow bridal shower albums. Gracie and I went to work early. Before I started, I opened a can of Diet Dr Pepper and checked the store's daily calendar. Dodie noted an appointment with Merrilee Witherow at eleven. It was only seven. I should easily be able to have the albums ready for her visit.

For the next couple of hours, I worked from the master list of photos, finishing the last few images. Dodie came in so quietly I didn't notice until she tapped my shoulder.

I looked up in surprise.

"I heard about Sheila taking Anya." Dodie's strong face was troubled.

"From Mert?"

"Not exactly."

That was a punch to the stomach. I steeled myself. "How?"

"Couple of CALA moms."

I groaned and laid my head on my arms. My worst nightmare: being the gossip du jour at CALA.

Dodie poked me. "I thought you could use a treat. Come on into my office." She had a small spread for me: a cup of Kaldi's coffee and a six-pack of Krispy Kreme doughnuts. Glazed Chocolate Cake. My absolute favorite. In fact, I love 'em so much that in years past, George piled them into a pyramid to create a "birthday cake" for me.

"Mert called me a short time later. I agree with her. You need a plan, sunshine. We'll discuss what to do about Anya this afternoon. Finish your goodies and get back to work."

I cross-checked the photos I'd printed. I still had a couple to enhance. I improved the brightness on two group shots and fixed the guests' red eyes, even though I was sorely tempted to leave Roxanne looking like the devil's own spawn.

Around ten I took a break and walked Gracie. Then I sat down and tackled the last three photos. Using the clone stamp I removed a wall clock that seemed to be growing out of Mrs. Witherow's head.

With a sigh of satisfaction (and the realization I do a lot of sighing), I started printing photos and checking off the guest's requests. Dodie interrupted me a little before eleven.

"You need to eat. There's a turkey sandwich and chips for you in my office."

I did as I was told. I didn't feel hungry or tired, just numb. Although my child and I had only been separated for one evening, the prospect of losing custody made it seem longer. The fact I couldn't contact her fostered a frantic loneliness and a disconnect from my body. Dodie's recognition that I wouldn't eat or take breaks without reminders surprised me.

She must have gone through this when her son died. She must have suffered the same sense of loss and emptiness. My child was my center. The fact I couldn't talk with her, couldn't leave her a message, couldn't build my day around when we'd be together, left me adrift.

I gobbled the food and took Gracie for a spin around the block. She, too, was depressed. Usually she thumped her tail eagerly when I came into the back room. Since Anya had been taken from us, my big dog only raised her head to look at me sadly when I walked in. We were in the same boat. Nothing much mattered. We were on autopilot.

By the time Merrilee showed up, I had finished the album base pages and an assortment of page embellishments. I'd long ago designed the title, but Merrilee's air of excitement told me she'd forgotten how it looked. As she turned pages, I adhered her photos, added embellishments, and created the album before her eyes. She was tickled pink with the finished product.

"I can't wait to show Mother," she gushed. "And to think each album will be personalized. I can't thank you enough."

Oh, but she could thank me. She could show her appreciation by telling me more about Roxanne's married lover. To soften Merrilee up, I gave her a gift. "As a small token of our appreciation, we printed two photos of you and your fiancé." I handed over the pictures of her and Jeff kissing.

Merrilee's face hardened. "Where did you say you got these?"

"From Roxanne's memory card. When we downloaded all the photos, they were there."

Merrilee huffed and puffed like a steam engine does. She worked her jaw back and forth. "These are NOT pictures of Jeff and me."

"But they are. I mean, that's you, right?"

"Wrong! See that mole over the woman's eyebrow?" She pointed to a teensy beauty mark in the photo. You could barely see it because Jeff's head was in the foreground and the photographer had taken the shot from behind him. All that was visible of the woman was a thin sliver of the right side of her face. Otherwise, the back of Jeff's head covered her features. It was an odd angle, the type of picture you might take if you were sneaking up behind the couple.

"I don't have a mole over my right eyebrow, but I can tell you who does! That's Linda. I wondered about her and Jeff. Now I know!"

"Maybe that's not Jeff. I mean, I was wrong about you."

"It's Jeff all right. He has a double crown to his hair. See?"

Merrilee flounced toward the front door. Stopping at the counter, she announced to Dodie, "The wedding is off. Throw the albums in the trash. I don't want any of them."

———

KIKI'S METHOD FOR PUTTING TOGETHER
AN ALBUM QUICKLY

Most people work one page at a time. If you want to get an album done quickly, there's a better way.

1. Start with a palette of papers and matching ribbon or fiber.

2. Choose a lettering system, such as rubber stamps, rub-on lettering, vellum preprinted phrases, sticker letters, computer type, or die-cut letters.

3. Create backgrounds for all your pages at once. Decide on a central design theme to carry through the album. For example, will you always run a strip of patterned paper vertically along the outside of the pages? Or will you divide the pages into quadrants and use different paper in each? Or will you put a broad strip of patterned paper across the midpoint of every page? Aim for consistency. You do not want to come up with a new look for every page.

4. Adhere your photos with a temporary adhesive. (This allows you to "play" with placement.)

5. Look at the negative space, the empty space around the photos. This space will determine the sizes and shapes of your embellishments. Note the average negative space size.

6. Create embellishments to fill those empty spaces, remembering to leave room for journaling. For example, if you have a twenty-four-page album, and thirteen spaces that are 4" × 6", you can safely make thirteen 3" × 5" tags or journal-

ing boxes. Mass produce your embellishments, remembering to duplicate several designs. In fact, you might wish to select a certain embellishment style and carry it through the entire album. For example, you might create a 3" × 5" tag with a silk flower and simply vary the journaling.

7. Be sure to leave space for journaling. These are SOFJ, Sites of Future Journaling.

8. Assemble the album.

THIRTY-EIGHT

"That's why I get a deposit," muttered Dodie.

"I can't believe it. And we thought we were being nice by printing those photos."

Dodie said, "I should know better. It never rose and it never flew."

Oh, boy. Dodie had dipped into her vast store of translated Yiddish sayings.

She continued her rant, "Like it's our fault her guy had a thing for her pal, Linda!"

The door flew open and Mert ran in. She was decked out in a lime green halter top with sequin trim, short shorts, and a pair of lime green wedgies. Somewhere in South America, a conga line dancer was missing an outfit. "How you doing, sweet pea?" She gave me a hug. "I brought you a gift."

First the Krispy Kremes and now this. It was my day to be treated like a birthday girl by my friends. The tissue-wrapped packet was soft and pliable in my hands. I untied the ribbon and unrolled a pink T-shirt with an embroidered emblem that read "Tough Tamales University" on top and "School of Hard Knocks" underneath.

"I wanted a real school logo. The lady at the shop borrowed the design from Harvard but used girlie colors."

"Wow," I said. What else could I say? It was pretty nifty. Official looking, too.

"Actually, all things considered, I was doing pretty well until a few minutes ago." I explained what happened with Merrilee and tried not to dwell on how much income had walked out the door.

"Don't that beat all. I know Linda's housekeeper. We're charter members of Toilet Bowl Cleaners United. We meet every third Wednesday at White Castle. It's a good place to try out new products." Mert scrolled down her cell phone directory and punched the send button as she headed for a quiet corner.

"Fortunately Mrs. Witherow already paid for the bridal shower albums. Maybe the others will still want theirs," Dodie said looking over the pile of leather-bound books sadly. "I'm not telling them the wedding is cancelled. That's Merrilee's problem, not ours. The deposit from Merrilee will cover the supplies we set aside for the other projects she wanted."

The profit I'd counted on was gone. Not only was I missing rent for the next three months, I still needed money for a new rental deposit.

Good thing I'd planned on stopping by Bill Ballard's office. August sure was far away. But if the buy-sell meant I was due some money, maybe I could borrow enough to live on until then. Still, I couldn't do anything until I read the papers.

I had no doubt that eventually I'd make enough money scrapbooking to provide for me and my daughter. But meantime, I couldn't make ends meet. Tisha seemed confident there was a lot of money in the business. Even if the fiscal year-end accounting showed only a small sum, that was more than I had now. I needed money desperately.

I had no idea how much Bonnie was going to charge for a visit to Family Court. Even if she kept having babies, and I kept making albums, I'd still owe for the supplies. And there was the money I needed as a deposit on a new place. My balance sheet was definitely skewed toward the minus side. Like the leaning tower of Pisa, I was dangerously off-center. How long could I survive without tumbling?

I picked up the Witherow bridal shower photos and sorted them into archival sleeves. Maybe the rest of the shower guests would want more customized work. Maybe all was not lost. Okay, so I could cross off Merrilee's wedding album and the album for Jeff's mother. But maybe Merrilee would still want help with Roxanne's memorial album.

I hoped so. Otherwise, I'd just lost a lot of business. A lot of money. Present and future. The more albums I did, the more business I generated. Every custom album included a tasteful sticker with my contact information on the back cover.

My spirits sank further as I tidied up the detritus of the ill-fated Witherow bridal shower album. Lately nothing had gone right for me.

"Well, well, well." Mert returned to my work area. "Stuff rolls downhill, and you, poor baby, stepped in a pile of it. Seems our little Linda is in a passel of trouble. Or as my daddy used to say, smart birds don't mess in their own nests. And if they do, they best better wipe their tail feathers quick-like.

"See, Linda was married once before to a poor boy. And she didn't much cotton to it. And Mr. Kovaleski was her hubby's boss man. Then she and Randy Kovaleski started swapping slobbers. And her first husband upped and D-I-V-O-R-C-E-D her and was going to name old Hot Pants Kovaleski co-respondent. Only, see, Kovaleski was married, too, and his wife woulda taken him to Birdland, where the sun don't shine, and there's doo-doo droppings on your window all day. But Mr. Kovaleski paid off Linda's first hubby to just go quiet into the sunset. Wouldn't you know it, old Linda got herself knocked up? Then Mr. Kovaleski found hisself paying a bundle to the first Mrs. Kovaleski to render their union asunder. By the time he got ready to marry Linda so's she could have his heir and a spare, he was already feeling a pain in his pants—and I mean his wallet. That's when he informed Linda she had to sign a pre-nup. And she did. Knowing her extracurricular activities, he made it heavy on the 'you better not mess around' lingo. In fact, I'd guess that if a picture's worth a thousand words, that one you showed Merrilee Witherow's worth a couple hundred thou or maybe even a million."

Mert's effusive use of metaphors had me a bit confused. "Come again?"

Detweiler had shown up in the middle of her dissertation. Mert went through her paces again, and Detweiler, thank goodness, understood everything she said.

"That, ladies, could be our motive for murder."

"How you figure?" Mert asked. Dodie joined us and was listening carefully.

"Those photos were on Ms. Baker's camera, right? She takes her camera to the shower to show Mrs. Kovaleski. Maybe she blackmails her. Maybe she's also collecting money from Mr. Jeff Spitzer. Maybe that's how Ms. Baker's been affording her fancy lifestyle the past six months—blackmailing people."

I dug in my purse for the paper Olivia gave me. On it were two names, Roxanne Baker and Linda Kovaleski. "Roxanne and Linda had lunch with George the day he died. I bet Linda paid to cover that up. She was protecting Roxanne. She couldn't take the chance her friend would be investigated for George's murder. If the police examined Roxanne's affairs too closely, they might uncover her little sideline: blackmail."

Detweiler said, "You downloaded the pictures from Ms. Baker's camera without her permission. Suddenly, Mrs. Kovaleski's got a problem. You've got the picture of her and Mr. Spitzer, the one she's been paying to keep under wraps."

"But Linda doesn't realize those photos are in four places: Roxanne's camera, the website, Kiki's computer, and the duplicate CDs. That's because Linda isn't a scrapbooker. She didn't understand the pains Kiki took to protect the images," said Dodie. "But Roxanne was a scrapbooker. She understood exactly what Kiki was doing. Knowing Linda was confused, Roxanne had to act quickly. She calls Linda and says bring me lots of money or I'll expose your affair with Jeff."

"That would explain the windfall," I said. "See, Roxanne told Merrilee she was coming into a bunch of cash. She said an 'investment' was paying off."

"The investment was blackmail money," said Dodie.

I was on a roll. I said, "Linda has to move fast. She tells Roxanne to meet her at the mall. That same night, Linda hires someone to steal my computer. Linda figures if she has my computer and the photos from Roxanne, she's covered."

"But the photos were on the website!" Dodie protested.

"Right," I said, "But Linda didn't understand how Snapfish worked! Remember? She came in here the day *after* my computer was stolen. She'd been up all night. Looked terrible. Once I walked her through the website, she raced out of here."

"Roxanne Baker was shot at close range. The killer was sitting next to her in her car. The murderer must have been a person she knew and thought she could trust. Linda Kovaleski would fit the bill perfectly," Detweiler said.

"Hold it!" Dodie put up a hand. "Why'd she want Kiki thrown in jail?"

"I can answer that," I said. "At first, Linda thought the pictures on the website were too small to see. After all, the identifying marks—her mole and Jeff's double-crown—are pretty subtle. But then I explained how I could fix them up. Make them clearer. And enlarge them."

"Her goal was to keep Kiki away from her work," Detweiler said. "Obviously, Kiki couldn't work on photos if she was in jail. So, Mrs. Kovaleski lied about seeing Kiki's gold Lexus leaving the scene of Roxanne Baker's murder."

Dodie asked, "Would Linda Kovaleski know you drove a Lexus?"

"Absolutely. I always saw her at carpool when I picked up Anya."

"After you got out of jail so quickly, she must have been really desperate. So she hired a teenager to break into your house again and steal the CDs," said Detweiler.

"Wow," said Mert. "That Linda Kovaleski's been one busy gal."

"Basically, I've been the victim of a one-woman crime spree," I said. "I'm glad we've got that figured out."

"Which reminds me." Detweiler pulled an envelope from his back pocket. "I wrote a letter supporting your bid to get Anya back. I never know about my schedule, and I didn't want to miss the chance to help." He handed it to me.

"I need to get right on this new information. The pieces fit, but all we have is speculation. I have to get Mrs. Kovaleski to admit she perjured herself. Your mother-in-law is using your incarceration to get custody of Anya. We have to prove you were set up." He gave my shoulder a quick squeeze.

I dreaded his leaving. For the first time, I really, really understood why people loved mysteries. While we were brainstorming who killed who, concentrating on life and death, I didn't have to think about missing my daughter.

"This new information is going to keep me busy," Detweiler said. At the doorway, he paused and gave the three of us a mock salute. "Ladies, Sherlock Holmes' Irregulars couldn't have done better work. The game's afoot."

"I just love a man who knows good literature," said Mert.

THIRTY-NINE

BETH, SHE OF THE nameplate fame, was on duty as receptionist for Dimont Development Inc. Today she wore a see-through blouse displaying most of her push-up bra. Once again, the phone was tucked under her ear, and she was issuing a steady commentary of, "Uh-huh, uh-uh, uh-huh," as I walked in. She was also painting her nails. I took a seat, but she didn't notice my arrival.

"Wow, that's really complicated," she said, not even looking up from her artistry. "How about you type that up and send it to us. In the mail. With stamps. That kind of mail. Oh. Like now? You want me to write it down? All of it? Gee, I'm not sure I have the time. I'm really busy. Okay, okay, let me find a piece of paper..."

Maybe this is just as well, I thought. I slipped past her and headed down the corridor to Bill Ballard's office. Gosh, it wasn't like I hadn't been in this place a zillion times. I'd be able to tell if I were interrupting an important meeting before I barged into Bill's office.

In fact, he was busily typing away—scratch that—pecking away at his keyboard, giving his index fingers a workout.

I rapped on the door frame, and his head jerked up.

"Hi. Sorry if I startled you. I happened to be in the neighborhood and thought I'd stop by."

Bill frowned. "How'd you get past Beth?"

I didn't want to get the girl in trouble. "She was really busy so I slipped past her."

His eyes narrowed.

Gee, I mused, why was he surprised? Surely he'd noticed a whole lot of filing (of nails) going on. I continued, "Do you have a copy of the buy-sell? I've left messages…"

Bill's mouth took a distinct downward turn. He paused as if counting to ten. Tisha's retelling of their marital woes hadn't included a bad temper, but I could see by Bill's reaction, he wasn't a guy who liked surprises. Vaguely, I recalled George telling me Bill was a control freak. Well, tough. I needed to know if he owed money to me and my daughter. If Bill didn't like my asking about what was mine, too bad.

He must have come to a similar conclusion. "Right. I've been busy. Important meetings. Just swamped. In fact, don't have much time now. Maybe we should make an appointment?"

He rose and moved to pull on his jacket.

I was being dismissed.

The old Kiki would have turned on her heel and gone along with his shenanigans. The new one wasn't so malleable. I sank into the chair across from his desk. "This won't take long."

"Hope not," said Bill, slowly sinking back to his chair. "By the way, you never said how you happened to realize you didn't have a copy."

Was he stalling? If so, why?

Didn't matter. I needed to appear bigger, tougher, and better advised than I was. "My accountant mentioned it." Okay, so I lied. No reason to tell him that his wife had clued me in. Things were obviously bad enough between them already. Wasn't Bill's forgetting to mention the buy-sell lying, too? I added, "He was a bit surprised you didn't hand over the agreement right after George died."

Bill had a lousy poker face. For an eye blink, he registered concern.

I decided to continue to apply pressure: "But I told him I was sure you'd come up with a copy."

He studied me. I could see the wheels turning. "Right. I didn't realize you had an accountant."

I said nothing.

Fingering a long line of file folders in the bottom right drawer of his desk, he tried to carry on a light-hearted conversation. "How about those Cardinals? You know, George and I bought season tickets. Planned to take our clients. If there are ever any games you and Anya want to see, let me know."

I'll never understand what made me say what I said next. Maybe a demon landed on my shoulder and whispered in my ear. Maybe I was feeling ornery. "That would be very nice. I'm dating a policeman, and he loves baseball."

Bill nearly fell out of his big, black executive chair. "A cop?" His fingers moved faster over the files. "No kidding? Gee, Kiki, I thought you had more class than that."

How dare he! That, I thought, took a lot of nerve.

He opened a file on his desk. Viciously pressing a button on his phone, he said, "Beth, get in here. Now."

I still smarted from his mean remark but I was determined to maintain my cool. "Honestly, Bill, I'm surprised at you. You and George and all your college pals never thought I had a lot of class. Personally, I respect law enforcement officials. They keep our streets safe."

Beth interrupted. Bill handed her a stapled set of papers. "Bring me a copy of that, right away. Don't forget to take the staples out before you feed it through the copier like you did last time," he snarled. Beth's eyes were big as Frisbees.

Bill pulled at his tie. A sleezy smile oozed over his face. "Don't misunderstand. We all appreciate the fine work of our men and women in blue. I'm only thinking of you, Kiki. You're used to the finer things in life."

I couldn't believe what I was hearing. I nearly choked. "Thank you, Bill. I didn't think anyone noticed what I was accustomed to. Why don't you tell me about the buy-sell agreement? Any idea what my half of all this is worth?"

His mouth flattened into a mean, straight line. "Not much. Thanks to your dead hubby. He borrowed against his share. Not only did he embezzle money from this company, but he cheated you. That's right, with all he borrowed, your portion of Dimont is a big fat zero. However, since you are so eager to see all this in writing—even though I tried to spare you the gritty details—here it is."

Bill took the papers from Beth and dismissed her with a curt nod of the head. He pushed the warm document toward me with a smirk on his face. "Read it and weep, Kiki. George left you nothing. He managed to squander his every dime—and some of my money as well."

I took the papers with a sinking feeling. Really, what had I expected? A sea change in my affairs? Not in this lifetime. I scanned the numbers. I was no accountant. However, the last page confirmed Bill's report. A promissory note was attached to the papers. On it was George's signature.

Bill's expression softened. "Honest, Kiki, I'm sorry about all this. I should have forced him to make sure you and Anya were provided for." He ran his hands through his slicked-back hair. "I swear, I thought I knew him like a brother. This all came as a surprise. What was he thinking? I ask myself that every day."

That made two of us.

Bill covered his mouth with a hand and stared off into space as if reviewing his memories. Covertly, I studied the man. Behind him, the monitor on his computer switched to the screensaver I'd seen so many months before. Lush trees stood against an azure blue sky. Sandy ground surrounded a stone base. A structure of white poles sat to one side of the scene.

Poles? That was a lighthouse!

"That's Cayman? The Cayman Islands? Did you go there with Roxanne?" I surprised myself. But it made sense, didn't it? Bill, the Cardinal lover, could very well be the man in the baseball cap. The married man who later dumped Roxanne.

He cleared his throat. "No. I mean, yes, back in our college days. The screensaver is a sort of memorial. Terrible about her death, isn't it?"

I could only nod. He was lying and we both knew it.

But who cared? Roxanne was dead, and Bill was about to pay for his indiscreet behavior in divorce court.

Once again I found myself wishing I could be magically transported to that tropical scene. I wanted to run away. How stupid I had been! I'd let myself believe there might be money for Anya and me. Why had I allowed myself to hope? Why had I pinned my hopes on this? It only made coming down to earth harder.

"Well," he said with a clap of his hands. "Okay, we're good to go, right? Hey, you know Britney and a few of her friends are going skating after school. Tisha asked Anya to come. Sheila said it was fine. I hope that's okay with you."

"I didn't know about it. It's ... it's nice of you and Tisha to include Anya."

"Yeah," he grinned. "Tisha caught up with Sheila at drop-off this morning. It's an impromptu thing, but what the heck. The girls'll have fun. And don't forget about those Cardinal tickets," he pointed his finger at me, clicking it like a gun. "I remember how much Anya likes baseball. Go Cards!"

FORTY

I left Dimont Development with my spirits dragging behind me like a gunny sack. I didn't stop to recheck the paperwork.

Later, I figured. I could read the legalese and feel sorry for myself. At a gas station I grabbed a free rental property magazine. Since I was going to be alone all weekend, I might as well start my search for another place to live.

Back at the store, Mert and Dodie wanted to talk about how hunky Detweiler was, and how I could use a good man.

Mert said, "That Detweiler's the type of man who'd stick by you thick or thin. Most men wouldn't have troubled themselves to type up a letter to help a woman get back her kid. In fact, most of them'd rather you be shy of a child, to tell the truth."

"You got that right," said Dodie. "He's one of the good guys, Kiki. You ought to hold on to him. Policemen get good benefits, you know. Great pensions, too."

I wasn't in the mood for any man, good or otherwise.

I was pretty disgusted with myself. Here I was a grown woman, and I should be fully capable of providing for me and my child. Instead, I'd left money matters to George. I hadn't exactly behaved like a responsible adult, had I? And come to think of it, wasn't that exactly how I got in this mess? By acting irresponsibly?

Once we decided to get married, we didn't spend much time talking about my accidental pregnancy. I felt guilty then, and I'd feel guilty until my dying day. It was never my intention to trap a man. And George knew that. In fact, he said, "I'm as much to blame as you. Guys want to believe this is all the woman's responsibility, but I made a decision to have sex with you. The consequences of sex can always be unwanted pregnancy. I was experienced. You weren't. I should have been more careful."

I'd argue, "But you were drunk."

He'd reply, "And so were you. Furthermore, I watched what went into that Purple Passion Punch, and you didn't. My frat was well known around campus for getting girls drunk, especially girls who hadn't any experience with drinking."

"But I should never have ..."

"Never have what?" he asked. "Gone to a party? Come on, Kiki, it was college. That's what college kids do. Never have gotten drunk? That's also what college kids do. Or never have trusted me? Okay, maybe that's where you made a mistake."

"You didn't have to marry me," I would respond.

"That's right," he had said. "I didn't. But I wanted a child. I knew even from the moment I met you that you were a kind and good person. It radiates from you, Kiki. That's why people find you so easy to take advantage of. We got married because we brought a new life into this world, and no matter what people say, the best way to nourish and protect a child is within the bonds of marriage."

We weren't soul mates. Ours wasn't a love match. We didn't have a burning desire for each other. But we had a friendship.

What happened?

———

After my visit to Dimont, I returned to the store. Gracie was hankering for a quickie walk. Dodie took one look at my face and asked if I was okay. I said, "Fine." She and Mert had a strategy for my day in Family Court. They were rounding up testimonial letters on my behalf. Bonnie promised to represent me.

Dodie'd clearly put a lot of time and effort into helping me. I thanked her profusely. And I felt sorry for her. She'd hired me and brought nothing but trouble on herself. I was determined to make it up to her.

"Let me take Gracie around the block real fast and then I'll work on a new class."

"First you have a new commission."

"Really?"

"Yes, Markie Dorring bragged about you to one of her friends in that ritzy 63124 zip code. Lila Gill? Lila brought in four boxes of photos. I told her you'd suggest a way to organize them into albums."

Dodie pointed to four big cardboard boxes. She agreed to mind the store while I worked my way through the photos.

Gracie and I went for a quick spin and I got down to business. Those boxes were great therapy. Ten minutes after feeling sad about the buy-sell and swearing off men, my mind was aquiver with ideas. I immersed myself in the project, letting it distract me from the weekend without my daughter.

My cell phone rang.

"Kiki? Bill Ballard here. Anya's had an accident."

"What?"

"She took a tumble while the girls were skating."

"Is she all right?"

Bill paused, "We think she broke her arm. I can't tell. She's a real trooper about the pain, aren't you, honey?"

I couldn't hear her response. He continued, "I'm taking her to St. Luke's. Meet me at the Conway Road entrance."

"I'll be right there."

Dodie listened to my problem and waved me off to the hospital. I left Gracie in the storeroom.

I didn't remember until I was speeding down Highway 40 that I wasn't supposed to have contact with Anya. I wasn't sure what to do. On the one hand, nothing was going to stop me from being with my kid when she needed me. On the other, I worried that by disobeying the Department of Social Services, I'd never regain custody. I wasn't sure who could tell me how to handle this, and I was frantic with concern. I tried dialing Mert but only got her answering system. I tried Bonnie. I didn't have her number memorized and wound up talking with Bricklayers Union Local 122. Finally, as I pulled off Highway 40 onto 141 North, I decided to call Detweiler. Maybe, I reasoned, a police escort would assure DSS I wasn't trying to flout their instructions.

Detweiler's speed dial was number 9 on my keypad. It's pretty tough to push the 9 with your right hand and drive with your left.

I set down the phone to turn onto Conway and make the nearly immediate left into the parking lot of St. Luke's.

Bill was standing beside his car, and he waved to me. As I pulled to a stop beside him, I grabbed my phone and hit number 9. The ringing was accompanied by Bill's gesturing for me to roll down the passenger window. I unlatched my seat belt and leaned over to hear what he had to say.

"Kiki, I'm afraid I have bad news. Open the door." He straightened to wait for me, his hand on the door latch. Bill was standing right up against my car.

"Detweiler," said the detective as the phone connected.

Bill filled my passenger side window: he was that close. I was trying to juggle the phone and unlock the door. "Just a minute," I told the policeman.

Bill hadn't heard the detective's greeting—or my response. He started to climb into the Beemer. My purse was in the passenger seat. I reached awkwardly over the gear shift to move my things. My left arm held my phone down by my side like the tilted pole of a tightrope walker, adding balance and keeping me from tumbling into the passenger seat.

"Where is—"

I glanced up and froze.

I was staring down the barrel of the gun. I raised my eyes to Bill's face. He smiled, settled into my car and slammed the passenger door.

"Scream and I'll kill you."

FORTY-ONE

"Anya? Where's Anya?"

"Forget Anya."

"Where's my daughter?" I insisted. My hand touched the top of the driver's door map pocket and I dropped my open phone inside it.

My guts went liquid, and my legs felt weak.

"But you called and said Anya was hurt—"

"Drive or I'll shoot you."

"Not without my daughter."

"She's fine. But you're going be dead if you don't drive." Bill shoved the gun into my ribs.

"Umph." I gasped at the sharp pain.

"Get on 40."

My hands were shaking. I thought I was going to puke. I was trying to turn the wheel but the ache in my side made it hard. Calm down, I told myself. Think! Cars passed us, their drivers on cell phones or talking to passengers. Clearly, I could not signal anyone for help without alerting Bill. Was this the end? Was I going to die? I gritted my teeth and made a decision: I wasn't going down without a fight. I had to let Detweiler hear what was happening!

"Tell me where Anya is!" I rolled to a stop.

Bill rammed the gun against me—hard.

I tried not to react because he seemed to be getting off on seeing me in pain. That, at least, I could control. If my pain excited him, I'd bear it stoically.

"She's skating with the girls. Now drive or I'll shoot."

"You'd shoot me?" I repeated this for Detweiler … if he was listening. I prayed he was.

"In a heartbeat." Bill jammed the gun into my side again.

"Umph." The sharp pain made me catch my breath. "Please, Bill. I'll do whatever you say. Don't shoot."

I prayed Detweiler was still on the line and could hear me. I repeated, "Please Bill. Please put the gun down. Don't shoot me."

"That's it. Beg. You wanna live? Do what I say. Or I swear I'll put a bullet in you."

"Promise me Anya's okay. Where is she?"

"As long as you do what I say, Anya's fine. She's with the other girls at the skating rink off of Manchester." He relaxed the pressure on my side a little. "But cross me, and I'll kill her. Got it?"

"Yes, Bill. Whatever you say." I figured my best bet was to make him feel powerful and in control. Without resistance, he'd let down his guard. We idled at the light before the ramp onto Highway 40. "Which way?"

"Babler State Park." As he spoke, he pressed down the door lock mechanism. I was locked in my car with a killer. But all I had to do was pull on my door handle and the lock would open. I realized that my knowledge of my old car was a point in my favor.

I played dumb. "I don't know the way to Babler State Park," I said the last three words extra loud.

"West on 40, exit Long Road."

"West on 40 and exit at Long Road," I repeated in a flat voice. I wanted to sound as obedient as possible. Acid rose in my throat. I swallowed hard. I had to think. Leaving St. Luke's had been a mistake. Dodie knew I was heading to St. Luke's. No one knew I was going to Babler, unless Detweiler was listening in. And I couldn't really count on that. As much as I wanted to cry, wanted to break down, I couldn't. This was a life or death situation—my life and my death.

"Why Babler State Park, Bill?" I tried to talk loudly. "What's at Babler, Bill?"

Bill pushed back the passenger seat and shoved the barrel of the gun into my side. "Don't mess with me. I'm not playing games. Roxie tried to mess with me, and I put a bullet through her head."

"You shot Roxanne?" Boy, and we had thought Linda Kovaleski was involved. Now curiosity competed with fear. What was this all about? Were they—he and Linda—in this together? Suddenly small clues formed a trail of bread crumbs: Bill saying he was buying the gift certificate for Tisha's birthday gift when she'd said her birthday had already passed, Bill foisting an attorney on me who conveniently "forgot" to tell me about the buy-sell, and Bill pretending his screensaver was a memorial to Roxanne.

His grin was cold and his eyes dark slits. "Yes. And she cried and begged just like you will. Don't mess with me."

The cruel timbre of his voice cut through me. "But why?"

"Why?"

"Was Roxanne a threat to you? Was she going to tattle on you to Tisha?"

"You are so stupid. I don't give a rat's rear end about Tisha. She'll do exactly what I say. She believes whatever I tell her, like when I said I was going to a conference last January and took off for the islands with Roxanne." Now he sat back, relaxed his shoulders and neck, and beamed with smug self-satisfaction. "Didn't you hear the news?"

"What news?"

"Tisha's pregnant. Again. So, she's decided to forgive me." The way he spat it out, the word "forgive" left a bad taste in his mouth. "She wants us to be a family."

Tears came to my eyes. I couldn't help myself. What, I thought, is so bad about being a family? Wasn't that all that really mattered in life? Being connected to other people by blood or love or both? I sniffled.

"Cut the waterworks." Bill rammed the barrel into my ribs again. He smiled as I winced. "Families. Kids. Who needs them? You wouldn't be in this mess if it wasn't for your precious little Anya."

I said quietly, "I don't understand. How did Anya get me into this mess?" Fortunately, Bill wasn't paying much attention to what I said. He was lost in a self-congratulatory fog.

He grinned. "Yeah, someone ought to appreciate my brilliance. Might as well be you, right?"

He was at ease in the passenger seat, moving it back to accommodate his long legs. Reaching over, he flicked the air conditioning to high, turned off the vents trained on me, and basked in the cold air. What a jerk.

"See, I'd been siphoning off money for years, a little at a time. A handful of small accounts won't raise red flags like large ones do. I set up a variety of accounts in the Cayman Islands. By the way, good call about me going there with Roxie—but that's getting ahead of myself. I've been building a bankroll and biding my time. Dimont has done okay, but we haven't hit the big one, you know?" He laughed. "At least we hadn't hit the big one until now.

"Along came Beth. I met her at the gym. Does she have a body that won't stop or what? Wow. It gets better. Beth has a doting daddy. And her daddy is a farmer who owns fifty prime undeveloped acres."

"Babler Estates, right?"

"Yep. Bingo! Soon Beth is eating out of my hand. She's talking about getting hitched. I tell her how I'd leave the old ball and chain, Tisha, except for the money. Beth says that's no problem. She introduces me to Daddy. Daddy, George, and I put together a deal. George goes to all those stupid zoning meetings. He figures out the utilities and yada, yada. We're ready to roll, except we're undercapitalized. George and I scrounge up two million each. He goes to Sheila and I hit up Tisha's father. Life is good ... then Tisha's dad gets a wild hair. He wants an outside firm to audit Dimont. To protect his investment," Bill said and shook his head. "This is bad news. The company's nearly two million light, and the whistle is going to be blown on my creative accounting unless I come up with the money fast."

We were driving along the western edges of St. Louis County, passing dense native greenery and occasional road kill. Those flattened, bloodied bodies gave me the creeps. They never knew what hit them. And neither did I, really. I'd never liked Bill, but I hadn't suspected him of all this wrongdoing, this depravity and deceit.

I wanted to live, and I was fast formulating a plan. For it to work, Bill needed to be involved in his story. "And you couldn't let that audit happen, right?"

"Right. But here's where Lady Luck winks at me. George and I hold two-million-dollar life insurance policies on each other—the buy-sell agreement. All I have to do is turn George into a corpse. I was working on a plan when Roxie came crying to me." Bill waved the gun at an overhead sign. "Get off at Long Road."

"What does any of this have to do with Anya?"

"Your little princess didn't like sharing Daddy. Anya asked George if he was planning to leave you. George said no—in front of Roxie. Told your kid he'd stay with you forever. Man, that ticked off Roxie something fierce. She and I bump into each other at a bar. Roxie spills her guts over a beer. Make that a case of beers. She'd turned into a sloppy drunk. But I'm always thinking." Bill tapped his temple. "I figure she and I've got a mutual problem."

Bill grinned. "I mention Roxie to George. He tells me he's going to give her a lump sum. A goodbye gift. I encourage him. I tell him that's a great idea. He does and she goes ballistic."

Wow, I marveled at how manipulative the man was. And he'd been my husband's best friend!

Bill continued his story. "Roxie's so angry, she's a nutcase. I'm seeing how this is good. Really good. I go comfort her. Let her cry on my shoulder. Tell her she deserves double what George offered her. I tell her he's done her wrong, wasting the best years of her life."

"So you killed your best friend." The words were out of my mouth before I had the chance to stop myself. A chill of fear ran down my spine. But I needn't have worried. Bill wasn't the sensitive type.

"Huh. Friendship is overrated. That and two bucks will get you a cup of coffee," Bill smirked.

He hadn't reacted to the sarcasm in my voice. I reminded myself that I had to keep Bill happy for a while longer. The happier he was, the more he'd relax. The more relaxed he was, the better chance I had of escaping.

He turned cold eyes on me. "I didn't kill George. I just helped Roxie along. She decided to give George a goodbye party he'd never forget. Did you know her old man was this genius plant-guy? And he was always yakking about plants to her. She knew a lot of poisons almost impossible to trace. Oleander. That's what she used. She slipped it into his drink at lunch."

Detweiler had been right. My husband had been poisoned. I'd read an article on a parenting site about oleander. A group of kids used the twigs for roasting hotdogs. They all died. Horrible deaths. I shuddered, thinking of the pain George must have felt. I mumbled, "So Roxanne murdered him."

"Yep. I didn't have to lift a finger."

"But she left her scarf behind."

"What a moron. I had to cover that up. See, hotel security pulled George's business card out of his pocket. They called me to ID the body. The manager pulled me aside. Said he wanted to protect Mr. Lowenstein's reputation. Showed me the scarf. I paid him to keep quiet. Couldn't take the chance of the cops leaning on Roxie."

"But she got away with it. And you got the buy-sell money. So why shoot her?" I managed to sound interested, not shocked. If I lived through this, I deserved an Academy Award. I had a plan, but it wouldn't work unless Bill was distracted.

"I had to. After George died, Roxanne got all weepy on me. She sobbed how she missed George. I had to shut her up. I took her to the Cayman Islands. I opened an account so she got a taste of the money coming her way. I promised her a payoff when the Babler Estates deal went through." He turned away from me briefly as we pulled onto Long Road. "Right at Wildhorse Creek."

Good. He was getting more and more confident.

"That picture of the two of you? Who took it?" I prayed Long Road was a long road. It isn't. Some jerk who names roads must have had a warped sense of humor. We passed McDonald's and a gas station, and idled at a light while my heart raced along with the car engine.

"The whole time we're in the Caymans, she was snapping pictures. She was as nuts over taking photos as my wife. Then this tourist wanted to be a hero. He offered to take a picture of the two of us. I complained, but snap! Now I had trouble. Couldn't get the camera away from her. She kept teasing me about how it was her security. And she was broke. Constantly. Always hitting me up for more cash. I mean, that woman could go through money like it was blow."

"So she blackmailed Linda Kovaleski."

"Hey, how'd you know that?" He was mildly surprised.

"I just guessed."

"Can't be because you saw her camera. I got it right here." He pulled Roxanne's missing Canon from his pocket. "She just couldn't

293

wait for the real money. And I couldn't let her ruin my forty-million-dollar payday. She was a loose end and I needed to tie her up."

A thought struck me. I said, "George didn't steal a half a million from the company, did he?"

Bill threw back his head and laughed. As he did, the gun moved away from my ribs. "You are so gullible. I should have told you it was a million."

My stomach lurched. This guy was a real whacko. I was alone in a car with a psychopath who had a gun.

My plan had to work. I couldn't trust Bill to leave Anya alone. He was well along the path to being a serial killer.

"Yes, I sure am dumb." I nodded weakly; my legs felt like Jell-O. My heart was going double-time and banging against my ribs. With each mile, I became more and more lightheaded. How was I going to save myself—much less make sure Anya was okay?

Bill's attention drifted toward the scenery. He stared out the window at the rolling hills, the spreading trees, and an old train car parked by the side of the road. The gun muzzle drifted from my ribs. His expression turned dreamy.

"What changed, Bill? It was all going so well for you. All that hard work and planning was starting to pay off." I wiped sweat from my chin. I could smell the fear oozing out of my pores.

"The cops started nosing around. They asked me how well I knew Roxie. Security cameras showed me visiting her condo." He ignored the scenery to give me a big smile. "But I'm one lucky guy. You showed up asking about the buy-sell. One look at your blank little face, and I thought, bingo! Then you noticed the screensaver. That sealed the deal. Do you know every lighthouse is different?

It's so guys out at sea can tell where they are." He sighed. "You came along just at the right time. This will be so sad. The police will find your dead body. You'll be holding the gun that killed Roxie. And her camera will be in your car."

I fought the nausea rising within me. I tasted acid in my mouth.

Bill sighed but didn't notice my distress. He was happy with himself, pleased with his progress. "It's a slam dunk. You lost your kid. Your life is in the toilet. You killed Roxie and you couldn't take the guilt. You decided to end it all."

"Right. That's my life in a nutshell." Oh God, I prayed, I know I'm a miserable excuse for a person, but please help me anyway. Help me be smart and strong. Help me find a way out of this. I want to live to raise my daughter.

"Turn onto 109." Again he waved his hand and the gun drifted from my ribs.

"Um, which way?" I had to keep him thinking I was clueless.

He waved his right hand to the south. The gun moved a little farther away from my ribs.

"I'll take Beth with me when I leave. I'll keep her as long as she's a good girl. The minute she gives me trouble, I'll ditch her. The stop sign is Babler Access."

As we turned onto Babler Access Road, Bill pointed to the sign. "See that? 'Dimont Development's Babler Estates. Luxury homes in a beautiful setting.' Right. Ha!" He threw the sign a big kiss.

While he looked away, I oriented myself. I had to get ready. I thanked Gracie that I knew the park well from our Sunday morning romps. My plan might work—emphasis on the "might"—if Bill continued to let his attention wander.

We passed the empty guard gate at Babler. It figured. Where was a guard when you needed him? What did he guard anyway? The trees?

"Tell me. Where are you planning on going? I mean, after you get the money from the development?" My fingertips set the cruise control at the twenty-five-mile-per-hour limit. Now I could take my foot off the gas pedal, and the car would keep going. I shifted my weight to the left very gently. I'd purposely left my seat belt unbuckled when Bill first hopped in. Slowly, imperceptibly, I leaned away from him and against my door. It was tricky because Babler's rolling hills go up and down, twisting and curving like a roller coaster. I couldn't lose control of the car—not just yet.

I tensed and relaxed the muscles in my right arm, testing them.

Bill's eyes grew dreamy. "Oh, I'm thinking—"

I slammed my right elbow into his Adam's apple.

"Gulch." He sputtered. His hands flew to his throat.

I poked his left eye hard as I could. My fingers sank deeply into a warm gelatinous substance.

I yanked my handle, automatically unlocking the doors. I thanked God and George for this old Beemer and all its quirks. The car veered wildly. Trees whipped by. We were on a collision course. I hurled myself out of the moving car, my shoulder hitting the asphalt hard. I slid along the pavement on my shoulder and side. The skin peeled from my body, burning and stinging. The impact jarred my teeth and knocked the wind out of me. I rolled and rolled, gasping for breath. The car—with Bill in it—kept going, heading toward the trees lining the road. I coughed and managed to get air into my lungs. My feet were moving as I scrambled along the blacktop. I scuttled away from the road, struggling to stand upright.

Every bit of me hurt. I didn't care. I ran.

The grounds sloped down sharply from the pavement. The woods were below me. I half-ran, half-crawled. I fell and rolled downhill. I struggled to my knees, to my feet. My calves burned at the sharp angle, the slant of the ground as I plummeted toward the dense forest. I didn't care how badly I hurt. I was running for my life.

I was nearly touching the trees now. The cool air of the shade beckoned me to come deep into the darkness, to hide, to disappear from my predator. I could smell decaying leaves. My arms stretched toward the dim shadows, reaching, almost touching, nearly there—

A bullet hit me.

FORTY-TWO

I NEVER HEARD IT. I smelled burning flesh and saw smoke rise from my right shoulder. My nostrils flared, and my leg muscles quivered. A blast of adrenaline fueled me like a rocket and I jumped into the air, moving forward, moving into the trees. I landed, half falling as my toes caught on a root. I hit the ground again, rolling and rolling down the hill. Head over heels. Each time my weight shifted onto my shoulder, a pain like when a curling iron touches your skin shot up my torso. The world flashed by me, green, blue, brown, green, blue, brown.

Bill yelled from somewhere above me, "You're dead! Hear me? You're dead!"

I scrambled into a clump of low bushes, parting rough undergrowth with my hands. Branches clawed at my skin. A shot zinged past me like a mosquito on speed. I dropped to my knees and grabbed tufts of grass to pull myself along. My shoulder pulsated with red licks of agony. I had to keep moving. "This is for Anya," I whispered. I pushed deeper and deeper into the grasses and vines.

Snot streamed down my face. I didn't stop to wipe it. I didn't dare look back. I heard Bill behind me, calling my name and cursing. The birds went quiet. Suddenly he quit yelling. His footfalls crunched somewhere in the distance but I couldn't calculate how far away.

"Give up! Give up or I'll … I'll make it take longer! I'll hurt your kid! You hear me?" Bill's voice rasped like a file on wood. He was obviously in pain and out of breath.

I thought about Anya and my hopes for our future. I wanted to see my little girl grow up. I wanted to help her get dressed for the prom. I wanted to meet the man she'd marry. I thought about my sisters. I vowed to make peace with Amanda and Catherine. I'd ask Mom to forgive me. I'd never forget her birthday again. I thought about Dodie and Mert. And Gracie, dear sweet Gracie— who would look after her? I pulled myself through the brush. I crawled on my belly. Three-leafed plants engulfed me. I was scooting through poison oak. I didn't care. My right shoulder was getting numb, but my arm still worked. I grabbed and pulled, scooting deeper and deeper.

Beyond me was a clearing. Should I run? Or stay hidden? Crunching noises told me Bill was close. Blood was trickling down my shoulder, streaking my arm, covering my hand and fingers. Even with the rush of fear, I was starting to feel weak. I didn't think I could outrun him.

"You're gonna pay! You hear me? You'll pay for this!"

I dug around in the bushes. My fingers discovered a couple of branches. They seemed sturdy, not too rotted, but bound tightly by vines.

Wiping blood on my pants so my hand would be dry, I began to pray. God, I mouthed the words, give me strength. That's what I learned from George. Jews don't pray to be delivered; they pray for strength. I had to stay tough. I tugged on a branch. It wouldn't move. I took a deep breath and pulled as I exhaled. The branch popped free, making surprisingly little noise. I ran my hand along it, feeling the knuckles of broken twigs, testing the heft and weight.

Leaves and small sticks crackled under Bill's shoes. I rested and listened. Thank heavens I'd poked his eye so hard. The undamaged eye would be watering in sympathy, making it difficult for him to see. Between the shade and the blurred vision, I could afford to let him get close. Picking out his form as he groped along, I watched him pausing to wipe his eyes on his sleeve. I pulled my legs under me and coiled into a balanced squat. I waited. I knew I could do this. Maybe I would die, but I wouldn't just lie down and die. I'd make him pay dearly for the privilege.

I judged him to be twenty feet … fifteen feet … ten feet … three feet.

I popped up.

Smack! I swung the branch with all the fury I could muster, feeling my abdomen ripple with the twisting, juddering motion. I hit hard and low. I aimed for his gut. I missed my mark a little, and thought I heard a crack of his ribs. But I got him.

Folding like a road map, Bill sank to his knees.

The back of his head wavered before me. His hands were splayed on the ground, which kept him from falling face down, and he still gripped his gun. I couldn't chance him rising and shooting me. I lifted the branch once more, fearful it would crack.

I ignored the pain shooting through my arm. In my mind, I was a batter at Busch Stadium. My stick hit the back of his head and bounced out of my control. Bill wobbled like a child's toy. Then he made a face-first dive into the detritus of the forest. I ran to him. Kicking his fingers, I sent the gun flying. I ran, dug through the leaves, and grabbed it, amazed at how hot and heavy it felt. I held it in front of me by my fingertips as if I were holding that two-headed snake. I watched the gun as though it were a living, venomous creature.

I stood there panting. My breath came in deep gulps. Bill didn't move. I held the gun in both hands, trained the sight on him, lined up the notches, and considered what to do next. The form on the ground didn't move. I cautiously stepped closer, pointed the gun at his back where I couldn't miss. My finger caressed the trigger.

I'd pretty much had it. I growled in anger and frustration, a grunting animal sound that tore at my throat. I was sick of complications in my life. Sick of people tossing me about like litter. I wanted to kill him. I really, really did. I wanted to know he'd never bother me or my child again.

The thought shamed me. He could do me no more harm, but, oh, how I wanted to finish him off.

FORTY-THREE

My feet didn't cooperate as I staggered toward the road. I was moving uphill, fighting gravity, and ignoring the pain, retracing the ground that earlier I'd covered so quickly. It seemed to take forever until the light changed, indicating the crest of the asphalt road.

I shoved the gun into my pants pocket, and hoped it wouldn't go off. I knew nothing about weapons. What if my fingerprints on the barrel got me in trouble? What if Bill came after me again? At least he couldn't shoot me. My shoulder and arm weighed as much as two concrete blocks and were just as agile. My legs felt weak, and each step was unsure. I was moving an inch at a time, my feet catching every root and branch.

I fell to my knees. Whimpering and crying, I crawled on one arm. Every other move forward, I'd slide backward. My shoulder hurt like it was on fire. Blood soaked my sleeve and trailed along my pants. My wound alternately ached and stung. Leaves and grass got in my mouth. I spit as I shuffled along on three good limbs.

In the distance sirens wailed, their tremulous notes changing back and forth, back and forth, louder and louder.

Detweiler is coming, I told myself. Detweiler is coming, and I'll be okay.

———

I woke up staring into a bank of fluorescent lights. The smell and noises told me I was in a hospital room. Mert was holding my hand. The eye makeup she applied with a trowel was smeared. Her mascara had melted into raccoon-like rings around her eyes. She looked awful. Her face was stricken, and her lips trembled. She patted my good arm, her hands roughened by work but gentled by affection. "The kid wanted to be here … but there's that DSS thing. Let me call her and tell her you're awake. She's tearing up Sheila's house pacing and worrying. You had us skeered as cats in a dog pound."

She leaned over, planted an awkward smooch on my cheek, and squeezed my hand. "By the way, you get an A-plus for the final exam, kid. You rose to the top of the class." Her voice was jaunty, but it was a false note.

Detweiler followed on her heels. "You okay?" His blue oxford shirt was decorated with small pieces of leaves along the buttons. A smear of blood across his chest brought back a memory. He was carrying me, holding me close, and my body was limp in his arms. It hadn't been a dream. His normally combed back-hair hung over his eyes, which were tense with concern.

I nodded. "Okay. I'm—"

"Shh. Your doc's on the way. After you were stable, he gave you a shot for the pain. You were lucky. The bullet nicked you. Ballard's a rotten shot."

"You get the gun?"

"Yep. Took it off of you. It wasn't registered."

"He killed Roxanne," I croaked.

Detweiler took a paper cup from the table beside my bed, held it to my mouth, and guided it to my lips with great concentration. Gosh, the water tasted good.

"Yeah, he used a nine-millimeter Glock on her. That's what we found on you. The crime scene crew is searching for casings." Detweiler set the cup down and tried to dab my mouth where I'd dribbled.

Watching him try so hard to be gentle and noting his awkwardness made me want to smile. He likes me, I thought to myself, he really likes me.

"Good grief, Kiki. What were you thinking? You took on a killer by yourself."

"Didn't have a choice," I whispered. My throat was surprisingly dry. "He said Anya had broken her arm at a skating party. I drove to St. Luke's—where am I?"

"St. Luke's."

"Back where I started." I sniveled. I was all out of brave. "He held a gun on me and hopped in my car." My voice cracked. Somehow it sounded worse to say it out loud than just to remember what happened.

Tears rolled down my cheeks. I began a series of hiccupping sounds as I moved from crying to blubbering.

Detweiler patted my forearm with an open palm, a motion like tamping down something. His eyes looked wet, and he sniffed.

"Yeah. But you're okay now, you hear? You're safe. You left your cell phone open. I heard it all. Enough to hang him. Or it would be … except…"

"Except?"

"He got away."

"What?"

"Looks like he got up and ran while we were helping you. Maybe had an accomplice. He's hiding somewhere. We're trying to track him." Detweiler's mouth was thin and pulled tight. And he cursed, saying stuff I'd never say. Almost never.

"I should have shot him when I had the chance." My lips turned down and trembled.

Detweiler leaned close. He took my hand and opened it. He planted a kiss in the palm and folded it closed. A warm glow flooded me. I tried to smile, but every inch of me hurt.

"No, honey," he said. His voice was surprisingly gruff. "You shouldn't have. You don't need that on your conscience. Trust me."

A doctor hustled Detweiler away. A nurse stepped forward with a pill in a cup. I gulped water and swallowed it. The doc and nurse conferred at the foot of my bed. Slowly, the world went soft and blurry. I quit hurting. And I slept.

———

"Mrs. Lowenstein, are you well enough for us to proceed?" Judge Parmenter adjusted her bifocals on the tip of her nose. All the better to stare at me.

A bright blue sling with cheery white piping secured my bandaged shoulder. My system's reaction to the poison oak began late

Sunday. Straight railroad lines of bubbling blisters ran up and down every inch of my body. My face was a gingham pattern of hatch-marks where plants had scratched and torn at my skin. The doctor at St. Luke had pumped me full of cortisone, which made me edgy. Absent-mindedly, I dug at my blisters, making them ooze plasma and scab over.

All in all, I did not look like a worthy candidate for parental custody.

"Yes, ma'am. My injuries are superficial. What's important is my daughter."

"Hmm." The dark-complected woman had a smooth forehead from which sprung a frizzle of hair. She peered at me over the top of her reading glasses. "And I'm to understand you had a near miss with a killer last week. Is that right?"

"Yes, ma'am."

"Is that related to this hearing?"

"I don't know," I said honestly. The judge cocked her head slightly in contemplation. I thought she must be a grandmother, because she had that look about her. I could imagine her both chastising and cuddling her offspring. Seemed she was in the perfect job. But would she empathize more with Sheila than with me?

Detweiler stepped forward and gave a brief explanation of Bill Ballard's behavior and attempt to kill me, while putting particular emphasis on my bravery. "Mrs. Kiki Lowenstein has been falsely accused and manipulated by those who will stop at nothing to cover up their crimes," he added.

The woman behind the bench stroked her chin. Her skin was the color of a Kaldi's latte, and her hair was white as whipped cream topping. She regarded me solemnly. Slowly, like a cartoon owl, she rotated her head to stare at Sheila.

"Mrs. Lowenstein, I want to be sure I understand. You predicated your call to Department of Social Services on the fact your daughter-in-law was incarcerated. Is that correct?"

"Yes, and she lives in a bad neighborhood, and she—" Sheila sputtered. In her crisp navy suit, she was the picture of a solid citizen.

Judge Parmenter waved her hand, "Thank you," and shut Sheila up before looking over her notes again. "How long were you in jail, Mrs. Lowenstein?"

"One night." I was afraid to say more. I got the impression Judge Parmenter didn't like people taking the bit and running.

"And that was because?"

"A woman named Linda Kovaleski perjured herself and testified she'd seen Mrs. Kiki Lowenstein leave the scene of Roxanne Baker's murder," Detweiler said. He was wearing a navy blazer, a white shirt, striped tie, and neatly pressed khaki pants. I looked like Indigent of the Year, Bawanna the Jungle Babe, but he exuded a crisp professionalism.

He added, "I'd like to submit a sworn statement from Mrs. Linda Kovaleski. She's presently out on bond, your honor."

Judge Parmenter took the proffered paper and read it slowly. The room was silent as we waited. "And you knew this, Mrs. Lowenstein? You knew this was a temporary situation?" The magistrate glowered at Sheila.

"Yes … but that's not my only reason for contacting the authorities. My grandchild is forced to live in a bad neighborhood. Their house has been broken into—"

"Your honor," interrupted Detweiler, "That's also in the statement. Mrs. Kovaleski paid people to break into Mrs. Kiki Lowenstein's home on two separate occasions."

"Like I said," continued Sheila, "that's a bad part of town, and it exposes my grandchild to unnecessary risks."

"Judge Parmenter, if the issue here is neighborhood safety, let me point out the city of St. Louis ranks in the top ten in the nation in crime. Does that mean we should remove every child in the city? I think not," Bonnie Gossage said. Fresh from feeding Felix, she was on a roll.

Judge Parmenter put up a creased palm as a stop sign. "That's enough, counselor." She shuffled pieces of paper from one pile to another. "I'd like to hear from—"

"May I talk?" Anya stepped forward. She was wearing a simple white blouse tucked into a knee-length black skirt. Her hair was pulled back into a ponytail and tied with a black-and-white polka dot ribbon. As sweet as she looked, her voice sounded strangely adult and serious. "I don't know the rules. I don't want to be rude, but I have something to say." She trained big blue eyes on the woman in the black robe, as she stood with her hands clasped, her fingers wrapped tightly together.

Poor baby, she had to be scared to death. If only we could have talked beforehand! I could have assured her everything would be all right.

Judge Parmenter smiled, crinkling her crow's feet at the edges of twin brown buttons. "I was just about to ask you to talk to us, young lady. My information says you are eleven. Is that right?"

"I'll be twelve next month. I know you might not think I'm old enough to know what's good for me. But I think you need to know … I mean what I want to say is …" Anya turned to Sheila and slipped one hand inside her grandmother's. "I love you, Gran, and I like staying with you."

My heart sank. Sheila could provide more creature comforts for Anya. Life at Sheila's was more stable, and Sheila didn't work. Sheila's neighborhood was safer, and her house would be a lovely place to bring friends. I bit my lip. Whatever happened, I would continue to love my daughter whether she lived with Sheila or with me. She would always be my baby.

Anya continued, "But the real reason you want custody of me is because you miss my daddy. I miss him, too. I hear you crying at night. Mom cries about him, too. But you had your time together while he was growing up. This is our time, Mom's and mine. You might not like her, Gran, but she's really pretty neat. Daddy told you that, and you wouldn't listen. I love you, but I want to live with Mom. I want all of us to be a family. Can't we try?"

———

A half an hour later, we were celebrating.

Sheila had taken the proceedings pretty well, all things considered. Judge Parmenter spoke kindly to her, remonstrated her for using the courtroom to solve family problems that we "clearly were qualified to solve" ourselves. The judge implied Sheila had acted on a misplaced concern for Anya's welfare. Her thoughtful assessment let Sheila save face, even while awarding me custody of my daughter. In summary, the judge said, "I see a host of people who love this child. As she grows, she will need all of you. For her sake, try to work together."

Mert drove Anya and me to Time in a Bottle. Horace, Dodie's husband, popped the cork on a bottle of champagne. I could instantly see why Dodie loved him. He had a tonsure that made his hair look like feathers on a baby bird's head. Horace came only to her shoulder, but he beamed with pleasure whenever she turned his way. "Now that's a hunk for you," Dodie whispered. "He might be short, but my Horace is a real man."

Mert poured a glass of sparkling cider for Anya.

I needed to tell Mert about the lights before I forgot. "I appreciate it, Mert, really I do, but I have to ask Roger to take the lights down."

"What?"

I recapped my conversation with Mr. Wilson.

"Dial him."

"Pardon?"

"Get that number. I'm going to call him up. Graduate studies at Tough Tamales University are now in session. Listen and learn."

Detweiler raised an eyebrow and stepped closer to hear.

"Mr. Wilson? This is Martha Grimes, attorney at law. I'm with Billem, High, and Offen. Right. I'm calling on behalf of my client, Kiki Lowenstein. You gave her thirty days notice, correct? She's happy to vacate the premises. You are aware of the break-ins? We'll be charging you with reckless endangerment." She paused. Dodie, Horace, Anya, Detweiler, and I pressed close to listen.

"That's right. You are familiar with Jacob versus Marley? You aren't? I'm quite surprised, Mr. Wilson. Most landlords are familiar with case law directly affecting their business." She sighed as if very disappointed.

"Shall I recap the case for you, or shall I simply serve you with papers?" She wore a petulant expression. I'd never heard her talk like this. Her voice was cultured, her diction impeccable.

"Valerie Jacob was an attractive, young, single woman like my client. She lived in an apartment complex without adequate lighting or security. Which, I might add, closely parallels our situation. Detective Chad Detweiler has made a security assessment of your property. Shall I put Detective Detweiler on the line?" She handed him the phone.

"Mr. Wilson? Detective Chad Detweiler, here. I specifically recommended to Mrs. Lowenstein that she have lights added for security purposes." He passed the phone to Mert.

"Now, I will proceed to recap the relevant case for you. Miss Jacob was assaulted inside her apartment. A jury found her landlord negligent. There were no security lights although she and other tenants had requested them. The property owner paid a three-point-five-million-dollar settlement to Miss Jacob. And she wasn't a young widow with a child. We'll use that case as the basis for our suit against you. My client has already suffered two break-ins. You want to expose her to more crimes. You already endangered her and caused her the loss of property she needs for her livelihood. And, her daughter will need ongoing therapy for her mental pain and suffering. Have a nice day."

She snapped the phone closed.

I gawked. "Holy shamoly. What have you done? Is that for real?"

Detweiler shook his head. He was trying to keep a straight face. "Billem, High, and Offen? You gotta be kidding me."

Horace covered his mouth to suppress guffaws as his shoulders bounced with barely restrained laughter.

Mert winked. "You betcha. I don't remember the names, but I read all about it in *People* magazine. Poor woman. Landlord wouldn't let her put in a porch light. Now we count. One Mississippi. Two Mississippi. Three Mississippi..."

We were at fifteen Mississippi, and I was hyperventilating when my phone rang.

"Um, Mrs. Lowenstein, I've been thinking," Mr. Wilson began.

"Yes?"

"Maybe I was too hasty."

"It's all right, Mr. Wilson. My attorney is excited about this case. She's contacting the news media tomorrow."

Mert gave me a thumbs-up.

"That's not necessary. I'd like you to stay in the property. I will even reimburse you for all the costs associated with the security lights."

"There's also the matter of my attorney's fees and my missing computer."

"Why not buy yourself a new computer, Mrs. Lowenstein, and send me the bill? And I'll take care of this month's rent. Are we square?"

"That sounds fair." I hung up and said, "Mert, what on earth would I ever do without you?"

Horace raised the green bottle. "A toast!"

"To the newest graduate of Tough Tamales University!" said Mert.

"To the bravest woman who ever escaped a crazed murderer!" said Detweiler.

"To my favorite employee," said Dodie.

"To the only mom at CALA who has a bullet wound!" said Anya. "Wow, Mom, that is way cooler than a tattoo!"

EPILOGUE

A COUPLE OF WEEKS later, I dropped Anya off at Sheila's.

"You go on in, darling, I'll be right there," my mother-in-law said to my child.

Every muscle in my body tensed. Since that day in Family Court, Sheila and I had treated each other with elaborate courtesy by circling each other like two dogs deciding whether to fight. Now she gestured to me to follow her into the living room.

"Police Chief Robbie Holmes and I are old friends," Sheila started.

I nodded.

Her eyes moved from my face to a picture of George on her mantel. Next to him was a picture of Anya, and next to that was a photo of Sheila and Harry holding Anya as an infant. "Robbie played a tape for me. A tape of your phone call to that detective." Sheila fingered an invisible spot on her sofa before adding, "That was smart of you. Very smart."

"I was lucky that I'd just called Detweiler, and Bill hadn't noticed. It was the only way I could think of to leave a message, in case ..." And I stopped. I was superstitious enough not to want to say "In case I died" out loud.

"No, you were smart. And gutsy. The man was holding a gun on you. And that monster used Anya ... my granddaughter! ... as bait to lure you into his trap. I can't believe it! My son's best friend! And his ... old girlfriend! I trusted them. Both of them. It's hard to believe, I ... I'm ... having trouble with it." Sheila was sputtering as she spoke, letting her emotions project the words from her mouth.

I nodded. It was hard to believe. All of it.

"Robbie says you never accepted the idea George died of natural causes. He tells me you asked questions from the beginning."

"George just had that medical workup, Sheila. And the circumstances ... well, they were too weird."

She said nothing. Tears made silver crescents in her eyes. Her lower lip trembled. I'd never seen Sheila cry. Not even at Harry or George's funerals. She was a great believer in a stiff upper lip. "And Robbie says you kept tracking down ... searching for ... the truth, even while you paid Bill to protect my son's reputation. That you were afraid George was being blackmailed. And all the while, that little—that Roxanne—she was behind it! And Bill! The two of them killed my son! My boy!" Sheila's hands covered her face. I noticed for the first time how thin she'd gotten, and how her shoulder blades made bad coat hangers under her clothes.

She cried and cried, stopping only to retrieve a cotton handkerchief from a pocket, before starting up again. I didn't know what to do. She'd never touched me. Never in twelve, almost thirteen, years. I'd never touched her. But I couldn't just sit on the other side of the room and watch her suffer. I moved slowly to her side. I knelt beside her and touched her shoulder.

"I'm so sorry," I said. It sounded terribly inadequate, but it was true. "I can't imagine what you are going through." I swallowed hard and steeled myself. She needed to hear what I had to say next, but I had no idea how she'd take it. "I want you to know that I loved George. I really did. Maybe I wasn't right for him, or maybe everything about us was wrong, but I did love him. I believed in him. He was a good man and a great father. Despite his relationship with Roxanne, he was a decent man. That's why none of this made sense. And I know how much you loved him. I try hard to be as good a mother to Anya as you were to George."

She lifted her chin. For the first time, I think, she saw me as a person, not an enemy. "How is your arm? I heard he got you. Good thing that monster wasn't a very good shot."

"I tried to make sure he didn't have a good target! And I'm fine. It was only a flesh wound, and it's healing. It was more scary than painful."

I returned to my leather wingback on the opposite side of the room.

Sheila squared her shoulders. "Obviously, I'm not a very good judge of character."

"That makes two of us," I said. "And now we have to go on. They're still searching for Bill—"

"I'm hiring a private investigator. Robbie has a few he recommends. I want them to find that weasel and bring him to justice."

"Sounds like a plan. Look, I need to get to work. Merrilee With-erow and Jeff Spitzer are back together again. I'm working on an album for her to give his mom."

Sheila's lips curved upwards and her eyes smiled, too. "Good. I'm sure that will make Elizabeth happy. Anya and I ran into her at the club. She told me she was desperate for a grandchild. I could tell she envied me my beautiful Anya."

For a minute, for the time being, we could put it all aside—the rocky start, the ugly first years, George's death, the DSS report—we had Anya and her future ahead of us.

"Okay. I'll be here first thing tomorrow to take her to the park."

"Babler?" asked Sheila mischievously.

"Heck, no. I thought we'd try Creve Coeur."

Sheila rose and we started toward the front door. "I suppose you're planning on taking that hulk of a watchdog with you. Anya told me how she scared your home invader."

"Good old Gracie. She was quite proud of herself afterward."

We stood awkwardly in the doorway, each wondering if we'd ever feel comfortable enough to give and receive a hug. The fragrance of Sheila's petunias was nearly cloying. The scent of her freshly mowed grass tickled my nose. My poor Beemer needed repair to the right bumper where Bill had swiped a tree trying to bring it under control. I smiled to myself and thought how fitting it was that both of us—the BMW and I—had clipped wings.

"Kiki," Sheila spoke my name in a tone she'd never used before. "I'd like things to be different between us."

"I'd like that too." I spoke to the denim-blue eyes that she'd passed on to George and Anya. "I really would."

Back in the car, I watched her wave from her porch. I raised my hand in reply. Maybe it could be different between us now. I sure hoped so.

I was nearly floating as I drove to Time in a Bottle. Thinking good thoughts, fantasizing about the future. My cell phone rang and I answered, "Hel-lo?" with a lift to the last syllable—a testament to my good spirits.

The voice on the other end was all too familiar.

"This isn't over. I'll make you pay."

THE END

50 FREE
digital camera prints

Get 50 professionally-developed prints from your digital camera.

plus...
- free online photo sharing and storage
- create personalized photo gifts
- easy-to-use photo editing software

110% quality guarantee!

To get your 50 FREE prints visit
www.snapfish.com/ScrapNScrap

get 25% off photobooks

Showcase your memories with our professional-quality photobooks, use coupon **ScrapNScrap** at checkout.

— CONTEST —

SCRAPBOOKER'S DREAM WEEKEND IN ST. LOUIS!

FIRST PRIZE

Two-night stay at the Sheraton St. Louis City Center, St. Louis, Missouri. Valid through February 2009 (value: $338), and dinner with Joanna Campbell Slan (priceless!). Plus a gift basket of scrapbooking books and St. Louis products worth $100.

Hotel stay is courtesy of the St. Louis Convention & Visitors Commission: www.explorestlouis.com.

SECOND PRIZE

A Premium Photo Book from Snapfish

THIRD PRIZE

Mrs. Grossman's Stickers Gift Package

ENTER THE DRAWING TO WIN!

To be entered in the *Paper, Scissors, Death* contest please fill out and mail the form on the next page. Entries must be received before November 15, 2008. Winners will be selected in a random drawing on November 30, 2008. Include your e-mail address, your postal address, and phone number so that we can notify you!

E-mail address: _____

First Name: _____

Last Name: _____

Phone Number (with area code): _____

Address Line 1: _____

Address Line 2: _____

City: _____

State or Province: _____

ZIP or Postal Code: _____

Country: _____

RULES

Winners will be selected at random. Enter as often as you like. All entries must be received before November 15, 2008.

- Important note: Coupon for hotel stay must be used by February 28, 2009.
- Entering the contest grants us permission to list your name as our winner, to add you to the Joanna Campbell Slan mailing list, and to receive information from our sponsors.

You can duplicate this page, or print out another copy of the page by going to www.joannaslan.com and clicking on **contests**.

Or copy and mail your entry to:

> *Paper, Scissors, Death* Contest
> 12033 Dorsett Avenue
> St. Louis MO 63043

Robert George

ABOUT THE AUTHOR

Joanna Campbell Slan is the author of twelve books, including seven on scrapbooking. She is a frequent contributor to the *Chicken Soup for the Soul* series, and her work appears in a variety of other anthologies. A world traveler, Joanna has led an interesting life, appearing before groups of all sizes as a speaker, meeting such celebrities as Jon Bon Jovi and Van Cliburn, and riding a camel to the pyramids in Egypt. Visit her website for tips on scrapbooking and to learn more about her work: www.joannaslan.com.

ACKNOWLEDGMENTS

You know how authors always thank this big list of people, and you wonder, "Did all these people help?" Well, the answer is: "YES!" (Not exactly a "cast of thousands," but close.)

You'd be amazed at the questions and problems you have as you work on a book, and the many times when your family and friends come to your rescue. (They can't hold your hand because you need it to type ...)

First of all, I have to thank my wonderful husband David Slan, my patron of the arts, my dearest critic, and my forever supporter. I also appreciate my son Michael for putting up with a working mom and listening to early drafts of my final chase scene. My sister Margaret Campbell-Hutts introduced me to scrapbooking years ago, and my sister Jane Campbell gave me medical advice (as did her friends Sally and Jon Lippert). My brother-in-law Mike Hutts loaned me his pancake recipe for my website and gave me advice on George's untimely death. (Those two activities are totally unrelated.)

Members of the law enforcement community assisted me as well. Thanks go to Lieutenant Lewis and Sergeant Cheryl Funkhouser of the Chesterfield Police Department, author and Detective (retired) Lee Lofland, Jerry Kramer of St. Louis County Justice Services, and Detective Joe Burgoon.

To kill George in such a sneaky way, I consulted Ruth Birch and Luci Zahray, aka "The Poison Lady." Don't mess with these women!

For information concerning the dogs in my book, I consulted with the Veterinary Group of Chesterfield, Missouri. Many terrific folks there offered assistance: Dr. Wayne Boillat told me how to knock out Gracie during the storm (don't try that without a vet's help!), Joan Logan shared her pet-sitting stories, Miki Boswell and Kari Murphy offered information on Great Danes. Kari owns Orion, a rescued uncropped female harlequin, who is the model for Gracie on my website.

Between writing and publication, WE, the two-headed snake, died. Her remains have been preserved and are on view at the World Aquarium, second floor of the City Museum here in St. Louis. Go to http://www.worldaquarium.org/we.php to see the tribute to WE. Special thanks to Leonard Sonnenschein for sharing WE with us and the world.

There is no Charles and Anne Lindbergh Academy; however, there is a Kaldi's Coffee Roasting Company, and I love their coffee! Go to www.kaldiscoffee.com.

Books have fairy godmothers: I wish to thank authors Emilie Richards, for a terrific idea and a first read, and Elaine Viets, for ongoing encouragement and career advice. Other early readers include Julia Kressig, Andrea Van Cleve, and Michelle A. Becker. Special thanks to Laura Bradford and Joe Richardson. The entire Greater St. Louis Chapter of Sisters in Crime has been of immeasurable assistance. Booksellers Vicki Erwin, Lynn Oris, and Wendy Drew gave me great advice. Shirley Damsgaard has been a great friend as well as a role model for any successful author. Sheila Glazov, my Jewish mother, kindly read my manuscript for errors, and Sonia Dobinsky of CAJE (Central Agency for Jewish Education here in St. Louis) also answered my questions.

Gerry Malzone of Steinway Piano Gallery of St. Louis answered my cries of "help" with graphics for promotional use. In fact, everyone at the store—especially our wonderful Pat Sonnett—helped with office support and enthusiasm for this project.

Jill Hafstad of Archivers and Tina Hui of Snapfish have offered invaluable support, proving once and for all that scrapbookers are the BEST people in the world.

David Jolly started working on my website when he was sixteen. (He's since graduated from college and has a "real" job, but he continues to serve as my webmaster.) Check it out at www.joannaslan .com. Be sure to sign up for my free ezine so we can stay in touch. Click over to the scrapbooking area for free templates, downloads, and tutorials. David and I are constantly adding stuff and upgrading. For tips on hobbies as well as cool contests, be sure to visit the Killer Hobbies blog at http://killerhobbies.blogspot.com.

I am proud to be a part of Midnight Ink. My publicist Marissa Pederson and artist Kevin Brown have gone that fabled "extra mile." Barbara Moore served as my acquiring editor. I was privileged to work with her.

The fates were smiling on me the day I met my agent Liz Trupin-Pulli of JET Literary Associates, Inc. I don't have the words to thank her, so instead I'll just have to promise to keep working really, really hard.

Any mistakes I've made, well, "I did it my way!" so all these wonderful people are not to blame.

Joanna

PS You can always contact me at my website www.joannaslan.com. I love hearing from you, and I'll make every effort to come to your book club or crop, either in the flesh or virtually.